---------------- ★ ----------------

"All right, everyone. Places, please." Evan looked around. "Where is Juliet?"

Donna made a face. "Making everyone wait, as usual."

Randi muttered, "Probably trying to steal someone else's shoes."

"Cindy, will you hurry her along?"

Cindy disappeared behind the curtains. Evan rearranged the contestants. "Now, ladies, I hope you remember your new dance. It looks absolutely perfect."

Cindy ran back, her eyes enormous behind her glasses. "Mister James, there's been some sort of accident. I think—" She had to stop and gulp for air before she could speak again. "I think Juliet's dead."

The girls gasped, and I thought Evan might faint. I hopped up on stage. "Show me."

Cindy led me backstage. Juliet Lovelace lay in a clump of white gown, her black hair in a tangle, her neck bent at an unnatural angle. I leaned down and felt for a pulse in her limp wrist. An extension cord was coiled near her body.

---------------- ★ ----------------

JANE TESH

A CASE OF
IMAGINATION

W❂RLDWIDE.®

TORONTO • NEW YORK • LONDON
AMSTERDAM • PARIS • SYDNEY • HAMBURG
STOCKHOLM • ATHENS • TOKYO • MILAN
MADRID • WARSAW • BUDAPEST • AUCKLAND

A CASE OF IMAGINATION

A Worldwide Mystery/July 2011

First published by Poisoned Pen Press

ISBN-13: 978-0-373-26760-6

This book is dedicated to
Gary Provost, teacher and friend

Acknowledgments

Thanks to everyone at Poisoned Pen Press for all their help and encouragement, and a special thank-you to Ellen Larson for her humor, insight, and computer lessons.

ONE

OKAY, WHEN YOU'VE TRIED everything and nothing works, it's time to get out of town. I stared at my phone, willing it to ring. A lost dog, a missing tooth, misplaced car keys—anything. On this nice July morning in Parkland, North Carolina, the office of Madeline Maclin Investigations might as well have been an Egyptian tomb: hot, dusty, and dead. I flipped through the desk calendar, finding it hard to believe it had been only a week since I'd solved the Lundell case. Nancy Lundell had been so pleased she'd promised to call all her friends and tell them about my services. Apparently, she had none.

My lack of clients wouldn't have been so bad except I could hear all kinds of activity from Reid Kent's office next door and knew he was doing brisk business without me. Around noon, he had the nerve to poke his head in my door and ask me about lunch.

"No, thanks." Why give him more opportunity to gloat? "It's Tuesday. I'm meeting Jerry."

Reid's grin widened and he made what I'm sure he thought were spooky noises. "Will he see success in your future?"

This wasn't worth a reply. It was worth a dirty look, though, a dirty look that didn't faze him. He parked his rear on my desk and gave his dark, carefully groomed hair a few pats as if walking all the way from next door had disturbed his coiffure.

"You know, Madeline, if this isn't working out for you, you can always come back to Kent and Ross."

"No, thanks."

"Think of this as a learning experience. Why struggle with your own agency when you can be a welcome addition to mine?"

"I tried that, Reid, and I prefer to be on my own."

"But you've had, what, two clients?"

"Three. And all three were very satisfied."

He gave me a pitying look. "Face it, Madeline. Nobody's going to hire a former Miss Parkland. I don't care if you've cut your hair short and don't wear any makeup. You're still too much of a distraction."

"I'm supposed to take that as a compliment?"

He leaned forward. "If you want to."

"Go away, Reid."

He laughed and hopped off the desk. "Oh, excuse me. I can see you've got way too much work to do."

I heard him laughing all the way back to his office. Damn it, Reid Kent was not going to spoil my day. He'd spoiled too many of my days already. That Miss Parkland crack was what passed for witty banter with Reid. Despite his doubts and the doubts of several of my friends, I was not going to believe that my looks had anything to do with my ability. Yes, I'd had a successful pageant career. I was determined to be just as successful as an investigator.

I slung my pocketbook over my shoulder and went out, pausing to lock my door. Even though I had nothing of value, I didn't want Reid or any of his toadies snooping in my office. A short elevator ride took me to the foyer of the Pressler Building. From there, it's a short walk to my favorite hangout, Baxter's Barbecue, one of the best little restaurants in this part of Parkland. Baxter's is very plain, with wooden tables covered with plastic red-and-white-checkered cloths, plastic forks and spoons, and cheap paper napkins. But the food is terrific: barbecue that melts in your mouth, tangy slaw, and crunchy hush puppies. I waved to Ellis and Betsy Stone, the owners, and slid into my favorite booth in the corner. I went ahead and ordered my lunch. Jerry would be late. He's always late.

Jeremyn Nicholas Fairweather. Sounds like the hero of one of those Regency romances, doesn't it? One of those tall, dark, dashing Lord Byron types, the kind of impeccably dressed man who can ride, fence, gamble, and dance, all with equal grace.

Jerry's not that. He's a slim, youthful-looking man of medium height with light brown hair and gray eyes. You'd never believe he belongs to one of the richest families in Parkland. His older brother, Des, is a world-class concert pianist. His younger brother, Tucker, grows prize-winning roses on the family estate. Harriet, the eldest, is haughty and distant. Jerry, however, is, well, different. He doesn't have a regular job. Right now, he was bunking with Buddy, one of his scruffy friends. And he's given up all claims to his share of the Fairweather fortune. I've yet to figure out why. I can only guess it has something to do with his so-called psychic ability, which he uses for all the wrong reasons.

He arrived ten minutes late, managing to look wind-blown even on a calm day, his hair in his eyes, his tie crooked. He tossed his jacket into a chair and sat down across from me. Jerry likes to wear suits, but has unfortunate taste in ties. The tie of the day was brown, with neon-yellow pineapples.

"Sorry I'm late. I was doing a reading for Constance Shawn."

"Again?" Constance Shawn is one of several rich old ladies who like to have their palms read. I'm sure the fact that Jerry, even at the grand old age of twenty-nine, looks young and cute has something to do with their insistence. "Isn't that the third time this week?"

"She asked me."

"You're such a pushover. What else are you doing today?"

He loosened his tie. "I have a séance at four."

I started to tell him what I thought about that when he reached into the folds of his jacket and brought out an envelope. "I also have a house."

"What?"

He took out a letter. "My uncle Val left me a house."

"I thought you didn't care about worldly goods."

"I don't, but this sounds interesting." He handed the letter to me.

"Who's Uncle Val?"

"My mother's brother. I think he only visited one time when I was little. He didn't like the idea of my mother marrying my dad, so he wasn't very welcome."

I scanned the letter. "This says he died two weeks ago and left you a house and some land in Celosia."

"I borrowed Buddy's VW. Let's go look at it."

"Today?"

"Sure. You're not doing anything, are you?" His expression changed. "Oh, sorry, Mac. That didn't come out the way I meant it."

"No, you're right," I said. "I don't have a case. I don't even have the hint of a case—unless you see something."

He paused, letting his large gray eyes focus on a point somewhere behind me. Then he crossed his eyes. "Nope. Sorry."

"I can't believe anybody buys your act."

He grinned. "What act?"

Betsy brought two large barbecue sandwiches, two orders of fries, and two large iced teas, plus a plastic basket loaded with fat hush puppies. She set everything on the table and wiped her hands on her apron. "You know, Jerry, I was wondering if you'd check on my grandma's knee. She seems to think there's some kind of demon interference that's keeping it from healing."

He avoided my skeptical expression. "Be glad to."

"She should be here in a little while. I'd really appreciate it."

"Okay."

Betsy moved on to the next table. I reached for the ketchup and poured it over my fries. "So now you're healing people. That's nice."

"Just a little laying on of hands."

"Good lord, Jerry, someday somebody's going to smack the hell out of you."

His look was pure innocence. "But if they believe, they get well. I'm saving them lots of doctor's fees."

"If you keep playing around like you're psychic, someday you're going to pay."

"Did you check with the Psychic Patrol on that? I haven't heard that rule."

"Shut up and eat."

The lush fat content of Baxter's barbecue calmed me down. I was all set to give Jerry a few more words of advice when he looked at me with his calm gray gaze and said, "What's the trouble?"

"If you were really psychic, you'd know."

He put his hand to his forehead and closed his eyes. "Give me a moment to get in touch with the cosmos. Hmm. Aah. Wait a second. It's coming in clear. It's a donkey's behind. No, no. It's Reid Kent."

"I am so amazed and astounded. How do you do that?"

He opened his eyes. "Reid Kent's an idiot. Is he going on about your beauty-queen days? Your looks are an asset. They always have been."

"I just want people to take me seriously."

"They will. They do. Just because your mother dragged you to every Little Miss in the South, there's no need to panic."

Jerry knew the story, of course. As a kid, I had been my mother's perfect little angel. I endured endless hours of practicing the correct way to walk and stand, the stiff ruffled dresses and overly teased hair, the ribbons, the nail polish, the curled eyelashes. At age thirteen, a "lucky growth spurt" shot me to my present height of five eleven (a good two inches taller than Jerry, as I often like to remind him) and saved me from Runway Hell. Mother was crushed that her baby doll was gone, and horrified by my taste for basketball and running track. Then, when I was nineteen and needed the money, I entered the Miss Parkland Pageant—my decision, not my mother's. I won. Mother was thrilled, and ready for the new campaign. When I refused to go on to Miss North Carolina, she practically disowned me. We've hardly spoken in the eight years since.

I took a sip of tea. "Mother never got over my defection to a normal life."

"Well, you don't have to take it out on everyone else."

"And you don't have to be a side-show act."

He pointed a French fry at me. "Touché."

I took another bite of barbecue, savoring the taste. "What does this house of yours look like?"

"The letter doesn't say. Probably the community eyesore. I could always sell it, I suppose."

"Let's go see."

"Are you serious?"

"As you said, I'm not doing anything right now."

He looked crestfallen. "Mac, I really didn't mean to say that."

I leaned over the table to give his arm a friendly punch. "I know that, you idiot. Haven't we been friends long enough?"

He smiled. "You're going to be a success. I sense it in the deepest core of my psychic being."

"If you're going to talk like that, I won't go with you."

He laughed. "Okay, okay. I'll try to keep it under control."

I'd been trying to keep something under control, too, trying to ignore the feelings I almost couldn't believe. Sitting here in Baxter's, surrounded by the comforting smells of fries and hush puppies, and looking at my best friend's smile, I knew in the deepest core of *my* being that I would go anywhere in the world with Jeremyn Nicholas Fairweather.

This was crazy. Jerry and I had been friends since we met in college almost ten years ago. It was just that friendly feeling, wasn't it? Lately, though, my heart had given a bizarre little jump every time he grinned at me. I found myself wondering what it would be like to brush his wayward hair out of his eyes, or take off that absurd tie—along with everything else he had on.

I was on the rebound from Bill. That had to be it. Even though my ex-husband was a lout who cared only for himself, I missed having him around the house. I missed the house, too. Maybe I was having separation anxiety. No Bill, no house, and certainly no career, the way things were going lately. Anyway, it wouldn't do to declare my feelings to Jerry, since the only thing he was interested in right now was his lunch. He'd wonder what had gotten into his old college buddy. I wondered, too.

After casting the demon out of Betsy's grandma, Jerry and I drove to Celosia, a small town about a half-hour's drive from Parkland. I'd been there a few times, mainly to check out the bookstore. As we crossed the town line, the scenery wasn't inspiring: pastures with drooping cows, little grocery stores, abandoned gas stations. Jerry's uncle's house was probably a shack with a washing machine on the front porch and scrawny chickens running in the yard. Closer in the houses were larger and nicer. We passed a modern apartment complex, banks, shops, even a small mall.

"Is this Main Street?" Jerry asked. "We need to find the offices of Mason and Freer so I can pick up the keys to the house."

"I think this is Main," I said. "I don't see any signs. I don't see much of anything. That could be Amelia Earhart over there, but I'm not really sure."

We drove past the Baker Auditorium, the Wayfarer Motel,

the public library, and a small park with swings, slides, and a band shell. At the band shell, a large group of people stood in clumps. I saw band members in uniforms, horses, convertibles, and clowns.

"Parade time," I said. "What's the occasion, I wonder? Annual Hayseed Festival?"

Jerry turned at the next corner and pulled into the gas station. He got out, unhooked the handle, and pumped some gas. Several men were standing around, so he asked them about the law office.

A lanky man in faded jeans and John Deere cap spoke around the wad of tobacco tucked in one cheek. "Down two stoplights and turn right. It's a big brick building."

I leaned out my window. "What's with the parade?"

"Beauty pageant this weekend. All the girls are riding in the parade."

I groaned. "Is there no escape?"

Jerry grinned. "I love beauty pageants. We'll have to hurry and check out the house."

"You got relatives here?" the man said.

"My uncle, Val Eberlin."

He almost choked on his tobacco. "Eberlin? Sheesh, he was a nut!" His face turned red. "Oh, sorry. No offense. Sorry."

"It's okay," Jerry said. "I didn't really know him. I'm here to see about the house." He handed the man the money for the gas.

The man gave him his change. "Not planning to live in it, are you?"

"Probably not."

"Yeah, well, sorry about the crack. He was a nice old guy, really, just, you know, weird. Had a great old car, though, a 1957 Chevy. Thing ran like a dream."

Another car rolled in, and the man went to speak with the driver.

Jerry got in the car. "Did you see how he reacted?"

"Yes, this is just peachy," I said. "A pageant *and* a nutty uncle."

By the time Jerry found the law office and parked in the small lot under a tree, people were gathering along both sides of the street.

"We might get to see the parade," he said.

"I can't think of anything more exciting."

I waited by the car while he went inside to sign some papers and get the key to the house. The crowd was an odd combination. There were grubby-looking families: skinny, untidy dads in overalls and caps, overweight, stringy-haired moms in sweat-stained clothes, and pale, skinny, barefooted children. Then there were young, upscale families: dads in expensive khakis and golf shirts, moms in designer jeans and gold jewelry, and children in name-brand tee shirts and sneakers. I know lots of people live in Celosia and commute to Parkland, so there's plenty of money in this little town. From the size of these families, Celosia was obviously a good place to raise children. This thought was even more depressing than the droopy cows. Bill and I had fought about children practically our whole marriage.

Jerry came out, holding up a large key. We were getting in the car when the strangled sounds of a high-school band made us stop, and to Jerry's delight the parade came staggering up the street.

"I've got to see this, Mac."

We found a spot and watched. Clowns tried handstands and cartwheels. Horses snorted and shook their heads. A group of young women in sparkly gowns rode by in convertibles. The signs on the cars read "Miss Tri-County," "Miss Little Acres," and "Miss Peace Haven." A bright red Corvette drove by, carrying a stunning brunette in white. The handmade sign on the side of the Corvette read "Miss Celosia

High." She was slender and regal with dark eyes set in a heart-shaped face.

The nearest native was a stout man in overalls and a cap with a picture of a fish. Jerry asked him about the brunette.

"Juliet Lovelace," the man answered. "Pretty little thing, ain't she?"

"Outstanding." Jerry watched admiringly as she rearranged the folds of her sparkly gown and shook back her long dark hair. "When's the pageant?"

The man eyed him, and then let his gaze travel up to my face. "New in town, ain't ya. The pageant's run by Evan James. Runs it every year, and every year, it's the first Saturday night in July, Baker Auditorium."

"Thanks."

Juliet Lovelace smiled an especially big smile at Jerry.

"Whew," he said. "Do you think she's more than eighteen?"

I shook my head. "Dream on, junior. 'Miss Celosia High,' as in high school."

"She is gorgeous."

I pulled Jerry away. "I don't think you need to be ogling the teenage girls, Mr. New in Town and Likely to Be Run Out on a Rail."

"No harm in looking, is there?"

"What about Olivia?"

"Oh." He grimaced. "That's over."

I couldn't believe the feeling of relief that swept over me. "Why? I thought you two were an item."

"An item on the marked-down sales table. She's after me to get my money back. That's all she talks about."

"Well, I'd like you to get your money back, too. Then you could give it to me."

"I don't want any of the family money. I think I've made that clear."

"And you have your super-secret reasons—unless you've told Olivia."

"No. That's another reason she's mad at me."

Movement caught my eye. I had to look twice to believe what I saw. "Jerry, are those protest signs?"

He looked. "Who would protest a parade?"

"I'm going to check it out."

A group of three women and one man had gathered beside a large oak tree at the corner. All four carried pieces of bright yellow poster board with black letters. When I got closer, I read the signs and had my second moment of disbelief.

"Pageants Unfair to Women" one read. Another read "We Are Not Hunks of Meat." The group stood tight-lipped and stony-faced while the crowd made a wide circle around them. Several people made unkind remarks or hustled their children past, glaring.

One of the upscale moms paused to scowl at the one man in the group. "Is there some reason you have to ruin everything? If you don't like pageants, you don't have to go."

"It's a free country," the man said. He was tall and good-looking, with dark hair and dark eyes.

She shook her finger at him. "Ted Stacy, you are not setting a good example."

"Excuse me, Mrs. Marsh, but I'm doing exactly that," he said. "I'm exercising my rights as a citizen of the United States to speak my mind about an outdated custom that degrades all women, yourself included."

"Well, I think you're being ridiculous."

"Since you were a former Miss Celosia High, I'm not surprised to hear you say that."

She turned and left, her back rigid with disapproval. Ted Stacy smiled at me. "Welcome to Celosia. Ted Stacy, protester."

"Madeline Maclin, private investigator."

His smile widened. "Really? Evan will be glad to hear

that. Celosia doesn't have any private investigators, and he needs one. He thinks we're sabotaging his silly pageant."

"Sabotaging?"

"You might want to talk to him. Evan James. He runs the pageant every year. There's been trouble at the auditorium lately."

"But we're not responsible," one of the woman protesters said.

Ted Stacy said, "We just want to make people think, although it's an uphill battle in this town."

"I'm Samantha Terrell," the woman said. "Are you new to Celosia, or just in town for the parade?"

"My friend and I came to check on some property he inherited," I said. "Val Eberlin's old house."

All four protesters looked surprised. "Is your friend related to Val Eberlin?" Samantha Terrell asked.

"His nephew."

"Well, old Val was quite a character," Ted said. "You'll hear all sorts of stories about him."

"What happened to him?"

"Heart attack. The mailman found him on the floor."

"Ted, we need to go," the other woman said.

He smiled at me. "Nice meeting you, Ms. Maclin."

I walked back to Jerry, who was waving at the other beauty queens. We stood and watched the parade until it was all the way up Main Street. The bands made up for their lack of tunefulness with a lot of rhythm, the flag team's snappy routine, and the vigorous drum beat. The clowns threw candy to the children. The beauty queens smiled and waved.

"Did you check out the main protester?" Jerry asked.

"Ted Stacy. He said your uncle was quite a character and died of a heart attack at home."

"Maybe I can get in touch with him in the house."

I don't know where he gets these ideas. "Will you stop talking like you can actually do stuff like that?"

"But wouldn't it be neat?"

"Let's take care of business so I can get home."

So we drove out to find Jerry's inheritance.

Jerry squinted at the faded road signs. "Mason said the house is just a little ways outside of town."

"Did he say what the house is worth?"

"Just that it was old and needed repair. He was more interested in whether or not I was going to stay."

"So am I."

"It might be nice."

Since the word "stay" is rarely in Jerry's vocabulary, I wondered what was going on. "Are you on the run from the local authorities?"

"Just the CIA."

Why did I think I'd ever get a straight answer? I glanced at the yellow fields bordered by tall wildflowers. A rail fence wandered haphazardly along one side of the road. On the other side, more cows stared blankly from green pastures. When I saw the large two-story gray farmhouse in the middle of an unkempt meadow, I knew it must be the Eberlin house.

"It doesn't look too bad," Jerry said.

"We're still far away."

"No, it's all right." He stopped the car to read "Eberlin" on the dented mailbox, then drove up the winding dirt driveway to park under one of the large shade trees spaced evenly around the house.

I got out and stood beside Jerry to take our first good look at the Eberlin house. If it wasn't haunted, it should have been. It looked dirty, drafty, and full of rats. I'd be sneezing all afternoon, and Jerry would be seeing Lord knows what in all the shadows. A few of the windows were broken, a few shutters hung crookedly. The wide front porch sagged. Several wooden rocking chairs were propped upside down against the porch wall.

But Jerry seemed pleased. "You know, a paint job, a few repairs, this place could be really nice."

"You're kidding, right?"

We went up the uneven steps. Jerry unlocked the front door. It swung open quietly at his touch; no squeaking monster-movie sounds. We stepped inside.

The house was cool and hushed. Sunlight and leaf patterns danced on the walls. A few silver cobwebs stretched in the corners of the tall windows and trembled in the breeze from the open door. Victorian-style furniture, dark, carved wooden chairs, and a sofa with gray cushions filled the large living room. The worn gray carpet had a pattern of faded pink roses and green leaves.

I tried the light switch. The power was still on. "Not bad, if you like gray. Nice marble fireplace. Furniture from the Plymouth Rock Collection. Might be worth something."

Jerry started up the flight of dusty stairs. "Be careful. There're a couple of loose boards here."

Upstairs, we found five bedrooms, three bathrooms, and a parlor. One of the bedrooms obviously belonged to Val Eberlin. The large four-poster bed had cream-colored sheets and blankets. Resting on the bureau was a silver comb and brush, a handful of change, a handkerchief, and a framed picture too faded for Jerry to recognize any of the people. The bedroom smelled musty. Eberlin's clothes hung neatly in the closet: white shirts, brown slacks, brown sweaters, and a heavy coat of beige tweed. Three pairs of brown shoes were on the closet floor, plus a walking stick and an umbrella. No other clues gave any idea what kind of man Jerry's uncle might have been. There were no pictures on the walls, no books, no souvenirs or knickknacks.

The other bedrooms were even more featureless: beds, chairs, rugs, curtains, lamps. That was it. In the bathrooms, we found towels, soap, toilet paper, and scrubbing brushes. In the parlor was another set of Victorian furniture with light green upholstery, a marble-topped table with a fancy green lamp, light green draperies, an old phonograph, and a bookshelf with leather-bound editions of classics like *The Count of Monte Cristo* and *Tom Sawyer*.

"Doesn't tell us a whole lot," I said.

"Maybe he stored things in the attic."

"Like an insane wife?"

He gave me a look and went up the smaller flight of stairs leading from the landing. He tried the attic door, but it was locked and the key didn't fit.

"Can't you pick the lock?" I asked.

"I'm out of practice."

"Didn't you and Jeff have some sort of daring escape act?" During our college days, Jerry and his friend Jeff West had tried several paranormal schemes, each one ridiculous. They'd also tried magic acts, usually making money disappear from people's pockets.

"I'd need my special keys." He dusted his hands. "Guess we save that for later."

"Seen enough?"

"I like it."

"You can't be serious."

"Let's check out the kitchen."

The kitchen was downstairs at the back of the house. It was large and complete with modern appliances. I sat down in one of the sturdy white wooden chairs at the matching table. "I thought we might be cooking over a wood stove."

Jerry checked the refrigerator, which was empty, and the cabinets, where he discovered some blue-and-white dishes. Then he stood for a moment, looking at the full view of the meadow from a row of wide windows with white draperies. He frowned.

"I wonder what he did. There's no TV, no sign of any hobby, no magazines. From the looks of the meadow, he wasn't a farmer."

"Maybe he traveled a lot. Maybe he wasn't home much."

"Maybe," Jerry said. He came to the table and sat down. He had an odd, preoccupied look that meant he was actually doing some serious thinking.

I wondered if he was considering staying in the house, if he might finally want to settle down. "What's on your mind?"

"I don't know. Something about the way the light's coming in."

"So do you have that special 'feeling'?"

"I'm going to stay overnight. We can go buy some groceries and a couple of toothbrushes. And we can check on the pageant."

"You just want another look at Juliet Lovelace."

"And you probably wouldn't mind another look at Ted Stacy."

"What about your séance?"

He looked at his watch. "Oops. I'll call and say the spirits weren't aligned. Borrow your phone?"

Jerry called and apologized for missing the big event. Then I took the phone and called to check my messages. There were none.

"This is getting depressing," I said.

"Can't get any worse."

"Don't say that."

A knock on the front door made us both jump.

"Must be the Welcome Wagon," I said.

It was something far from welcoming. Jerry opened the door. There stood a petite platinum blonde, hands on hips.

"Oh," he said. "Hi, Olivia."

Olivia Decker is a very pretty young woman, but she's eternally pissed about something or another. She works for a law firm, so she's always dressed in beautifully cut suits that show off her figure. Today's suit was black. So was her mood. Her green eyes narrowed.

"You inherited a house and didn't tell me?"

"I didn't know until today. How did you find out?"

"My associate asked me if I was going to help you with the details. I told him that was the first I'd heard of any property in Celosia. Then a Mrs. Amelia Farnsworth corners me in front of the office to ask why you missed her appointment. Seems she had something important to ask her dear departed husband."

"I just called and explained things to her."

"You should have called and explained things to me."

Jerry held up both hands. "Wait a minute. Skip back a couple of days. Aren't we over?"

"Not necessarily." She came in, looking around as if appraising the room. I could see the dollar signs dancing in those green eyes. She glanced my way. "And what's she doing here?"

"Nice to see you, too, Olivia."

She ignored me and continued to inspect the room. "This has real possibilities. You are planning to sell it, aren't you?"

"No, I'm planning to keep it," Jerry said.

She faced him, eyes wide. "Keep it? You give up the Fairweather Mansion, but you want to keep this rat trap?"

"I'm going to set up shop. Psychic Shop."

"Oh, for heaven's sake. When are you going to stop? You can't make a living doing séances. Why don't you take your share of your family's money? You're entitled to it."

Jerry's voice was cold. "This has nothing to do with my family."

"Of course it does. I don't have to be a trained psychiatrist to see what's going on here."

"I don't want to talk about my family. I've told you."

I hoped Olivia would push further into the taboo subject so Jerry would get angry and make her go away, but she realized her mistake and softened her approach.

"Yes, you did, and I apologize. I'm just, well, puzzled about your intentions."

"I like this house. I want to fix it up."

I could tell by her expression she'd decided to humor him. "Okay. Let's talk about what it would cost."

Olivia can go on for hours about expenses and profits. I didn't want to look at or listen to her. "Jerry, I'm going to town for groceries."

"Okay, thanks," he said, but his eyes were on Olivia.

I HAD ANOTHER REASON for going back into town. Maybe there was something to the pageant sabotage. Maybe Evan James really could use my help. No harm in asking. Besides, did I really want to hang around Uncle Val's house and watch Jerry and Olivia kiss and make up?

We had passed Baker Auditorium on our way into town, so after a brief stop at the gas station to ask the attendant for directions, I found my way to the large brick building. I parked the VW in the shady parking lot and went inside. I smelled a faintly charred smell, as if there'd been a fire. The auditorium, which looked as if it would seat about four hundred, was cool and dark. Soft gray walls and darker chairs blended with the carpets and velvety curtains that framed the stage. On stage, the twelve pageant contestants, dressed in lurid outfits of magenta, pink, and Day-Glo orange, attempted a disorganized dance number, which was set in Venice, complete with cardboard gondolas. A large man in a green caftan shouted instructions.

"No, no, Miss Peace Haven! To your left! Left! The other way! Miss Tri-County, you are two steps behind. Girls, look alive! The pageant is Saturday night!"

A voice near my elbow said, "May I help you?"

I looked down. A small woman with dark eyebrows and overlarge glasses peered up at me like a raccoon from a hole.

"I'd like to speak with Evan James."

"Are you here about being a judge? We already have our judges."

"No, I'm here on other business."

She hurried down the aisle and held a brief conversation with a thin man who stood and walked up the aisle to me. With his blue suit and a yellow polka-dotted scarf folded around his neck like an ascot, he looked ready for tea at the Kentucky Derby. He had a clipboard in one hand and a yellow handkerchief in the other, which he used to wipe his brow and sparse brown hair. When he saw me, he did a double take.

"Madeline Maclin? Miss Parkland, if I'm not mistaken!"

The little raccoon woman followed him. She looked at me with new respect.

"That was some time ago," I said.

Evan James shook my hand. "But I never forget a queen. We're delighted to have you."

"Before you get too delighted, I've traded in my tiara. I'm here to investigate your reports of sabotage."

He blinked as if unable to process this information. "You're not here as one of our visiting queens?"

God forbid. "I'm a private investigator, Mr. James. I understand you're having some trouble, and I'd like to help if I can."

He sighed and perched on the arm of the nearest seat. The little woman sat across the aisle. "This pageant's been nothing but trouble," he said. "One disaster after another. You can probably smell the smoke. The other day, one of our curtains caught fire. I just managed to catch it before the whole thing was destroyed. We were sent the wrong outfits for the opening number. Our musical director got sick, so I had to hire Percy." He indicated the man in the caftan. "He and I do not share the same vision for this pageant, that's all I can say about that. And now, for the first time in the pageant's history, we have protesters. I can't believe it. My pageants are always clean, decent family entertainment. The girls in this town look forward to being in the show. We give out nice cash prizes and beautiful trophies and crowns. What's to protest?"

"You think someone is sabotaging the pageant?"

"What else could it be? As for hiring an investigator." He gave me a long considering look. Was he just seeing me as a visiting queen? He surprised me. "Yes. I think that's an excellent idea."

Shrieks of outrage came from Percy. His caftan billowed as he raised his arms. "Don't you girls realize people are going to pay to see this? Do you want to look like idiots? Try it again."

Evan James spoke to the little woman. "I'd better go smooth some feathers. Ms. Maclin, we'll discuss the details later, but if you can get started right away, I'd appreciate it. The pageant's in four days!"

"Of course. I'll need to have a look around."

"Certainly. Cindy, will you answer any questions she may have?"

Cindy turned to me with an eager expression. "Where would you like to go first, Ms. Maclin?"

"Madeline, please. I'd like to have a look backstage."

While Evan James had a tense conversation with Percy about yelling at the contestants, Cindy pulled back the stage left curtain and showed me the charred edge.

"If we keep it pulled back like this, the burned places hardly show. There's no way we could buy a new curtain in time for the pageant. It was really lucky Evan was working here that evening and smelled smoke."

"When was this?"

"Last evening."

"Evan was the only one here?"

"As far as I know."

The curtain was thick heavy velvet. I picked up the burned end. "Did anyone call the fire department?"

"No. He was able to put the fire out. It was just smoldering, he said. Our insurance will cover the damage, so it's really more of an annoyance than anything."

"Do you have any idea what could have caused the fire?"

Cindy shook her head. "I thought maybe a light overheated, but the lights are all there."

She pointed to the rows of lights above us. I looked around for electric cords or outlets that may have overheated, but the floor under the curtains was bare. "Is there anyone who might be unhappy with Evan about something? Someone with a grudge?"

"Oh, no. He's a very nice man, just a bit single-minded about pageants. If he had his way, we'd have a pageant every month."

I repressed a shudder. "What about Ted Stacy and the other protesters?"

She looked surprised. "I don't know. This looks more like a prank, something kids would do."

"Are there kids in town who'd set fire to curtains?"

"Not that I know of personally, but Celosia's a small town. There's not much for teenagers to do. Maybe some of them snuck in here to smoke and drink and got carried away."

"Isn't the theater locked at night?"

"Yes, but it's an old building, and we don't have an alarm system. If somebody really wanted to get in, they probably could."

Evan James called for Cindy to assist him for a minute. I continued my inspection of the backstage area. It was cluttered with candy wrappers, wood shavings, odd pieces of wood and plastic, and a few scraps of duct tape. The smells of wood and paint made my stomach roll. Memories surfaced of my pageant days—huddled in the dark with dozens of other little girls, our stiff dresses keeping us apart, my smile glued on, ready to walk out into that blinding white light, terrified that I'd stand with the wrong foot in front, or forget to turn the correct way and give the judges that one last flash of teeth.

Brrrr! Those days were over! I concentrated on the floor of the stage. Like most backstage floors, it could use a good sweeping. Dust bunnies rolled in the sawdust as I walked behind the back curtain past stacks of lumber, ladders, paint cans, and music stands. Chairs were stacked in one corner, and several loops of rope and electric cords hung from brackets set high in the wall.

Cindy returned. "Are you finished here, Madeline?"

"Has anyone checked those electric cords?"

"They aren't connected to anything. They're just up there out of the way. Did you need to see anything else back here? The dressing rooms?"

"Yes, thanks."

The dressing rooms were small with long counters and lighted mirrors. The contestants had crammed every inch with gowns, shoes, makeup, and beauty utensils. The smell of perfume and hair spray made Cindy wave her hand in front of her nose.

"I don't know how they stand it."

I took some deep breaths, too, but for another reason. I was going to have to do something about these pageant flashbacks. "Could you show me the rest of the building?"

Cindy led me back out on stage and down some steps to the auditorium. She pointed to a room high up in the back wall. "That's our light booth." We went up the aisle to the lobby where she pointed out another room. "Box office there, restrooms on either side. That's everything on the first floor. Evan's office is upstairs. The judges are meeting there."

"I'd like to meet them."

Cindy led the way up one flight of stairs to an office on the second floor of the auditorium and introduced me to the judges: Benjy Goins, a local DJ, a weary-looking man with scruffy hair and a full beard; Kimberly Dawn Williams, a former Miss Celosia, a heavily lacquered blonde wearing too much eye shadow and too much perfume; and Chuck Hofsteder, a chubby, good-natured man who'd judged several local beauty pageants.

"I remember when you won Miss Parkland," Hofsteder said. "Pleasure to meet you, Ms. Maclin. Thought for sure you'd go on to Miss North Carolina. What happened?"

"Change of plans."

"Well, you sure could've taken the crown."

Cindy passed out some sheets of paper. "Updated agenda. Interviews start today. Tomorrow, we'll finish interviews and have dinner at the country club. The pageant's at eight Saturday night. I'll have a list for each of you."

"Anyone promising so far?" I asked the judges.

"Miss Celosia High," Hofsteder said. "She's got quite a lot of stage presence. Miss Peace Haven looks good, too. I'd say it's quite a nice crop of girls."

I never got used to the casual way everyone referred to pageant contestants as "girls." How's your girl doing? Is your girl up to standard? Our girl's not feeling well. That sort of thing. This girl got really tired of the pet-shop attitude. Come on, old girl. Let's go for a run.

"Are you staying at the Wayfarer?" Hofsteder asked.

"No, a friend of mine has a house here, so I'm staying with him. You probably know it. Val Eberlin's place."

His broad face fell. "Really? You're staying there? At night?"

"During the day, too," I said. "How haunted is it?"

"Well, there've been a number of rumors about the place."

"Such as?"

Hofsteder seemed reluctant to elaborate. "Odd noises, strange shapes, that sort of thing."

Kimberly Dawn Williams leaned toward me. "Did I hear you say you were staying in Val Eberlin's house? It's nonsense, all of it. Val was a very nice gentleman, just a little eccentric."

"Wasn't there half the time," Benjy Goins said.

"What about all those lights in the attic?" Hofsteder said. "I had some people on my street ready to swear he was a mad scientist."

Kimberly Dawn dismissed this notion with a wave of her pink-tipped hand. "Nonsense. When he went off on his trips, he had timers on the lights."

"Not that any burglar would bother that house," Goins said.

"Excuse me," Cindy said, "could we get back to the pageant and leave the useless speculation for later?"

Chuck Hofsteder grinned and said to me, "There's another rumor going around that Evan James is not the one in charge here."

A short while later, when Cindy was certain they knew everything they needed to know, the judges were sent off to prepare for their interviews. I went back out through the auditorium to discuss the details of my assignment with Mr. James. He was sitting in the front row. Percy had set up a video camera on a tripod to film the dance. The contestants were making their way through the choreography with varying degrees of success. Miss Tri-County couldn't dance at all. Miss River Valley Falls kept the beat, doing interesting things with her arms. As for Miss Celosia High, she was perfect. Elegant. Graceful. Coordinated. She caught my eye and gave me a look I had seen many times in many pageants. This young woman was a shark, and she would win if she had to savage everyone in her path.

Percy waved his hands above his head as if signaling a jet plane to land. "Stop, stop, stop! Girls, for heaven's sake. All of you come around here and look at yourselves. I guarantee you'll be absolutely shocked."

They crowded around the camera to watch the playback. Some of them snickered.

Percy drew himself up. "Think it's funny, do you? I did not choreograph a comedy routine. Look here. Juliet is the only one dancing in time to the music."

Juliet Lovelace looked smug. The other contestants straightened and moved away from the tiny screen. They didn't say anything, but their dark glances and rigid posture telegraphed a world of hate for Miss Celosia High.

Percy seemed oblivious to this show of resentment, or maybe he just didn't care as long as they performed up to his standards. He clapped his hands. "Now let's try it again."

When Evan James saw me, he got up. "I must apologize for all the disorganization today."

"That's all right. I know how pageants can be. Cindy was very helpful, but I'd like to speak with the contestants."

He checked his watch. "Oh, dear. They're really busy today with dance rehearsal and interviews. We're on such a tight schedule. Could you speak with them tomorrow, say, around 1:30?"

"That would be fine."

He shook my hand. "I can't tell you how relieved I am having a real queen on the case, Ms. Maclin."

A real investigator, I wanted to say, but I smiled and thanked him.

I LEFT THE VW BUG in the theater parking lot and walked down Main Street heading for the bookstore—Georgia's Books. I hoped that Olivia had steamed back to Parkland, but if she stayed and if she and Jerry were going to argue all night, I'd need something to read.

I stepped inside and went over to the magazine section that stretched the length of the store. There were several customers in the broad aisles. Two women hunted through Georgia's vast array of crochet and needlework magazines. Teenagers slouched against the back wall of the comics section, checking out the latest *Spiderman, Black Orchid,* and *Anthrax Monthly.* Another customer collected his weekly supply of tabloids. A woman and a small boy selected a birthday present from the children's books.

Georgia Taylor, a slim woman who looked to be in her sixties, checked the display of best sellers in the front window, keeping her eye on a big ugly man in the classics section. He wore a cape over his gray suit, so I figured he must have been in the parade. The man gave me a brief nod and strode up to the counter, the cape swirling behind him. His domed forehead sloped back into a tangle of wild gray curls that wobbled as he gestured. His prominent teeth flashed.

"A word with you, Hayden, if you please!"

The man behind the counter was a very nice-looking young man, about Jerry's size, with dark brown hair and blue-green eyes. "What is it this time, Prill?"

Prill tossed his curls. "How can you continue to ignore the contributions of the Futuristic Literary and Universal Feelings group? We are the mainstay of this pitiful little town's cultural development, and we have yet to be featured in any display in this miserable excuse for a bookstore. I have repeatedly told you of our accomplishments, and you repeatedly ignore them! What's the world coming to when a legitimate literary organization cannot get the slightest bit of help from other institutions devoted to the fine arts?"

"Prill, I've explained—"

"And to think of all the work we've done in this provincial wasteland! Poetry readings in the park, poetry teas, round robins, socials—" He broke off. "Have you read *Destinies,* by our vice president, Emily Nesp?"

"Yes, I have and—"

"Then you must admit the work is superior to Tebling's drivel." He gestured with a large, well-manicured hand to the poetry section, where poet John Tebling's best-selling volumes were artfully displayed amidst ribbons and dried flowers.

"It's a pleasant enough piece, but—"

"Then display it! Promote it! Good heavens, sir, do I have to think of everything?"

"Will you let me finish a sentence?" When the big man gave a slight begrudging nod, Hayden said, "I've told you a dozen times we have limited space and many other works to consider. And frankly, I think Miss Nesp's work is a bit overdone."

Prill had just enough chin to quiver with indignation. "Overdone!"

"There are a lot of meaningless words strung together."

"Meaningless! Those phrases are dynamic! 'The tearing limb of gratitude.' 'Blocks of Justice wrapped in faithful timeliness.' 'Fragrant withering spasmodic bells.' Excellent phrases, sir! Magnificent!"

Hayden looked around for support, but Georgia hid behind the rack of postcards. The other customers melted into the background. "Just what exactly is a tearing limb of gratitude?"

"I shouldn't have to explain anything to you. Good heavens, man, you're a poet! You're one of us."

"Not really."

Prill leaned on the counter. "Still stuck, are you? Serves you right. You're a stumbling block for those of us climbing the ladder of success, a high wind assailing our delicate skimmers of fancy."

He paused as if expecting applause. "Does no one around here appreciate true talent?" He turned back to Hayden. "So, how long has it been?"

"Three months," he said.

Prill made a face. "Well, I didn't come here to talk about your troubles. What about FLUF? They deserve recognition."

He called over his shoulder. "Georgia, I know you're back there. You are no help whatsoever."

"Don't look at me" came a voice from behind the postcards. "I just own the place."

"Hayden, I expect you to pull strings for me."

"I can't pull strings for you or anyone else," he said. "Sorry."

"Then what good are you?"

Hayden laughed. "I'll buy you a drink."

Prill flipped back his cape. "An offensive attempt at compromise, and one I shall accept. I warn you, though, I intend to continue to plead my case." He looked around, saw me, and said, "Young lady, are you a poetry lover?"

"I like it well enough," I said, "if it makes sense."

"Are you familiar with the work of Emily Nesp?"

"No, I'm sorry. I've never heard of her."

He glared at Hayden. "You see? If you'd had her work out where people could see it, this charming young visitor to our fair town would've been able to ascertain for herself the beauty and wonder of Miss Nesp's verse."

I could tell Hayden was trying not to laugh. "I read mysteries mostly," I said.

"Ah, then maybe you can help Hayden solve the Mystery of the Writer's Block. Wouldn't that be nice, Hayden? Georgia, I must fly. I'll meet you across the street, Hayden. Don't be late."

He sailed out. Georgia chuckled. "I hope Gregory didn't scare you off. He's all wind."

"He was very entertaining," I said. "I'm Madeline Maclin."

"Georgia Taylor. I think I've seen you in the store before."

"Yes, I try to stop in whenever I'm in town."

"I'm Hayden Amry," the young man said.

"I actually do solve mysteries." He had a wonderful smile. "So if you have one…"

"I don't think you can help with this one. I haven't had an

idea in three months. I'm beginning to think I'll never write anything again."

"Now, now," Georgia said, "none of that. He tends to get depressed," she said to me. "All that artistic temperament. It's unhealthy."

Hayden smiled at her obvious concern. "It wouldn't be so bad except Shana's on the best-seller list every week. It compounds the failure."

"Shana?" I said.

"Shana Fairbourne. That's my wife, and that's her display over there."

I turned to look at the large display of paperback books featuring bright red covers with stylized gold flames around embossed hearts. Shiny gold letters proclaimed in bold letters "*Flames,* the Provocative New Novel by Shana Fairbourne, Best-Selling Author of *Suppressed Desires.*" I picked up one of the books. Shana Fairbourne's picture was on the back. She was a stunning redhead.

A gorgeous wife. Okay. Talk about suppressed desires.

"'Fairbourne' was Shana's agent's idea," Hayden said. "He didn't care for Fields, Shana's maiden name. Too plain, he said. And Amry was too odd. Thank goodness Shana had an exotic first name, or they'd have to invent one."

"I'm sorry to say I've never read any of her books, either."

"They're what the industry calls 'bodice rippers,' big sprawling sex stories set against some historical background."

The kind of book I never read. "And what do you write?"

"When I write, I write short poems that take me months to finish."

Not something I'd read, either. "Well, I'm sure you'll get inspiration again."

"Thanks," he said. "Are you in town for the pageant?"

"My friend and I came to see about the Eberlin house. His uncle left it to him."

I was surprised to see Hayden Amry turn pale. "My goodness. He's not planning to live there, is he?"

"Is there something wrong with it?"

"Now, now," Georgia said to Hayden, "don't start putting ideas into her head. Ms. Maclin, Hayden believes in ghosts, but I don't. You have a big old house outside of town so naturally everyone invents stories. Val Eberlin was a very nice man. He was in here often. I was very sorry to hear he'd passed away."

"Can you tell me anything else about him? Jerry only met him when he was a child, and there aren't many clues at the house."

"Well, I know he liked cornflakes. Tessie Newall down at Food City says she never saw somebody buy so many boxes. He was always real polite, paid with cash. Let's see. Occasionally he attended First Baptist Church. He always bought Girl Scout cookies from Averall Mercer's niece. Just a nice man."

"Yes, he was," Hayden said. "I apologize. The house has always looked a little scary to me."

"It looks scary to me, too," I said.

Georgia straightened the stack of free bookmarks on the counter. "The nephew's name is Jerry, you said?"

"Jerry Fairweather."

"And what does he do?"

As little as possible. "I guess you'd say he's a sort of consultant."

"Well, he's welcome in Celosia, and you, too, dear. Are you a consultant, too?"

"In a way. I'm a private investigator."

Hayden smiled. "So you weren't kidding about solving mysteries."

"Actually, I'm looking for work, if you hear of anyone needing my services. I was just talking with Evan James about the trouble he's having with the pageant."

Georgia shook her head. "Pageants. Silly things."

"I don't know much about them," Hayden said, "but if you can help Evan, that would be great. He worries about every little thing."

"Like someone else I know," Georgia said.

A small, hunched man slid two copies of *TV Guide* onto the counter and spoke to Hayden in a low voice. "Hear you have ghosts."

"Yes, I do," he said. "How did you find out?"

The man tapped his forehead, his long mustache drooping. "The alien network is always humming with news." He nodded wisely and looked both ways before adding, "Want my advice?"

"Yes, of course."

He lowered his voice even further. "Bread crumbs."

Okay.

"Any particular kind?" Hayden asked.

"White works best. You sprinkle them near all entry ways. Ghosts won't come in."

"Thanks, I'll try it." He rang up the magazines and put them in a bag.

The man handed him several limp, faded dollars. "I'm going to a high council tonight. I'll ask them what to do, and I'll stop by some night. How about Friday?"

"I'd appreciate that, Bummer."

Bummer nodded again and went out. Georgia came around to the register. "Mr. Stevenson was quite chatty."

"He was in the mood to talk, I guess."

"He likes you, Hayden. You're always so patient with him."

"Well, I feel a little sorry for him," he said. "Nobody believes his stories about being abducted by UFOs. What if he's telling the truth? Stranger things have happened."

"Is his name really Bummer?" I asked.

"He likes to be called that," Georgia said. "He tiptoed through one too many mushroom fields in the Sixties, dear."

She patted Hayden's arm. "I'm so glad I have Hayden to handle all my eccentrics."

Another customer came to the register, and Hayden went to help her. I found the magazine I wanted, paid and left the store.

Across the street from Georgia's Books was a drug store remodeled to resemble a drug store of the Fifties, complete with soda fountain, juke box, ceiling fans, and booths with red vinyl seats. I sat down on one of the red vinyl stools at the counter. Gregory Prill got up from a booth and sat on the stool beside me.

"Allow me to buy you a drink, Ms. Maclin. I must atone for my boorish behavior in the bookstore."

"No problem," I said.

He snapped his fingers at the girl behind the counter. "Annie. Two Cokes, please, and make them sing."

Annie rolled her eyes. "Yes, sir."

Gregory Prill fixed his bulging gaze on me. "Now, then. Tell all. No secret is safe in Celosia. You've been seen on the street, so the town is abuzz. Who are you, and who is the cute man with you?"

I handed him one of my cards. "Madeline Maclin of Madeline Maclin Investigations. The cute man is my friend Jerry Fairweather, Val Eberlin's nephew and new owner of the dreaded Eberlin house."

"Nicely put." He frowned at the card, looked at me, and frowned again. "You know, my dear, I think I've seen you. I do enjoy frequenting these little beauty pageants, and if I'm not mistaken, you were once a queen."

Once a queen, always a queen. "Miss Parkland."

"I knew it." His frown took in my tee shirt, jeans, and sneakers. "But, my dear, this ensemble is so not you. Are you in disguise?"

"Let me put it this way," I said. "If I never see another pageant, it will be too soon."

"Ah," he said. "Burnout. Understandable." He turned my card around in his long fingers. "This is a serious business, then. You're for hire?"

"Yes."

Annie brought our Cokes. Prill thanked her and passed me a straw. "Good. I have a job for you."

Two jobs in less than an hour. Could my luck finally be changing? "What can I do for you?"

"Not for me, for Hayden. The poor boy's convinced his house is haunted."

And two haunted houses in less than a day.

"Why would he think that?"

"Because he sees things that aren't there. Dinosaur monsters, ghostly women outside his window."

Hayden needed to meet Jerry.

Gregory Prill reached beneath the folds of his cape and pulled out his wallet. "I want you to find out what's going on in Hayden's house. Something's set him off, and I'm certain it isn't a ghost. If someone's playing a trick, it's a very cruel one. What's your fee?" I told him, and he handed me some money. "A retainer, if you will."

"Thank you," I said. "This is my first case of ghostbusting, but I'll do my best."

Gregory Prill, oddly enough, fixed me with his big goldfish eyes and said something I didn't realize I wanted to hear.

"I know, my dear Madeline. I have every faith in you."

TWO

I STOPPED BY the first grocery store I saw and bought milk, cereal, apples, cookies, and candy bars. On second thought, I added bread, peanut butter, ham slices, and cheese to my cart, as well as a carton of cola. Then I decided to visit the local Walmart and buy a few necessities. With two cases to work on, I needed to stay in town. Maybe the Eberlin house wouldn't be so bad for a couple of days.

It was about 7:00 PM when I got back to the house. I was relieved to see that Olivia's car was gone. Jerry was sitting on the front porch. He hopped up to help me with the bags of groceries.

"Wow! What's with all the stuff? Did I look that hungry?"

I handed him the drinks. "I'm happy to report I've got two cases, so I'll be staying over, at least for tonight, if that's okay."

"That's great. So, did the pageant guy hire you?"

"Yes, he did. It looks as if someone doesn't want the pageant to go on." I tried to make my next question sound casual. "Is Olivia coming back?"

"I don't know. She went on for a while about what it would cost to fix the house. Then she had to get back to Parkland to work on a brief or something."

He didn't seem too concerned. Maybe acquiring the house was the final blow to their relationship. If that was the case, and Jerry wanted to stay here, then I definitely wanted to stay here. I could learn to love this old dump.

We carried the bags into the kitchen. I put the milk and

apples in the refrigerator while Jerry found places for the cookies and candy on the counter. He opened the ham and cheese to make a sandwich.

"You mentioned two cases, Mac. What's the other one?"

"You'll like this. I stopped by the bookstore, and I met local poet Gregory Prill. He hired me to find out if his friend Hayden Amry's house is really haunted."

As I'd expected, Jerry's eyes lit up. "Another haunted house?"

I sat down and reached for the bread. "If this detective thing doesn't work out, I could always have a second career as an exorcist."

"I know all about exorcisms! You could be my sidekick."

"I was kidding, Jerry."

"I wasn't," he said, and for a moment, I could've sworn there was something more than friendship in his eyes. Maybe Olivia had pushed too hard. Maybe she wouldn't be back. Maybe he was finally seeing me as more than just good old Mac. Then he said, "I really need somebody to carry all the extra equipment. You have to make an exorcism look flashy."

I covered my disappointment by getting up to get a cola. "I doubt Hayden Amry's house is haunted. He seems to be a nice guy, just a little nervous."

"We could do an exorcism if you think it would make him feel better."

"I'll handle it, thanks."

Jerry took a bite of his sandwich. "What age is this guy?"

"Our age."

"Buck-toothed and spotty?"

"No, he's quite handsome."

"Great. That makes two possibilities in town."

What was he talking about now? "Possibilities?"

"For you." When I frowned, he said, "Mac, it's time you let yourself have a little fun. I know Bill was a louse, but not every man's like that."

"I don't really want to talk about this," I said. Not now. Not when I'm sitting across from the man I want. The one incredibly obtuse man.

"That protester, Ted Stacy. He looked like your kind of guy. Somebody who hates pageants as much as you do. Or this Hayden fellow. He works in a bookstore. You read books. A match made in heaven."

"He's married." Jerry as matchmaker was a more frightening idea than Jerry as exorcist. "Stop trying to fix me up."

"Okay."

"I don't pressure you to marry Olivia, do I?" God forbid. When he raised his eyebrows, I had to ask, "Do you want to marry Olivia?"

"Well, I'm not ready to make that leap yet. She is a bit hard to please."

At least he could see that. "If she's hard to please now, she's going to be hard to please later."

He took another bite of sandwich and chewed awhile. Then he said something that really alarmed me. "She might be worth it."

I didn't want anything else to eat. "It's been a long day. I'm going to pick out a bedroom."

"You can have Uncle Val's."

"No, thanks. That's for the lord of the manor."

I took my Walmart purchases upstairs and decided on the largest of the four guest rooms. I wasn't exactly sleepy, but I wanted to sort things out. Today, I'd quit one job and found two more. Today, I'd tried to escape my pageant past and failed. But I was here in the house with Jerry. Maybe not in the same bedroom, but that was another problem for me to solve.

EARLY THE NEXT MORNING a bizarre noise made my eyes pop open. For a moment, I had no idea where I was; then I remembered I was in the large guest room upstairs at the Eberlin house, haunted-house number one. The bizarre noise sounded again. I realized it was a rooster crowing. And now a chorus of tweets and chirps and hoots greeted the rising sun. Ah, the peace and quiet of the country. I burrowed back under the covers. I'd slept well and I hadn't been eaten by rats.

I must have drifted back to sleep because the next sound I heard was *"Scintille, diamant"* floating up the stairs. Jerry was brought up listening to classical music, so he's fond of opera, of all things. He knows several by heart, and if I don't stop him, he'll start at the beginning and sing one all the way through. Not that he can sing like a real opera singer. His voice is midrange and usually in key, but I've heard *The Tales of Hoffmann* too many times. He also likes one called *Paul Bunyan,* which is kind of obscure and actually pretty funny, but I didn't want to hear that, either.

Better put a stop to it right now.

I rolled out of bed. Time to get up and check my messages.

No messages.

Maybe there was something wrong with my phone. I put that at the top of my list of things to check when I got back to Parkland.

My Walmart items included underwear and a tee shirt that said, "Welcome to Celosia." I slid on my jeans and the tee shirt and went downstairs, being careful to step over the loose boards.

Jerry must have gotten up with the sun. The dusty rug from the foyer hung over the porch railing. The wooden floor glowed with a warm golden shine. He was dusting the mantel and singing something about trees.

"Shut up," I said.

"Thought I'd paint this room light blue," he said. "You can help."

"I have cases to work on, remember?"

He gestured with his dust rag. "This place is perfect. It's already spooky and mysterious. It's just right for séances and readings. I'll clean it up and start advertising. 'Come to Eberlin House and Find Your Future.' It'll be brilliant."

"If you want it to be spooky and mysterious, don't paint it light blue." I yawned. "I need to find out why I'm not getting my messages. I thought I'd return Buddy's car and pick up mine."

He followed me into the kitchen. "Did you eat all the apples?"

"No."

"Well, they're all gone, and the cereal, too."

I peered into the cabinets. "All that stuff I bought?"

"The cereal and a whole bag of apples."

"Do you suppose some kids got in? It's probably a rite of passage to spend the night in this house." I checked the back door.

"I'm sure I locked it," Jerry said. "But whoever took the stuff left the cookies and candy bars."

Maybe Celosia was home to a roving gang of bored teenagers. "Kids today. What gets into them?"

"No more of my food, that's for sure." He sat down at the table and opened the jar of peanut butter. "If you're going to Parkland, will you pick up some of my things?"

"Where can I find your things?"

"At Buddy's."

"Anything else you want me to bring you?"

"More food."

"How about a welcome mat and a birdbath? One of those ceramic deer, perhaps?"

"I need some blue paint and some brushes."

"Got any cash?"

I don't know how he does it, but despite having turned his back on the family treasure chest, Jerry always has a wad of bills in his pocket. He handed me about fifty dollars. "That oughta do it. Buy a little something for yourself, too."

"You're too generous." I put the money in my pocket. "Where did all this come from?"

He took a bite of his sandwich and indicated his mouth was too full to answer.

"It's not from some scam, is it? You haven't been playing with Jeff again, have you?"

Jerry shook his head. I wasn't sure I believed him, but then again, Constance Shawn had just paid for a séance. "Okay, well, I'll see you later. Don't let the rats get you."

"Same to you," he said.

PARKLAND'S MORNING RUSH was over, but there was still a lot of traffic. After the calm of the countryside, I found it distracting. Going into my apartment, I felt a touch of claustrophobia. Had it always been this cramped and dark? True, it had been my idea to move out and let Bill keep the house, but I regretted leaving the large sunny house with its deck and front porch. Regretted leaving the house, not Bill. He couldn't come to terms with the fact that I was not a mother and never would be.

I slumped in the armchair and stared at the blank wall in front of me. I hadn't put up any pictures. Bill was a good photographer, and all the pictures in our house had been portraits he'd taken. Unfortunately, his favorite subject was children. He had photos of little girls making sandcastles and little boys hanging by their knees from tree branches and children feeding ducks and babies discovering their toes. He thought this would inspire me. It just made me thankful the children in our house were framed and on the walls.

Maybe I should have been more sympathetic. Maybe I should have explored the possibility that I wouldn't have become like my mother, that I would have been patient and kind and understanding with a child of my own.

Maybe this little fit of pity was because I was tired and discouraged and because Jerry had all the insight of an amoeba.

I let myself wallow for about ten minutes, then I shook it off. Didn't I have not one but two cases waiting for me in Celosia? I took a shower and washed my hair. I exchanged the Celosia tee shirt and jeans for my favorite yellow shirt and gray shorts and packed my suitcase for an extended stay in the country. I could commute from Parkland, but, dammit, I wasn't going to give up on Jerry, and I wasn't going to give up on me.

Feeling one-hundred-percent better, I called Buddy to thank him for the use of the Bug. "It's parked in front of my apartment."

"Thought Jerry had it," Buddy said.

"He's staying in Celosia to take care of some business."

Buddy's the type of big sloppy man most people would call a redneck. He's proud of the label because most people also misjudge his intelligence. He knew right away what was up. "Another one of those stupid schemes of his?"

"I'm going to try to talk him out of it."

"Why does the boy think he's psychic, anyway? There's no money in it."

"Sort of like the detective business."

"Yeah, how's that going for ya?"

"Pretty good. I've picked up some work in Celosia. I can stay with Jerry while I investigate."

There was a pause, and then Buddy said, "That's a right good idea."

I wondered exactly what he meant by that. "Jerry says he left his things at your house. Shall I come get them, or do you want to bring them when you pick up the VW?"

"I'll bring 'em. Give me about twenty minutes."

I went out to my light blue Mazda. I had tossed the overnight bag in the back when a black Infiniti pulled up beside me and a voice said, "Madeline, hello!"

Nancy Lundell waved from her window. "Have you been out of town?"

"Just for the night," I said.

She adjusted her Ray-Bans. "I thought maybe you'd moved."

"No."

"Well, my friend Alexandra has been trying to reach you. She wanted you to investigate something about a will. I don't know the details."

"Has she been trying to call me? I think there's something wrong with my phone."

"Yes, she called several times, and then she went over to your office yesterday, but you weren't there."

Hell. "Please tell her I'm sorry I missed her. I'm heading over there now."

"I think she's already hired Kent and Ross."

I could feel the heat rising up my neck. "Okay. Maybe next time."

"And my girlfriend Gloria tried to reach you, too."

Another car drove up behind the Infiniti and honked for Nancy to move along. "Let me give you her number." She dug in her purse and handed me a card. She gave me another wave and drove off.

An ancient pickup wheezed to a stop behind the Mazda, and Buddy hopped out of the passenger seat. He had on the standard redneck uniform of overalls and tee shirt, his scraggly hair poking out from under a baseball cap. He pulled two duffel bags and a box from the back. Then he gave the side of the truck a slap and hollered, "Thanks!" to the driver, who put the truck in gear and roared off down the street.

"Is that all?" I asked. I knew Jerry traveled light, but this was spare, even for him.

Buddy picked up the duffel bags. "This is all he kept at my place. Where you want it?"

I opened the trunk. "In here, thanks."

Buddy heaved the bags into the truck. He picked up the box. "This is mostly books."

"It can go on the back seat."

Once Jerry's belongings were safely stowed, Buddy wiped his hands on his overalls and tugged his baseball cap tighter on his head. "So you're headed for Celosia, huh? Not much to do over there."

"Not much for me here, either, Bud."

"Saw Bill the other day. Got him some pale little hottie."

"I know."

He grinned, showing crooked teeth. "Take three or four of her to make one of you. I like 'em tall and feisty."

This is Buddy's idea of a compliment. "Thanks, Buddy." I gave him the VW keys.

"So you're staying with the detective business," he said.

"Yes. There's very little chance for advancement in the pageant world."

"Got a friend who's a detective. It can get dangerous."

"I think I can handle it," I said.

Buddy nodded. "I know you can. Just be careful."

"I will, thanks."

He jerked a thumb toward my apartment building. "Gonna move out?"

"I don't think so. It depends on how things go in Celosia."

"You get ready to move, let me know. I'll come help you."

"Thanks."

Buddy gave another gap-toothed grin. "Jerry still seeing Olivia?"

"Apparently."

"She's a mean little squirt."

"I believe she won Miss Mean Little Squirt in '82."

"Always knew the boy wasn't right. Tell him he better treat you like he should."

"He does. We're really good friends."

Buddy's little eyes twinkled. "All the same, if you need me to straighten him out, you give me a call. If the boy wants to communicate with the dead, I can arrange that."

I DROVE TO MY OFFICE, which was still hot and dead. But my phone and the answering machine were alive. No messages. Time to call the phone company and see what was going on. Maybe there'd been a power outage.

"Thought I saw you come in." Reid grinned from the door. "It's hot in here, Madeline. Can't you afford some air conditioning?"

I was determined not to let him rile me. "Just checking my messages."

As usual, he parked his rear on my desk. "Oh, you got some cases?"

"Two."

"At the same time? A true test of your detecting skills."

"They're in Celosia."

"A hotbed of crime."

"Legitimate cases."

"Some farmer lose a cow? Grand Theft Bailer?"

"I'm not going to discuss my cases with you. I just stopped by to pick up some things."

He got up. "Well, good luck. There's quite a backlog of cases next door should you run out of things to do."

"I'll keep that in mind."

The phone company said there hadn't been any service interruptions lately. They'd be happy to send somebody by tomorrow to check my phone, but suggested the problem might be in the answering machine and I might like to return it. I called Nancy's friend Gloria and left a message, apologizing for missing her and asking her to please call again.

I was almost to my car when I realized I'd left Gloria's card on my desk. I'd need it if I wanted to try to get in touch with her from Celosia.

When I came down the hallway, Reid was coming out of my office. He stopped, his expression pure guilt.

"What were you doing in there?" I asked.

"Just stopped by to see you."

"I locked that door."

He tried to bluff his way out. "It was open."

I was absolutely sure I'd locked the door. I'd even jiggled the doorknob. "You've been going in my office, haven't you? You've been intercepting my messages and then erasing them."

"Why would I do that?"

"Because you're a sneaky bastard, that's why. You've been stealing my clients so I'd think I was a failure and come back to you."

He knew he was caught. He grinned. "Is that so bad?"

I pushed past him into my office. I looked around and decided there wasn't a damn thing I couldn't live without. "That's it," I said. "I'm leaving."

"Leaving?"

"You can come in here as much as you like. Hell, you can dance naked on the desk. It's all yours."

He followed me down the hall. "Madeline, come on now. It just shows you how desperate I am to have you back."

"I'll find another office, and you can find somebody else to cheat."

"It was just a joke. I'll give you one of my clients."

I stopped and whirled around. He skidded to a stop. "You're not going to give me anything. I'm going to make this work on my own terms."

"Like your marriage?"

I swung out, but he jumped back. My fist barely missed his nose.

"Okay, okay," he said. "Violent beauty queen on the loose. Go ahead and leave. When you get tired of playing detective, I'll take you back."

I knew if I said anything else, I'd explode. Then I'd be facing murder charges. I left Reid still grinning that shit-eating grin, got in my car, and drove to Baxter's parking lot where

I sat, my hands gripping the steering wheel, until I stopped shaking. Another part of my life blown to hell.

When I'd calmed down, I went inside, sat at a table, and had a barbecue sandwich and a Coke. Okay, now, things are not that bad, I told myself. You weren't making a go of it next door to Kent and Ross. You'll be better off somewhere else. Plus you have two cases in Celosia. Concentrate on that. Everything will be fine.

Everything was fine until I saw Olivia Decker.

She came toward me like a small locomotive in full steam. With a loud scrape, she pulled out a chair and sat across from me. She folded her arms on the table and gave me the full force of those green eyes.

"Okay, what's the deal in Celosia?"

I didn't need this aggravation. "There isn't any deal, Olivia. I have a couple of cases there, and Jerry wants to fix up the house."

"Exactly why I'm suspicious. Have you ever known Jerry to want to fix anything? There's something about that house he's not telling me."

"Well, he's not telling me, either."

She looked as if she didn't believe me. "He tells you everything."

"No, he doesn't."

She slapped her black leather pocketbook on the table and rooted around for her checkbook. "Oh, you two are such buddies, I'm sure he'll tell you if you ask. In fact, I'm so sure, I'm going to hire you to find out."

I had my sandwich halfway to my mouth. I put it down. "What are you talking about?"

"He has to be getting money from somewhere. Maybe his uncle left him more than just the house." She opened her checkbook. "What's your fee?"

"Olivia, why do you care?"

Her green eyes widened. "You know how I feel about Jerry."

"Aren't you over?"

She waved her hand as if dismissing the thought. "Just a little lovers' quarrel. I still don't understand why he doesn't want any part of the Fairweather fortune."

But you'd love to get your hands on it, I thought.

"So then he inherits this house and the land, which must be worth quite a lot, and decides to keep it. You see the mystery?"

The only mystery here is what does Jerry see in this woman? Of course, he's always been attracted to the perfect little fairy-tale-princess types. "It's probably just a whim. You know he doesn't settle on one thing for long."

She was getting impatient. "You want this job, or not?"

Olivia's one of these people who thinks money can buy anything. "I'm not going to spy on Jerry for you. Just ask him what he's doing. If he cares enough about you, he'll tell you."

She put her checkbook back in her pocketbook and stood, giving the chair another scrape. "You know something? He does care enough about me. I'm going to make damn sure of that."

I didn't want to think about what she meant.

Betsy was halfway to my table when Olivia whirled out, almost bumping into the waitress.

"I was coming to see what she wanted," Betsy said.

"She wants me to find out why Jerry's decided to keep this old house he's inherited."

She pushed Olivia's chair back under the table. "What would Jerry do with an old house?"

"I have no idea."

"Could be he's thinking about settling down?"

We gave this a few seconds and then both started laughing.

"Nah, he's just fooling around," I said.

Betsy folded her arms and gave me a long, hard look. "And when are you going to stop fooling around?"

"You mean about being a detective? I'm serious about it, Betsy."

"I don't mean that. I mean, when are you going to let Olivia Decker know she has some competition?"

Why are my feelings so obvious to everyone except Jerry? "She already sees me as a threat."

"Well, she should. You need to step up your campaign, girl. Think of this as another beauty pageant, only there's a better prize than some cheesy crown and a bunch of roses."

First Buddy and now Betsy. I'd heard just about enough helpful suggestions for one day. "Thanks, Betsy. I'll have two sandwiches and some fries to go. Could you pack them in a cooler, please? It may be a while before we eat them."

She nodded as if satisfied she'd set me straight and went back to the kitchen. No need to explain to Betsy that one of the many reasons I left the pageant world was I didn't have the killer instinct necessary to claw my way to the top. I wasn't going to fight Olivia Decker for Jerry's affections. If he couldn't see me as a lover, what the hell was I supposed to do about it?

I WENT BY the hardware store and bought several gallons of blue paint, rollers, and brushes, then stopped at Super Food and loaded up on groceries. On the drive to Celosia, I felt as if I were leaving a whole world behind. Maybe I could find an office in Celosia. Then I'd be closer to Jerry.

There it was again. Closer to Jerry. Jerry and I had always been close. Close friends. Maybe there wasn't anything more to our relationship. I didn't like Olivia or any of the other little gold diggers he managed to attract, but that was because I had his welfare at heart, that's all. Besides, after my disastrous marriage to Bill, I certainly wasn't looking for husband number two. Jerry would make a terrible husband. He didn't have a job, he was always late, he was a junior conman.

He was also kind, easy-going, and fun to be with. Who else was on my wavelength, who could really almost read my mind?

Time to give myself a sermon. Damn it, don't let your imagination run away with you. Concentrate on your cases. That's the only reason you're going back to Celosia.

I LEFT PARKLAND at 1:00 PM and got back to Celosia around 1:30. My first stop in Celosia was the Baker Auditorium. When Evan James saw me, he hurried up, twisting his yellow handkerchief in his hands.

"Thank goodness you're here! Come look at our set!"

Venice was in ruins. The gondolas lay on their sides, shipwrecked.

"When did this happen?"

"We came in at one o'clock for the interviews and found it. Percy says it probably just fell overnight, but I believe we were sabotaged!"

Percy strolled over. Today, he was wearing a blue caftan that billowed like a sail. "James, don't exaggerate. The set wasn't constructed properly. I told you that."

"Then who demolished the gondolas? They didn't get that way from just falling over. The girls are going to be crushed. The pageant is tomorrow night, and we have to have a dress rehearsal today. It's vital!"

"We'll have one, don't worry."

Evan blew his nose on his handkerchief. "I just don't know how much more of this I can stand. Have you found out anything, Madeline?"

"Not yet. It's important I talk with the contestants."

"Juliet, Donna, and Randi have their interviews today. I'll ask them to come speak with you when they finish."

"The judges, too, please."

Evan blew his nose again and hurried up the aisle. Percy followed me as I examined the ruined set. He was still complaining about how the disaster upset his plans.

"Can you imagine having to work under these circumstances? Why do I even bother? The girls will forget everything I've taught them."

Behind the fallen scenery were electric cords fastened down with duct tape. Venice had been painted on flats held in place by bar weights. Someone had removed the weights, and the flats had toppled over onto the gondolas, which perished under the weight of the painted waves. I picked up one of the weights. It wasn't that heavy.

"Who has a key to the building, Percy?"

"Evan, of course. I don't think anyone else does."

"How late was the building open last night?"

"Well, I finally got the girls to walk in a straight line, and then Evan sent them home to practice their talent. I don't know how he expects me to have the opening number ready by showtime. I left around nine, I think."

I set the weight aside. "Who's got it in for you?"

He clasped his large hand to his heart. "Me?"

"Well, this is your show. Somebody might be jealous."

"The world is jealous of my talents, but there's no one in this provincial little hick town with enough brain power to mastermind my downfall."

This guy and Gregory Prill needed to get together. "Does Evan have any enemies?"

"No one I can think of. No one wants his job. They're very happy he wants to do it every year."

"How do you know Evan? Are you originally from Celosia?"

"Good Lord, no. I live in Parkland. But everyone in the pageant world knows Evan. He's been at this for years. I'm surprised you've never heard of him."

I'd forgotten what an insulated little world Pageantland could be. "So you're doing this job as a favor?"

Percy looked insulted. "I don't do favors. I wanted to show Celosia what a real pageant looks like." He frowned at the mangled gondolas. "Apparently, my efforts are not appreciated."

"How about the contestants? Did you turn down some young woman who had her heart set on becoming Miss Celosia?"

He shook his head. "Evan said he had twelve girls audition, and he and the pageant committee took all twelve. They can't afford to be choosy for such a small pageant. If the girls met the age requirement and paid the entry fee, they were in. Of course, one would think that at least half of them would have some sense of rhythm. I really don't know if I care to keep beating my head against that particular wall." He looked down at the piles of curled cardboard. "Not that there's much wall left in this dismal place. Ah, here's our lovely Miss Celosia High now."

Juliet Lovelace came down the aisle, smiling and posing as if the auditorium were full of adoring fans. When she saw the remains of Venice, she stopped. "Wow, Evan said it was a mess. What happened?"

Percy gestured, the folds of his caftan flapping. "Venice is no more."

She came up to the edge of the stage. "Did somebody do that on purpose?"

"I'm afraid so."

"Can it be fixed?"

"I have no idea. It's not my problem, is it? I'm not a stagehand."

She smiled up at Percy and batted her long eyelashes. "Did you want to talk to me?"

"Me? No." He gestured toward me. "But I believe Ms. Maclin would like to have a few words with you."

Juliet frowned as Percy sailed up the aisle. Then she turned and looked me up and down. "So you were Miss Parkland? That must have been some time ago."

"Forty years. I age well."

She blinked. Then she got the joke. "What I meant was, I hadn't heard of you."

"Miss Parkland was my farewell appearance."

"You weren't interested in going on?"

"I'd had enough fun."

This went by her, too. "It really isn't fun. It's work. You have to stay in shape. You have to practice your song. You have to learn stupid dance routines. What did you do for talent?"

"I played the kazoo."

Whiz. Right over her head. "I'm singing this old song from the Forties. It suits my voice."

"Juliet," I said, "do you have any idea who'd want to sabotage the pageant?"

She glanced at the stage. "You mean, do this?"

"And try to burn the curtains."

"Lots of people. Everyone's jealous of me—Donna and Randi, especially. Then there's Ted Stacy and his protesters. They think anybody who participates in a pageant is some kind of traitor to all women."

"Who stands to gain the most if the pageant's cancelled?"

"I guess that would be Donna. She's always coming in second to me. She hates it."

"Where were you last night?"

"At home, practicing my song." She gave the stage another long look. "Do you think the pageant will be cancelled?"

"I don't know."

"This could've been just an accident."

If someone accidentally moved all the weights and pushed the flats over.

I thanked Juliet. She started to go and then paused as if

she wanted to say something else. Then she shrugged and went up the aisle.

Donna Sanchez was the next to enter. Her reaction to Venice's demise was much more vocal. She flew down the aisle to inspect the damage.

"Oh, my God! Who did this? This is horrible!" She turned to me, hands on hips. She was a dark-eyed brunette with a smooth olive complexion burning red with indignation. "Who's responsible for this? It's Juliet, isn't it?"

"Why do you say that?"

"Oh, she'd do anything to keep me from winning."

"Or coming in second?"

Donna smiled a grim smile. "Juliet told you that, didn't she? She's forgetting cheerleading squad and debate team. I totally blew her away on both, plus I've got a full scholarship to Wake Forest, and I think she's going to study Nail Polishing 101 at Parkland Community College."

"If you've got a full scholarship, why bother with the pageant?"

"Well, to spite Juliet, mostly. She thinks she's got it sewn up, but I'm going to blow her silky lace panties off."

An interesting visual. "If the pageant is cancelled, who benefits?"

"Nobody. Well, maybe Mr. Stacy and his friends could gloat a little."

"Do you really think Juliet is responsible for these incidents?"

"I wouldn't put it past her. But she's not running me off. I'll come put this scenery back together myself if I have to."

"What did you do after rehearsal last night?"

"Evan suggested everyone go home and practice their talent."

"And that's what you did?"

"Yes. Juliet thinks her singing is so wonderful, but everyone says my character ballet is the best they've ever seen."

Donna didn't look like a ballerina, but that never stopped the character ballets. "How about this afternoon when you came in? Who was here?"

"Juliet, Randi, and I had to be here by one o'clock for our interviews."

"What about the other contestants?"

"Six had interviews yesterday. The remaining three come later this afternoon."

Randi Peterson was also shocked by the sight of dead Venice. After commenting sadly on the Venetian disaster, she gave me a determined stare. "There's no way anyone's scaring me away with these silly pranks. I'm here to compete and to keep Juliet from winning. She doesn't deserve the crown or the good name of Miss Celosia."

"Why not?"

Randi had brown curls and hazel eyes under high, perfectly plucked brows. The brows went up even further. "Because she's a bitch. Can't you tell?"

"There's at least one in every pageant."

"Whoever wins Miss Celosia is supposed to represent our town. She ought to be someone good, don't you think?"

"Good like sweet and kind?"

"Well, yes. Isn't that the whole idea? Who wants a Miss Celosia who's bragging about her special designer gown with the one-of-a-kind sequins and looking down her nose at everyone and chasing after every good-looking man in town?"

"Is that what Juliet's doing?"

Up went those brows. "You've met her. What do you think?"

I thought Juliet Lovelace looked capable of anything, but that didn't mean she'd actually do anything. "It's possible."

She gave an unqueenly snort of laughter. "You got that right."

"What's your talent, Randi?"

"I've written an original poem I plan to recite."

"Were you practicing your poem at home last night?"

"Yes, I had my whole family pretend to be the audience so I could practice in front of a crowd. Would you like to hear it?"

Lord, how many of these awful recitations had I heard? "I'd love to, Randi, but I need to speak to the judges."

"That's okay. You'll hear it Saturday night."

After she'd gone, I sat down for a moment in the front row. Randi and Donna had been genuinely shocked by the ruined set, but I couldn't read Juliet's reaction. Maybe she was so confident she'd win the pageant, a collapsed Venice didn't worry her. Unlike Randi and Donna, who were determined that the pageant go on as scheduled, Juliet seemed unconcerned about the future of Miss Celosia.

Evan came down the aisle, wiping his brow. "Are you ready for the judges now, Madeline? I told them you were officially investigating these disturbing incidents, and everyone's agreed to help you as much as they can."

"Thanks, Evan."

He took a deep breath and blew it out. "They're waiting for you in my office. I've got to find Percy. He's being very difficult."

Chuck Hofsteder, Kimberly Dawn Williams, and Benjy Goins were sitting in Evan's office. Chuck offered me a chair.

"You're not seeing the Miss Celosia Pageant at its best, Madeline. I apologize."

Kimberly Dawn Williams got out her compact and added another layer. Whoever supplied her with eye shadow was making a fortune. "I still can't believe you gave up the pageant circuit, Madeline. It's opened so many doors for me."

"I had other interests," I said.

"But isn't the detective business dangerous?"

"So far, I've managed to stay out of any gun battles."

She finished larding on the blue eye shadow. "I don't imagine Celosia would have any sort of battles."

"You're not concerned about this latest break-in?"

She shook her head. Not a strand of hair moved. "Just some kids playing pranks. We've had some trouble with vandalism at the high school, too. Evan's making sure the building is locked."

"Did he call the police?"

"I don't think we want any more negative publicity."

"I've noticed how quickly news gets around in Celosia. He can't keep this kind of thing a secret for long."

Kimberly Dawn turned to Chuck. "How is Evan handling that, Chuck?"

"He had Chief Brenner come by," Hofsteder said. "He advised Evan to keep the door locked."

She rolled her eyes. "How helpful."

"Well, nothing was stolen. Amps, microphones, CD player, all sitting here. All that video equipment Benjy brought from the TV station, untouched. Brenner's thinking some kids got in, got to horsing around, and knocked down the set."

Kimberly Dawn looked satisfied. "That's it, then. The show will go on."

"Let me ask you about this show," I said. "Who stands the best chance of winning?"

Chuck was so eager to answer, he almost raised his hand. "We all know Juliet can be a little difficult, but strictly off the record, she's our best chance at winning Miss Parkland this year. Seriously, I think that girl could go all the way."

"And we've got a little score to settle with Dixley," Benjy Goins said.

Dixley's a town about the size of Celosia, located a few miles south of Parkland.

"You have a rivalry with the Miss Dixley Pageant?"

"It was an absolute scandal the way their girl took second place at Miss Parkland last year," Chuck said. "She didn't have a tenth of the talent our girl did. Those judges were blind and tone deaf."

"So, unofficially, you feel Juliet is the best choice."

Kimberly Dawn didn't look as pleased as the men. "We're not just going to give her the crown. She'll have to prove she's worthy."

"I think her talent is the best," Benjy Goins said.

"Did anyone stay here last night to practice her talent?"

"No, Evan sent them home. He doesn't like to wear everyone out."

"Did any of you stay?"

"We weren't needed last night, so, no, we weren't here."

"Do any of the contestants smoke?"

Kimberly Dawn looked appalled. "They'd better not!"

Chuck pointed to Evan's desk. "Evan's the only one who smokes, and he's trying to cut down. He keeps a pack in his desk for emergencies."

At that moment, Evan, with Cindy in tow, came in, wringing his handkerchief and mopping his brow. "I can't decide if I'm upset or not," he said. "Percy has quit. He says the girls are impossible to teach. He says it can't be done. Now, I'm really quite glad to be rid of him, but he was also our accompanist."

"Don't worry," Benjy Goins said. "I know someone who plays piano for the Sunday-morning gospel-hour radio show. He'll be happy to do it."

"Thank you, Benjy." Evan James looked at me entreatingly. "Tell me you have some idea who is behind all this."

I had to admit it looked like minor vandalism. "Just keep everything locked, like the police said."

I could tell he was disappointed I didn't have the criminal in hand. He sighed. "Very well. Benjy, please have your friend come over right away so I can show him what needs to be done."

As Evan started up the aisle, I followed and kept my voice

low. "If you'll give me a key and let me keep surveillance tonight, I may surprise someone."

"Excellent," he said.

"Only don't say anything to anyone, not even Cindy."

On my way to my car, I encountered drama in the parking lot. Evan was in earnest conversation with Percy. I couldn't hear what they were saying, but from the way Evan was strangling his handkerchief and Percy was flapping his arms like a condor attempting takeoff, I could tell the conversation wasn't going in Evan's favor.

I got into the Mazda and had reached for the key when Kimberly Dawn and Juliet walked past. Kimberly Dawn's voice was tightly controlled.

"What do you think you're doing?"

Juliet gave an elegant shrug and kept walking. Kimberly Dawn caught her arm and made her stop. "You're not going to make any trouble, Juliet, do you hear me?"

Juliet calmly removed the woman's hand. She smiled a superior smile. She leaned forward and spoke right in Kimberly Dawn's face. "I will if I want."

I expected Kimberly Dawn to give her a lecture on manners, but the older woman stepped back. Juliet gave her a little wave and walked on. Kimberly Dawn stood for a moment, fists clenched. Then she noticed me sitting in my car.

"Oh, Madeline. Did you hear that?" She wiped her palms on her skirt and fussed with her hair. "Honestly, the nerve of that girl!"

"What was that about?"

She stooped a little to speak into my window. "That girl thinks she can do anything she likes. I—" She glanced over to Evan and Percy. "Good heavens, do I have to fix everything? Excuse me, Madeline."

As she hurried over to the men, I wondered if Juliet had been caught doing something destructive to the stage. And if so, why Kimberly Dawn would want to protect her. I started the Mazda and drove out of the parking lot, passing Juliet in her car. She was still smiling.

I DROVE OUT TO the Eberlin house and parked the Mazda under one of the oak trees. Carrying a couple of bags of supplies, I nudged the door open with my foot.

"Jerry, I got the stuff you wanted."

Jerry was asleep on the sofa.

"You lazy bum," I said. "Here I think you're working and you're goofing off." I stopped. Jerry was lying very still, and there was some sort of towel on his forehead. I put the bags down and gave the sofa a little shake. "Hey, what's the matter?" Jerry blinked up at me. "What happened? Here, don't go back to sleep. Talk to me."

He got his eyes open. "I fell."

"Fell? Fell where? Are you all right? Did you break anything? Let me have a look." I lifted the towel. "Well, you took a nice chunk out of your forehead."

Jerry looked around. "Where's the girl?"

"Save the delirium for later, will you? Do you remember what happened?"

"I tried to get into the attic. The door was stuck. I came back down the stairs. I must have tripped on one of those loose boards."

"Let me fix a better bandage." In the kitchen, I got some ice cubes out of the freezer and wrapped them in a dishcloth. While Jerry was holding this to his forehead, I went out to my car where I keep a first-aid kit.

When I came back, Jerry was sitting up. "That feels much better."

"Let me have another look." The cut was more of a scrape and didn't look as deep as I'd first thought. "Keep the ice on it for a while, and then I'll bandage it. Does it hurt?"

"A little."

"I can take you to the emergency room if they've got one here."

"No, I'm okay."

"I've got some aspirin in my overnight bag."

"That might be good."

I found the aspirin bottle. Jerry took two pills and leaned back on the sofa. I pulled a chair closer.

"Tell me again what happened," I said.

"I cleaned this room awhile. Then I ate something. I thought I heard some noise in the attic, but I couldn't get the door open. When I started back down the stairs, I saw this girl outside, and that's when I fell. I remember I tried to grab the railing, but it broke off in my hand."

I hated to think of him lying here all day. "When was this?"

"Sometime around three, I guess."

"Tell me about this girl."

"She was outside by the trees." He rubbed his eyes. "I just caught a glimpse. I thought she was a ghost."

"Probably just a neighbor."

"From where? The next pasture?"

"Okay, so she was a ghost. Happy now?"

"Thrilled." His eyes were clearer. "And how was your day?"

"Not to take anything away from your adventure, but I feel as if I've fallen down a flight of stairs, too. Want to know why I haven't had any messages? Reid's been erasing them."

"What?"

"Intercepting them, taking them for his own, and then destroying the evidence."

"I hope you hit him in the eye."

"I tried. But he won't have Madeline Maclin to push around anymore. I've moved out."

"Good," Jerry said. "It's about time. Did you bring any food with you? I'm starving."

"Just some Baxter's Barbecue."

"You are my new best friend."

"I'm your only best friend."

He smiled, and again I felt that odd quiver inside. Did he want more than friendship? Did I?

At the moment, all we wanted was barbecue and fries. I bandaged the scrape. Then I unpacked our food. Uncle Val didn't have a microwave, but everything heated up in the stove. We took our feast out to the porch. We sat in the rocking chairs and watched the sun gleaming over the meadow.

"This girl I saw," he said, "she was beautiful."

"Of course she was."

"I must have been distracted."

"Sounds like it. You don't suppose your uncle was cooking up magic mushrooms in this house?"

"I think he was a mad scientist, and his experiments have gotten loose."

"Well, why don't I have a look in this attic?"

I went up the stairs, being careful to step over the loose one, and on up the smaller flight of steps leading to the attic. The door wouldn't budge. I knocked. "Anybody home?" I listened, but there wasn't a sound.

I went back to the porch. "I think the girl must have been one of your fairy-tale ladies—which reminds me, Olivia tried to hire me today to find out why you want to keep this house."

"I told her. I wanted a place to hold séances."

"This is what you plan to do with your life?"

"For now." He looked out across the meadow. "She was that interested, huh?"

"She was her usual intense self."

Jerry put his barbecue sandwich down. "I wonder."

"What?"

"Nothing," he said. "Maybe she does care about me. I mean, if she went to all the trouble to find you and hire you."

I didn't like the way this conversation was heading. "Finding me is no problem. I'm nearly always at Baxter's."

"She can be really sweet."

I couldn't tell anything from his expression. I had to ask him. "Do you love her?"

"Maybe. I really missed her."

I kept my gaze on the golden fields. "You think the two of you have a future?"

He didn't answer for a while. When I looked back at him, he shook his head. "You know her as well as I do, Mac. Would she ever want to live out here in the country?"

I had a hard time keeping the joy out of my voice. "Not in a million years."

We ate for a while in silence. Then Jerry said, "Maybe she was a ghost."

"Who?"

"The girl I saw."

"Maybe you hit your head just a little too hard." I passed him another Coke.

"I saw her first—then I hit my head." He carefully touched his forehead. "Which has stopped throbbing, by the way, thanks to my excellent health-care provider."

"You're welcome."

"See, Mac? You can do it all. How's the Case of the Purloined Pageant coming along?"

"It's become the Case of the Pulverized Pageant. Somebody trashed the set. The police say it's probably kids, but I'm not so sure. I'm going to stake out the place for a few hours tonight and see what happens."

"Could be the ghost of a former contestant, someone who was robbed of her rightful title."

I chuckled. "Do you sit around making this stuff up, or does it just come naturally to you?"

"You forget, I'm in the séance business. I'd better come along and try to make contact."

"Are you sure you feel up to it?"

"It's better than waiting here alone for Ghost Woman to make another appearance."

I started to say no, then reconsidered. It wasn't a good idea to leave someone with a head injury alone overnight, and of course, I always enjoyed Jerry's company.

"Okay, partner, I'll deputize you. But you can take it easy for a while. I'm not leaving until eleven."

"Aren't they rehearsing tonight? I can't think of anything more relaxing than watching beauty queens."

"The choreographer has quit, and the set is on the floor. I don't think they'll have much of a rehearsal."

The phone rang. I went into the living room to answer it. Gregory Prill's booming voice said, "Madeline Maclin, have you found any ghosts yet?"

I felt guilty I'd neglected his case. "Not yet. I apologize."

"Well, don't fret. I realize you're busy with the pageant. I'm calling to let you know Shana Amry is back in town. She's been on tour, promoting her latest book. She'd love to meet you, say, around noon tomorrow, at Georgia's?"

"That would be fine, thanks."

"I think the two of you will get along splendidly. Until later, then. Ta, ta!"

I'd never actually heard a grown man say, "Ta, ta!" I was still grinning when I came back to the porch.

AROUND ELEVEN, we drove into town and parked several blocks from the theater. We walked around to the stage-door entrance. I used my key to unlock the doors. Inside, the auditorium made strange creaks and breathing sounds. I turned on the backstage work lights. Most of the set had been re-assembled, although the gondolas were pretty much a loss. "Venice lives again."

"Ah, the old country," Jerry said.

"Did you ever go to Venice?"

"We took the Grand Tour when I was little. I don't remember much."

"Find someplace to get comfortable. I'm going to look around."

Jerry sat down in the front row while I prowled backstage. Everything looked the same. When I stepped onto the stage, he clapped and whistled. I gave him a pageant wave and a big fake smile.

"Brings back fond memories, doesn't it?"

I sat on the edge of the stage. "Memories of screaming mothers and crying girls."

Jerry had seen a tape of me in one of the Little Miss Parkland pageants. "I especially like the big hair."

I ran my hand through my short curls. "Yeah, I miss all the teasing and the hair spray. Sleeping in rollers is good, too."

"And now you're Macho Mac, Defender of the Poor."

"And where has that gotten me? Sitting in an empty auditorium."

"Waiting to snag an unsuspecting Venice-destroying pageant-hater."

I grinned. "Who's not going to make an appearance if we're out here yakking. Let's find a better hiding place." I looked around. "How about the light booth? We can see everything from up there."

We climbed the narrow metal stairs to the light booth. The wide window gave us a complete view of the stage and auditorium. I found the light switch that turned off the work lights. The dim blue glow of the lamp in the booth gave us just enough light. I perched on the stool in front of the control panel and looked down into the shadowy auditorium.

Jerry sat on the floor. "What have you got so far?"

"I still haven't ruled out kids. The curtain was just singed, and the scenery easy enough to reassemble. It's as if someone wants to make a mess, not cause real damage."

"Any clues?"

"Evan's the only one who smokes, and I doubt he set fire to his own theater. He doesn't seem the kind of person to burn the one thing he's crazy about."

In the dim light, I thought I saw Jerry wince. "You okay?"

His expression was odd, but then again, it may have been the faint light. "Yeah, just a twinge. What else do you know?"

"After a short rehearsal last night, all the contestants were sent home to practice their talent."

"That's what they say."

"But all these young women want to win the pageant. Why sabotage it? It's puzzling."

"What about your other case, the one with the haunted house?"

"I haven't even started on that one. Maybe Hayden's ghost is responsible for the pageant mishaps." I sighed. "I really don't have much to go on right now."

"You'll figure it out."

"Thanks."

He leaned back against the wall and gave me a serious look. "I have to tell you I'm jealous of you, Mac. You've always known what you wanted to do with your life."

"Not really. I knew what I didn't want to do."

"As for me, I have no idea."

What brought this on? "That's never bothered you before."

"You know Des has had a hard time composing lately. The last time I talked with him, he said he'd had a real breakthrough. Not only is he writing music like crazy, he's featured soloist with the Parkland Symphony and has a big tour planned."

"So?"

"Life has finally settled for him. And did I tell you Tucker's getting married? He tells me he's found the girl of his dreams. I'm just wondering."

"Wondering what?"

"Moving here, starting over. Maybe I'm due for a breakthrough, only I don't have anything to break through." He yawned. "I know what the answer might be, though."

"Figured it out already?"

He nodded. He smiled at me. "Maybe it's time I thought about settling down."

I didn't know what to say. "Did you have to fall down the stairs to have this revelation?"

He feigned a serious expression. "Sometimes it takes a brush with death to realize what life is all about."

"Have anyone in mind?"

"Olivia wouldn't have come to Celosia if she didn't care. Maybe she's the one."

Damn. "Is she ready to settle down?"

"I'll have to ask her."

"Remember how she feels about the Fairweather fortune. Won't your lack of money be an issue?"

He thought a moment. "I think she'll get over that."

"Can you really trust her, Jerry?"

"I'd like to." He yawned again. "You know, you're the only one I really trust."

That was something, at least. "Thanks."

"From the beginning, you were interested in me, not my name or my money. I've had plenty of girlfriends, but you're a true friend. I can't say that about anyone else." He slumped down further and closed his eyes. "Wake me if anything exciting happens."

As he settled into sleep, I wondered if I was crazy to care this much about him. A true friend. Great. That's just great, Jerry. Why can't I be the girl of *your* dreams?

THREE

NOTHING HAPPENED. No thrill-seeking teens, no ghosts, no-body returning to the scene of the crime. While Jerry took his nap, I took my flashlight and made the rounds, check-ing all entrances. I didn't see any way anyone could get in without breaking a window. I didn't see any signs of forced entry. Around 1:00 AM, I roused Jerry and took him home.

The next morning, I called and left another message for Nancy Lundell's friend Gloria, giving her my cell-phone num-ber. For now, I had enough work in Celosia, but it would be foolish to ignore a possible case. When I finished, I went into the kitchen for cereal and found nothing. I'd bought two new boxes yesterday, and I knew I put them in the cabinet. What was going on?

I made some toast and poured a big glass of orange juice, which I took up to Jerry.

"You doing all right?" I asked.

His eyes were halfway open. "Just barely. You want to breathe a little quieter?"

I set the plate of toast and the glass on the nightstand. "That bad, huh?"

"And not even a wild party to forget." He slowly sat up. "Ow. I must have landed on every part of me."

"No chance you zipped downstairs during the night and had a bowl of Sugar Pops, is there?"

He gave me an incredulous look. "You mean it happened again?"

"Well, we are staying in the dreaded Eberlin house, Mystery Home of Celosia. Apparently, our ghosts think breakfast is the most important meal of the day."

Jerry took two aspirin with a gulp of juice. "This house really is haunted, Mac."

"By cereal-loving ghosts? That's pathetic. Post Toasties Ghosties, maybe? Sugar Coated Spooks?"

"All-Bran Poltergeists."

"Eeeeuww."

"Well, you gotta keep them regular, or they'll start throwing furniture."

I handed him the toast. "I think you're feeling better. Will you be okay by yourself?"

"Sure," he said. "Who are you grilling today?"

"I've made appointments with Benjy Goins, local DJ, and Ted Stacy. And Gregory Prill asked me to meet Shana Amry at Georgia's around noon to talk about Hayden's ghost."

"Hmm."

"What's that 'hmm' supposed to mean?"

"It was just a 'hmm' of interest."

"Trust me, I'm not ready to hop into another relationship."

"Not even with Tall Ted?"

"We'll see." I had to get out of there before I leaped into bed with him. "What are you doing today?"

"I'm going to paint."

I had a vision of coming home to find him with his head stuck in the pail. "Well, please be careful."

AT THE LOCAL TV and radio station, Benjy Goins was in the middle of his radio show, "Benjy's Big Hits." As far as I could tell, "Benjy's Big Hits" consisted of a lot of three-note thumping and loud, unintelligible voices shouting to the beat.

Goins took off his headset and came out to the lobby of WCLO to meet me.

"Morning, Madeline. Great stuff, huh?"

"Rockin'."

"You a Noxious Fumes fan?"

"Since nineteen fifty-five."

He looked at me blankly, then got it. "Don't know them, do you?"

"Not exactly my style."

"Yeah, I would imagine you're into cool jazz."

He could imagine what he liked. "I wanted to ask you a few questions about the pageant, if you've got time."

He turned to check on the large clock in his studio. "Got a bank of commercials running. It'll be five minutes at most."

"You run a radio and TV studio yourself?"

He grinned. "Well, it's not much, as you can see. I do local news, sports, stuff like that. As for the TV studio, we have a local-access channel on a cable station out of Parkland. Six hours a day."

"I would imagine you feature pageant news."

"The pageant is big news." He pointed toward a video camera on a tripod and a stack of video cassettes. "And big business, for Celosia, anyway. I get my assistant to videotape the pageant and sell copies to all the girls' relatives."

"Do you sell a lot of copies?"

"You bet. It's the event of the year."

"So who'd be against the pageant?"

"Nobody's against it except Ted Stacy, and he's just making a statement. He's not the kind of guy who'd sneak around at night knocking over some cardboard walls."

"Is there that kind of guy in town?"

"If there is they're just doing it for kicks. Not much to do in Celosia."

I recalled what Jerry had said about former queens. "Evan doesn't have any enemies? Women who were rejected for the pageant years ago?"

"I don't know about that."

"How many women have been in the pageant?"

"Just about any good-looking teenager growing up in this

town has been in the pageant. It's like homecoming queen or head cheerleader. They make it, they usually leave town." He looked at the clock. "You really ought to ask Kimberly Dawn. She's the historian. She's knows every little detail about the Miss Celosia Pageant." He glanced at the clock. "I gotta go."

I thanked Benjy and went out. If he made a profit off the pageant, it seemed unlikely he'd have anything to do with the incidents at the auditorium.

BENJY'S IDEA of talking to Kimberly Dawn was a good one. She might tell me, the former Miss Parkland, more in private than she would be willing to say in front of her colleagues. I got her address from Cindy, and headed over.

Kimberly Dawn received me—there's no other word—in the living room of her home on Crestwood Street.

"My dear Madeline, I was just about to have some tea. Won't you join me?"

She indicated a fancy chair with an embroidered cushion. I sat down. "Thanks."

She settled herself in another chair. Tea in Kimberly Dawn's house meant hot tea served in thin china cups. "Lemon?"

"Just sugar, thank you."

"How about a cinnamon wafer? These are superb. I get them from Francie's in Charlotte."

I took a wafer, remembering to hold my pinky up. Kimberly Dawn floated a tiny slice of lemon in her tea and sat back. In her pink suit, she looked just as stiff as the furniture. Her long fingernails gleamed pink. Even her toenails, peeking out from her pink sandals, were the same bright color. Middle-Aged Barbie.

"I know why you're here, Madeline. It's about this pageant problem, isn't it?"

"Yes. I'd really like to know the history of Miss Celosia."

She beamed. "I can tell you whatever you want to know."

"Start at the beginning."

She set her cup on the end table. "Well, in 1985, a very enterprising woman named Alexandra Newsome decided that Celosia should have its own pageant and send the winner to Miss Parkland. She organized a committee, ran the pageant, and our first Miss Celosia, Carolyn Buford, was in the top ten that year. As you can imagine, that got everyone very proud and excited. Since then, we've had sixteen top-ten girls, including myself, and a second-runner-up. You might remember her. Phyllis Mayfield."

"Oh, yes." No one who heard her jazz version of "O Caro Mio" ever forgot Phyllis Mayfield.

"An excellent contestant. So, we've had a pageant since the mid-Eighties."

"When did Evan James come in?"

"He's been our pageant coordinator since 1990. He's a bundle of nerves, but he always manages to have a good show. It is simply criminal the way things have been lately. He doesn't deserve all these headaches."

"Is there anyone who would have a grudge against him or the pageant committee? Someone who felt she should have won?"

Kimberly patted her solid helmet of hair. I was surprised it didn't go "clang!" "Of course, there were hurt feelings and petty jealousies along the way, but I honestly can't think of a girl who would lower herself to destroying scenery. It goes against the Miss Celosia Code."

"You have a code?"

"A standard of rules and behavior. Every girl signs the agreement. Rule One states that each contestant will conduct herself in a manner befitting the ideals of Miss Celosia. Those ideals include fair play and a gracious attitude in defeat." She picked up her teacup and took a sip. "We have to draw the line somewhere."

"Would you say all the contestants in this pageant are following the code?"

"To be perfectly honest with you, Madeline, this is the most fractious group of girls I've ever seen. They've hated each other since grade school. Yes, they all signed the agreement, but I don't think they know the meaning of 'gracious attitude' in anything."

I took another wafer. They were thin, but pretty tasty. "Yesterday, Chuck said that he thought Juliet was the best choice."

"We have to choose the girl we feel has the best chance to win Miss North Carolina. Right now, unfortunately, that girl is Juliet Lovelace. She does well in interview. She has an excellent figure. Her talent is strong."

Kimberly Dawn's tone was bitter. I said, "But you don't want her to win."

"No, I don't. But who else do we have? Donna Sanchez has no talent. Randi Peterson doesn't even know who our president is. Karen Mitman has no stage presence, no confidence. The rest of them are just as flawed." She sighed. "I have to put personal feelings aside and go with the best contestant. It won't be the first time." She reached for the teapot. "More tea?"

"No, thanks."

She poured another cup for herself. "Honestly, some of these girls are so unprepared. I've had to instruct them on how to stand, how to turn, how to present themselves in the very best light possible."

"Are you a professional pageant coach?"

"I've done some coaching, but I'm also exploring other avenues. Commercials, for example. I've done several for some very prominent local businesses. I've also done some modeling. Have you ever considered modeling?"

I'd been approached by several agencies, but I wasn't interested. I'd served my time on stage. "No, not really."

She smiled. "I think you'd do very well. Like me, you're tall and you've kept your figure." She gave herself an admiring gaze. "Do you know I'm the same size as most of the Miss Celosia contestants? I've even lent some of my gowns to the girls."

"I'm sure they were happy to have them."

"Well, this pageant means a lot to me." She gestured to a corner cabinet. "Let me show you my memorabilia."

I knew we'd get around to her glory days. We walked over to the corner. Inside the cabinet was a large framed picture of Kimberly Dawn in all her pageant finery, an overly beaded gown with padded shoulders and a frilly neckline. Her tiara and trophy sat in the center with her Miss Celosia sash draped carefully around the trophy. On the bottom shelf were framed newspaper clippings of the event.

I felt a moment of nausea. My mother has an entire room full of stuff like this chronicling my years on the Little Miss circuit. Kimberly Dawn waited for a response, so I said, "Very nice."

She kept her eyes on her treasures. "I just wish these girls took this pageant as seriously as I do. They don't realize what a positive effect being in this show can have on their lives."

Or how it can crush and warp their little minds.

"The only reason most of them want to win is to beat Juliet Lovelace," she said. "It's not the purest of motives."

"So it's doubtful any one of the contestants would've torn down Venice?"

"Unless she hates Juliet so much she's willing to destroy her own future."

I didn't see winning Miss Celosia as a step toward the future, but I didn't say so.

"Are you sure you won't stay for more tea, Madeline?"

"No, thanks," I said. "I've enjoyed this, but I have to be going. I have an appointment."

"Please feel free to stop by anytime," Kimberly Dawn said.

"There's just me rambling about this big old house. I always enjoy company."

I was surprised there wasn't a Mr. Kimberly Dawn. She was wearing several rings set with overlarge diamonds.

She saw me looking at her hands, and knew what I was thinking. "I noticed you aren't married, either, Madeline."

"Divorced."

"Me, too. Nathan and I had a parting of the ways five years ago. He did not support me in any of my endeavors. Was your ex-husband against your pageant career, as well?"

"We couldn't agree on many things."

"You must stop by again, and we'll swap horror stories."

I thanked her for the tea and the information. I didn't tell her I wasn't keen on sharing divorce details.

MY NEXT STOP WAS Ted Stacy's office.

Ted Stacy worked for Arrow Insurance, just a short distance down the street from Mason and Freer. His secretary, a very young woman, smiled and told me to go right in. Stacy's office was burgundy and forest green and decorated with pictures of fish. A huge mounted swordfish hung on one wall; fishing trophies stood in a glass case on the other.

Ted Stacy stood to shake my hand and offered me a seat in front of his desk. "Good morning, Madeline. What can I do for you?"

"Nice fish," I said.

He settled in his burgundy leather swivel chair. "Atlantic Beach, two summers ago. Do you fish?"

"Sometimes." Bill had been crazy about fishing. "Freshwater, mostly. Bass, crappie."

"There's a great little lake about five miles from here. I'd love to have you join me some Saturday."

"Thanks." I had to admit that sounded like fun. Ted had a ready smile, and those dark eyes were attractively warm. "I stopped by to ask you about the pageant."

He frowned. "Is this about that trouble yesterday?"

"Trouble?"

"This is Celosia. Everybody's heard about the damaged scenery."

"Then you know your group is under suspicion."

He didn't seem too concerned. "Well, since my group consists of me and three soccer moms, I think Evan better look elsewhere. I know Tessie and Amy were playing bridge Tuesday night, and Samantha took one of her daughters to a gymnastics competition in Mayfield. As for me, the mastermind, I was here, catching up on some reports. You can check with Missy. She had to help me."

"Missy's your secretary?"

"Summer intern. I have two or three each year."

"Why are you really protesting the pageant?"

He leaned forward, his hands clasped together. "I really don't care if those young women want to be in a beauty pageant. I just don't like the way the pageant feeds into the peer pressure in this town. My niece—" He paused as if deciding how much to tell me. "My niece is recovering from an eating disorder. You see, practically every teenage girl in Celosia feels she should enter the pageant, and if she's not pretty enough or thin enough, she feels worthless. The pageant is the only reason my niece stopped eating, and then she was too weak and thin to enter."

"I'm very sorry," I said. "Is she going to be all right?"

"Yes, thank God. I just don't want that to happen to anyone else. How are these teen girls going to make informed decisions if they hear only one viewpoint? You know what I'm talking about. You got out of the business, didn't you?"

I wasn't surprised that he knew about my pageant background. By now, I assumed my history and Jerry's were all over town. "I didn't have a choice when I was younger, but later, I entered the Miss Parkland pageant for the money."

He sat back, satisfied with my answer. "And that's the way

to do it. If these girls are old enough to make a decision, they need to see both sides of the picture."

"The favorite seems to be Juliet Lovelace."

"Good for her. She's a very strong person. She can probably survive. But someone like Karen Mitman should never have entered."

I hadn't met Karen Mitman. "Why is that?"

"She's a lovely girl, but very timid, very sweet. I'm sure being in the pageant was her mother's idea."

"I can relate to that."

Ted's phone rang. "Excuse me." He picked it up. "Yes, Missy? All right. Tell him I'll be just a few more minutes." He hung up. "I'm sorry. I've got an appointment with a client."

I got up. "No problem."

Ted stood and walked me to the door. "There's a really nice restaurant just up the road. I'd love to continue this conversation over lunch."

I was genuinely sorry to turn him down. "I'm afraid I already have plans."

"Some other time, then. May I call you?"

I gave him my cell-phone number. "That would be nice."

We shook hands again, and he held my hand a while longer. Looking into his warm, dark eyes, I thought, it doesn't look like my chances with Jerry are good—why not see where lunch with Ted Stacy might lead?

"I hope to see you soon, Madeline."

I could answer with all sincerity, "I'm looking forward to it."

SHANA AMRY WAS ten times more beautiful than her photo. Her long red hair shimmered with golden highlights, and her remarkable tawny eyes gleamed like the eyes of some rare tiger. She had on red shorts and a white shirt open at the neck to reveal a gold heart-shaped locket. A large red canvas bag hung over one shoulder. She smiled a perfect cover-girl smile.

"You must be Madeline Maclin. Prill described you perfectly."

"I can't imagine what he said."

"He said, 'You'll know her right away. She's tall, dark, and gorgeous, and looks like she could take on anything.'"

I laughed. "That's generous."

"I'm Shana Amry, and if you're willing to take on anything, then you're the right person for this job." She looked at her gold wristwatch. "I'm meeting a friend for lunch. Please join us. We can talk over cheeseburgers, unless you're a fan of salads."

"Not when there's a cheeseburger around."

"Great. Deely makes the best in town."

We walked a short distance along Main Street and turned down a side street to a small diner called Burger World. Deely was a happy-looking man with a wide smile.

"Afternoon, Shana."

"Deely, this is Madeline Maclin. Madeline, meet Deely Thomas, the best fry cook in town. We want two with everything, Deely, and special fries."

"Yes, ma'am."

We sat down at a small table near the window.

"My friend should be here in a few minutes," Shana said. "Her name is Delores, but everyone calls her Twenty for reasons she won't explain. Don't worry about the fashion disaster. She's harmless."

Twenty arrived in a cloud of perfume. Tall and model-thin, she was dressed in a bright fuchsia-and-lime-green polka-dot dress, clunky lime platform shoes, and a strange sort of pillbox hat with a yellow feather.

"Hello!" She plopped down in the other chair and extended a hand. She was wearing lace gloves and a stacks of brace-

lets. "Welcome to Celosia! I'm Twenty, only really I'm not."
She laughed at what must have been a standing joke.

"Nice to meet you," I said. "I'm Madeline Maclin."

"So you're the detective. I find this all very exciting."

"I'm going to do what I can."

"I suppose Prill told you Hayden's ghost story."

Prill had mentioned a ghostly woman Hayden had seen
outside his window. "It sounds pretty bizarre. This ghost
woman—what does she look like?"

"Very spooky," Shana said. "Hayden says she's glowing
white with black eyes and a black heart on her forehead. Oh,
and there's a dinosaur."

"A dinosaur?"

"Well, the way he describes this creature, it sounds like a
dinosaur." She sighed. "Hayden has too much imagination.
He grew up in such a neurotic home it's a wonder he has any
sense at all. His dad left one day without any explanation,
and his mother is the worst hypochondriac you'll ever meet.
I've cured Hayden of most of his irrational fears, but this is
something new."

Twenty waved her hand. All the bracelets clacked together
like castanets. "Speaking of irrational, don't get me started
on my current boyfriend. He's hopeless."

"How about you, Madeline?" Shana asked. "That's a very
nice-looking man in town with you."

"Jerry and I have been friends for years."

"Friends make the best kind of husbands."

"I don't think that kind of relationship is in our future."

Twenty leaned forward. "I hear he's fixing up the Eberlin
house. Is he actually going to live there? It's falling down,
isn't it?"

"It's actually in pretty good shape," I said.

"Celosia's a nice town," Shana said. "I didn't think I'd like
living in such a small town, but it's the perfect environment
for writing."

"And for Hayden's nerves," Twenty said.

"He just wasn't cut out for a big-city nine-to-five job. Georgia's Books is just the place for him." She salted her fries. "What does Jerry do?"

"Not very much."

Twenty took the salt shaker next. "Isn't his last name Fairweather? He's not one of *the* Fairweathers, is he?"

"Yes."

"My gosh, what's he doing with that old house, then? I thought they had a mansion somewhere in Parkland."

"Jerry's decided to leave all that behind. He thinks he's psychic, so he'll be holding séances in the Eberlin House."

"Oh, my Lord," Shana said. "Don't tell Hayden, or he'll be over there all the time. He believes in all that stuff."

Twenty clapped her hands. "Oh, I do, too! Let me know when he's ready to call up the spirits."

"Save your money," I said.

"But wasn't Val in tune with the cosmos?" Twenty said. "Weren't there all sorts of tales about ghosts and monsters?"

Shana's expression was skeptical. "And time tunnels and alternate universes and mutants. Sometimes a small town can be a little boring and people have to make up their own fun."

I passed the ketchup. "But you believe something really is disturbing Hayden."

"I'd appreciate it if you'd investigate. If you find nothing, that would be just fine. In fact, why don't you and Jerry come to dinner tonight? You can see what I'm talking about."

"Thanks."

"You can come, too, Twenty."

"Sounds like fun! What about Prill?"

"Madeline has probably had enough of Prill."

"No," I said. "He's interesting."

"He's odd," Shana said, "but he's one of Hayden's best friends. I think it's because they have puzzling fathers.

Hayden's just decided to leave one day, and Prill's never speaks to him, even though he lives right here in town."

"Jerry's mother and father died in a fire when he was very young," I said. "I don't exactly know the details."

"Well, the men can start their own little club now, can't they?"

"And you'll have to join our club," Twenty said. "It's a great club. We have no officers, no committees, no dues. We meet whenever we feel like it."

They laughed, including me in their humor. I thought it might be nice to have some real girlfriends. Years in Pageantland had taught me to be wary of friendly smiles and promises, and I certainly wasn't likely to get chummy with Olivia Decker. But Shana was comfortable enough in her own beauty, and Twenty was happy to be quirky. They might be the very friends I needed.

"Well, as long as there's no pledge, initiation, or secret handshake, I'm in."

AT THE HOUSE, Jerry had managed to get paint on practically everything except the wall.

"You're not much of a handyman," I said. "Why don't we leave this to the experts?"

"I can do this."

"Yes, but it'll look like hell. Where's the phone book?"

"Under the newspaper."

"Celosia has a newspaper?"

"The *Celosia News.* Check out page four."

I folded the paper back to page four. A photo showed a small child holding a tomato the size of a beach ball. "Now that's news."

"You know you're in the country when overlarge vegetables are featured prominently in the media."

I scanned the want ads. "Why don't you get a real job? Burger World is hiring."

"I'm holding out for an executive position."

The For Sale ads included musical instruments. "Here's a nice piano for sale. I know you can play."

"No place to put a piano."

"That huge parlor."

"That's my séance room."

I put the paper down. "Why don't you forget that and come down to the theater and help me look for clues?"

He brightened. "And meet all the beauty queens?"

"Miss Lovelace is seventeen. I checked."

"Miss Lovelace is quite lovely, but my heart belongs to Olivia."

Ouch. "The heart she continues to stomp on?"

"The very same."

I knew exactly how that felt. "What brought this on?"

"She called this morning. We've had a long talk," Jerry said. "She's really concerned about me."

I tried to make my voice sound pleasant. "How can you tell?"

"She's thinking of moving out here."

This time, I honestly felt my heart hit my shoes. "Here? To this house?"

"Plenty of room."

"She's leaving her job?"

"It's just a half hour to Parkland."

Olivia Decker. In this house. With Jerry. "You have to be kidding."

"It could happen. That's why I want to get the painting done."

"But she hates the country, doesn't she?"

"That's what I thought, too. Then I remembered she grew up on a farm."

"She did?" I try not to remember details of Olivia Decker's life.

Jerry attempted to paint in the corner and succeeded in

getting paint all over the molding. "Besides, you don't like the rural life, either. You've always said you prefer the city."

"Not now. Not after Reid Kent screwed me over."

Jerry sat back on his heels and looked up at me curiously. "You're thinking of setting up an office in Celosia?"

"Why not? There seems to be enough crime to keep me busy." And I'd be near you. Lord, I almost said that out loud. In fact, I'd be right here in this house. Not Olivia. Me. I'd be here when you fell or caught cold or had to hide from some unhappy dope who'd paid money for a phony psychic reading.

The realization hit me hard. My phantom maternal instinct had surfaced like an Eberlin house spook. Not only would I go anywhere with Jerry, I wanted to look after him.

He was still looking up at me, and I think I would've done something seriously romantic, but there was a knock on the door, and Jerry got up to answer it.

Two men stood on the porch, one tall and red-haired, the other shorter and darker. Both had sour expressions and squinty eyes. They didn't look like men you'd be glad to see, but Jerry was delighted.

"It's my arch foe and his faithful sidekick! Hi, guys!"

If Geoff Snyder's hair weren't already red, Jerry's greeting would've turned it that boiled-lobster color.

"Fairweather, just what the hell do you think you're doing? You can *not* start one of your séance scams in Celosia!"

Jerry wasn't fazed by this attack. "It's not a scam. I'm providing a valuable service to the community."

I thought Geoff's face couldn't get any redder, either. I was wrong. He and his brother Sean were on a crusade to stamp out anything remotely psychic. Luck, chance, fate, whatever you want to call it, they're against it.

"You miserable little charlatan. I'll have you arrested for fraud. I'll have this house condemned!" He started forward, fists clenched.

I stepped up to meet him. "Hold on."

He stopped, glaring. "You keep out of this, Madeline."

"What Jerry does in his own home is his business."

Sean Snyder put in a few words. "Don't tell me he's got *you* fooled, too."

When I took a step toward Sean, he ducked behind his brother. "No, I know it's hokey, but I don't let it affect my blood pressure. What are you two doing here? Aren't there enough psychics in Parkland for you to harass?"

Sean peeked out from behind Geoff. "Our aunt Flossie Mae lives in this town, and we won't have her lured by your black magic."

"It isn't black magic," Jerry said. "It's white magic. The good stuff."

He wasn't helping the situation. "Jerry."

He looked at me, all innocence. "Geoff and Sean haven't even been to one of my séances. How do they know? I'm very entertaining."

Geoff and Sean looked like twin rockets about to go off.

"Everyone calm down," I said. "Geoff, if you don't want your aunt to come here, just tell her. Jerry isn't going to drag her into the house."

"She's very stubborn," Sean said. "If we tried to warn her, she'd come here just to spite us."

"Well, don't warn her. There's really nothing to warn about."

Geoff Snyder shook his finger in Jerry's face. "I swear, if she gives you one penny, I'll beat it out of your hide."

Jerry reached in his pocket. "Why don't I give you a penny now and save you the trouble?"

"Come on, Sean."

The Snyders stalked down the porch steps to their car, got in, and drove away.

I turned to Jerry. His eyes were sparkling. "Why do you bait them like that?"

"Because they're so damn serious about everything."

"Geoff could wipe the floor with you."

"No, he couldn't."

"You've spent so much of your life running away, I doubt you know how to make a fist."

He did, threatening me with a grin. "Come on, give me your best shot."

"Go get cleaned up. We're due at the Amrys' by seven."

IT DIDN'T TAKE HIM LONG to get ready. After I convinced him his plain gold tie would look much nicer with his dark suit than the tie shaped like a rainbow trout, we drove out to Autumn Fields.

The Amrys' home was a beautiful redwood house with a wraparound porch, set deep in a lush woodland. Shana met us at the door, radiant in a short red dress and gold jewelry. I heard Jerry gulp.

"Gosh," he said under his breath as she led us through the living room to a candlelit dining room. "If I'd known the women in Celosia looked like this, I'd have moved here years ago."

Hayden was in the dining room, rearranging the silverware. Twenty was helping him, oddly attractive in a short silver-and-lime-green kimono, red leather boots, and fishnet hose.

She came forward, her hand extended, bracelets jangling. "You must be Jerry Fairweather. Aren't you brave to sleep in that haunted house?"

"I'm hoping it's haunted," he said. "I think it would be fun."

"Well, you sound like my kind of guy."

No, he's my kind of guy, I wanted to say, but caught myself. If I started reacting to every innocent remark, my little secret wouldn't be secret for long.

Shana said, "Twenty, why don't you sit at the end, and I'll put a man on either side of you."

"Just the way I like it," she said.

I sat next to Jerry and across from Shana. She raised her wineglass. "A toast, please, to new friends."

"To new friends," we all said. We clinked our glasses and drank.

"To new helpful friends," Twenty said. "I just had the most amazing brainstorm. Jerry, you and Hayden would be perfect for my fashion show. Please say you'll be in it."

"A fashion show?" Jerry said.

"I've been after Hayden for months, but I bet he'll do it if you will."

Jerry looked to Hayden for an explanation. Hayden grimaced. "She wants me to model some suits."

Shana joined in. "And I told her that was all right with me if she didn't mess with his hair."

Twenty sighed. "Oh, come on. I just want to spike it up a little. It's not like I'm going to color it blue or something."

Jerry grinned. "You can spike mine. It's already out of control."

"Really? That would be so cool!" She leaned over to press Hayden's arm. "Come on, Hayden. I won't do anything to your hair. Just come model a couple of suits. You'd look so good in black."

Hayden didn't look convinced. "So you want me to wear a suit and walk around in front of a bunch of people? This sounds suspiciously like a Mr. Celosia Pageant."

"Oh, my, no. This is a legitimate fashion show of Antoine Largen's new fall line."

"Fall? It's July."

Twenty looked at me and shook her head. "They have no clue. Guys, in the fashion world, you have to be months ahead."

"Well, I'll do it," Jerry said. "Just tell me when and where."

"Excellent! We have a rehearsal in two weeks, and the show is the last day of July. I have a dark blue suit that would look great on you, and a gray that you were born to wear."

Hayden was still thinking about it. "Two suits? That's all?"

"Yes, dear, a dark blue and a black. Please say yes. I may put you and Jerry in black at the end. You'll look good together because you're the same height."

"I think Hayden's a little taller," I said, and Jerry gave my arm a punch.

I had noticed similarities between Hayden Amry and Jerry. They were about the same size. They both had youthful faces brightened by expressive eyes. But Hayden had a distracted air; he seemed anxious, even about something as simple as modeling a few suits. His every move was careful and deliberate. I vastly preferred Jerry's cheerful demeanor. His movements were quicker, more decisive, and he certainly smiled more. As much as I admired Hayden's blue-green eyes, whenever Jerry looked at me with his calm gray gaze, I still felt that sudden jump in my pulse.

Suddenly, something made us all jump, a jarring noise from somewhere on the front porch.

"What in the world was that?" Shana said.

"Are you expecting company?" I asked.

"No. Hayden?"

He was already on his feet. Another thump. "I'll go see."

"I'll come with you," I said, and Jerry followed me.

We stepped out onto the porch. A mild breeze sent a few leaves scurrying across the lawn. The moon shone faintly behind the clouds. Nothing else. No movement in the forest.

"Theo?" Hayden said.

A shape darted around the corner of the porch, small, humped, alien.

Hayden reacted with alarm. "Oh, no. Another one!"

The shape was too large for a dog and moved with a curious sideways motion. It headed toward the back of the house.

"Another what?" Jerry asked.

Hayden spoke in a panicked whisper. "She's sent something after us, an evil creature to do her bidding, a familiar, a demon."

Jerry brightened. "A demon? Hot damn."

We followed the shape. It stopped at one of the side windows. It was bigger than I'd first thought, and it was hunched over the sill doing—doing what? It moved on, heading for the dining-room windows.

Hayden was shaking. "How can we stop it?"

Something crunched under our feet. I bent down and touched a grainy powder. The same substance was all over the window frame.

"Is it cocaine?" Jerry asked me.

"Why would anyone sprinkle it on the window sills?"

"We have to stop this creature," Hayden said.

The figure turned the corner of the porch and halted just before the light spilling out of the dining-room windows. We heard Shana call, "Hayden, is that you thumping around out there?"

He cried, "Don't come out!" but she had already pushed open the French doors and stepped out onto the porch, face to face with the mysterious prowler. Twenty was right behind her. Shana screamed. The creature swerved, saw us coming up behind, and made a mad dash past Shana and Twenty into the dining room.

Shana ran after it. "Get out of my house!"

Twenty came next, shouting for Shana to leave the burglar alone. We ran back around the porch and in the front door, hoping to intercept the creature. We did better than intercept. We ran right into it. Yellow light flashed as if a gigantic camera had taken a group shot. When my vision cleared, I found everyone on the floor. Shana was coughing and waving smoke away with one of the sofa cushions, her dress smudged and her hair in wild disarray. Twenty was charred around the edges, her face outlined in smoke, her hair and clothes so tangled, I could hardly tell where hairdo began and outfit ended.

Jerry blinked from his soot-smeared face. "Is everybody okay?"

Hayden was sitting on the creature. "Bummer!" he said in surprise.

At first, I thought he was making an astute observation. Then I saw he was talking to the man I'd seen in the bookstore.

"What are you doing here?" Hayden asked him.

The little man was shaken. "Told you I'd come. Get rid of the ghosts, remember?"

The grainy substance. Bread crumbs.

Hayden glanced at Shana. She'd gotten to her feet, her hands on her hips and fire in her eyes. He stood and pulled Bummer to his feet.

"This is Friday, ain't it?" Bummer said.

"No, this is Thursday. My wife and I have dinner guests, as you can see. What the hell was all that light and noise?"

Bummer took a pack of firecrackers out of his pocket. "Loud noises scare 'em away, too."

"Don't tell me you thought we were ghosts," Shana said.

Jerry wiped his face with his handkerchief and grimaced at the streaks of black. "What's going on? What kind of ghosts do you have around here?"

Shana's voice was tightly controlled. "This unfortunate man is a town character and one of Hayden's many screwball friends. This was a cute little prank, Mr. Stevenson, but I think you'd better go now."

"Want me to come back tomorrow?"

"No," Hayden said. "Did you walk all the way over here?

Let me take you home, and you can explain what to do. I'll handle it from there."

Bummer shrugged. "Well, all right, if you think that'll do it."

"It certainly will," Shana said.

Hayden drove Bummer home. By the time he came back, we had cleaned our faces and attempted to straighten the living room.

We sat down at the dining-room table to finish our dinner. Shana poured everyone another glass of wine. "Honestly," she said, "you see what I have to put up with? Hayden, explain again why he was here."

"He got the days mixed up."

"He got the days mixed up. You were planning to explode firecrackers in the house, only not today?"

"No, there weren't supposed to be any explosions. I thought he was just going to sprinkle some bread crumbs." The minute the words left his mouth, we knew he was doomed. Shana's eyes narrowed to dangerous slits, and when she spoke, her voice was deadly calm.

"Bread crumbs?"

"It sounds crazy. I know it does. Bummer was only trying to help. You know how he is."

"No, but I know how you are. You're insane."

"Hayden," I said, "what did you mean when you said, 'Oh, no. Another one'? Have you been bothered by prowlers?"

"And who's Theo?" Jerry asked.

Hayden glanced at Shana, who sighed. "Go on and tell them the whole ghost story." He hesitated. "Go ahead. It'll be like dinner and a movie."

"All right." He stood and paced as if to work up his nerve. "It's like this. I've seen two ghosts in this house. One is a woman. She calls herself Portia. She's very beautiful, but she's very eerie-looking. She has very black hair and eyes like black holes. She's been telling me the oddest story."

Jerry sat up straighter. "Wait a minute. Does she wear a long white dress?"

"Yes, a sort of old-fashioned gown."

"I've seen her! Mac, that's the ghost I saw yesterday."

"Please don't encourage each other," Shana said.

Jerry was thrilled. "Black hair, black eyes, white gown. That's her."

"Was there another ghost with her?" Hayden asked. "It would look like a large lizard or dinosaur."

I could tell Jerry was disappointed he'd missed that one. "No, just the woman."

"The other ghost is Theo. He's trying to keep Portia from harming anyone. They're old enemies. She's told me all of this."

Jerry was full of questions. "Are they always together? Where did they come from? When did you first see them?"

"I think they came from an alternate universe."

"Oh, man, this is great! Where's the portal?"

"It must be somewhere in the woods."

The two men must have sensed our disbelief, because they stopped talking. When they paused to look at us, I'm sure my expression mirrored Shana's.

Hayden said, "Well, that's what Portia told me."

Shana sighed again. "Where did we go wrong, Madeline? Jerry looks so normal, and I really thought I'd married a sane man."

"But this is perfect," Jerry said. "I need some ghosts for the house."

"Not Portia," Hayden said. "She has an awful lot of teeth."

"Teeth?" Jerry said. "She looked beautiful to me."

"Oh, yes. At first, she looks beautiful and serene. But don't let her kiss you. Her kisses are so cold."

"Oh, now she's kissing you?" Shana said.

"The other night when I was so cold. You remember."

"You kicked all the covers off."

He shivered. "It was that first nightmare. I get cold just thinking about it."

Jerry gave me a worried glance, but Shana rolled her eyes. "I think we've bored our guests long enough with this nonsense. Let's have cake and coffee and try to salvage some of the evening."

Then Hayden said something else. "I was thinking Cynthia Riley could perform an exorcism."

Shana went so still I knew this had to be a major Foot-in-Mouth Moment.

"Oh, that's perfect," she said. "Cynthia Riley can come waltzing in anytime she likes, and you call it an exorcism?" She pushed herself up from the table and pointed a finger in his face. "You bring that woman in here and I'll skin you alive."

"Shana, for goodness sake," Hayden said.

"I've seen the way she looks at you! I don't have to be psychic to know what's on her mind."

I exchanged a glance with Jerry. This conversation was rapidly getting out of control.

Hayden said, "But I don't care anything about Cynthia Riley. That's ridiculous. Now who's having a problem with her imagination?"

Twenty's eyes went wide. She gave a nervous little giggle. Shana's face was as red as her hair. I thought Hayden was well on his way to becoming a ghost, but Shana took a deep breath and smiled.

"Why don't you write this story down? I think that would cure anyone's writer's block."

He gave her an apologetic look. "I promise I won't hire Cynthia Riley."

"Thank you."

"You could hire me," Jerry said brightly.

"Thank you, Jerry." She gave Hayden a sidelong glance.

"But since there are no evil spirits in our house, you'd be wasting your time. Hayden, sweetie, would you get the dessert?"

When Hayden went into the kitchen, Shana explained that he'd been chosen to write a special poem for the dedication of the new elementary school, and she thought that was preying on his mind.

"Nightmares I can take. Nervousness, a little stress, okay. But when he starts inviting his loony pyromaniac customers to the house to sprinkle bread crumbs, I simply have to draw the line."

"But I saw Portia, too," Jerry said. "Maybe I'm picking up vibes from Hayden."

I ignored this. "When did he start seeing these ghosts?"

Shana folded and unfolded her napkin. "About a month ago, he started hearing Portia. Then he started having nightmares about her. I have to confess I'm worried. If he could just start writing again, I know that would help. He puts too much pressure on himself."

Jerry hadn't given up. "What if I hold a séance here at the house and tell Portia to get lost?"

"No," Shana said. "I don't want anyone encouraging him."

"Here we go," Hayden said, returning with a large cake. "Hope you like chocolate."

To be a good guest, Jerry limited his conversation to his remodeling plans, but I could tell he really wanted to discuss communicating with Portia. We finished our cake and coffee. Shana saw us to the door. "I'm sorry the evening exploded," she said, "but you got an excellent demonstration of why I'm so worried."

"I'll come back tomorrow morning and look around," I said. "It's probably the same pranksters who keep stealing our cereal."

"But why target Hayden? He's never done anything to anyone."

"They might be trying to get to you."

"Me?"

"Somebody's who's jealous of your success might want to disturb your life so you can't concentrate on your writing. The best way to do that is by attacking someone close to you."

She was plainly taken aback. "I can't imagine anyone who'd do that."

"That's what I can find out."

"I'll see you tomorrow, then. Good night, Jerry. Don't let anything get you, either."

"I won't," he said. "I've got a real good bodyguard here."

"I'M FLATTERED," I said as we got in the car.

"What?"

"Your remark to Shana."

"Oh," he said. "I know you can take care of yourself and me. We'll catch this weird woman or whatever she is." Then he quoted from *Ghostbusters:* "'We have the tools; we have the talent.' Or you do, at least. That was pretty impressive back there."

It was my turn to say, "What?"

"Well, you sounded very professional."

"Thank you." My cell phone beeped. "Hello? Oh, hello, Ted." I avoided Jerry's eye. "Lunch tomorrow? That would be fine. Okay, I'll meet you there." I turned off the phone.

Jerry sang, "'Here comes the bride.'"

"Don't be ridiculous. It's just lunch."

He started the car and drove down the Amrys' driveway. "But don't you see, Mac? It isn't just lunch. It's Fate. You were meant to find Reid Kent messing with your answering machine. You were meant to come to Celosia and find the man of your dreams."

I'm sitting in the car with him, I wanted to say. "Ted Stacy is a suspect."

"Even better. When you clear him of all charges, he'll be

really grateful." He wiggled his eyebrows. "Or you could get lucky tomorrow."

"You'll be lucky if I don't smother you in your sleep tonight."

"Listen to your friendly neighborhood oracle. I still say it was meant to be."

Some oracle. He couldn't see past the best friend. "Just promise me one thing."

"Sure."

"Don't go as far off the deep end as Hayden. He needs serious help."

Jerry drove toward town. "Yeah, maybe he's believing a little too much. But what if it's true? What if there really is an alternate universe?"

"Then you'll be the first one to fall through to the other side."

"I'd like that."

He sounded serious. "Why?"

"Maybe things haven't gone the way I planned."

Things definitely hadn't gone the way I'd planned. "You actually had a plan?"

"I just imagined life would be different, that's all."

"Different how?"

He stopped at one of Celosia's few stoplights and looked at me. "The same, I mean. I thought everything would stay the same. I knew my brothers and I would all grow up and probably move away, but the house would always be there. My parents. Everyone well and happy."

He rarely spoke of his parents. "I'm sorry, Jerry."

The light turned green. He drove down Main Street and turned at the corner. As we left the town behind and headed out into the warm darkness of the countryside, he said, "I thought I might be something, you know. A doctor or a lawyer or even a scientist for NASA. Something important and useful."

"It's not too late. You could still be whatever you wanted to be."

"That's just it, Mac. I don't know what I want to be. And it is kinda late. Benjamin Britten was only twenty-six when he wrote *Paul Bunyan.* I'm way behind."

"You're planning to write an opera?"

"You know what I mean."

"You think you'd find the answer on the other side? Is that why you keep playing with all this psychic stuff?"

"Des is psychic, and so is Tucker."

I'd never seen any indication of this. "What makes you say that?"

"Well, we were all there when—" He stopped.

"When what, Jerry? What's the big family mystery? Can't you even tell me?"

"No," he said. "I'm not sure it really happened."

"Don't go all Hayden Amry on me."

He wasn't going to say anything else about it. "That's why the Eberlin house is perfect. This séance thing is just right."

"I think it's just going to get you into trouble."

"And you can bail me out."

"Oh, so that's why I'm along."

Even in the darkness of the car, I could see him smile. "That's not the only reason."

My heart began to beat a little faster. "Oh?"

But Jerry's answer wasn't what I'd hoped for. "I need you to kick Geoff Snyder's butt for me."

Damn him and his occult nonsense. If he hadn't been driving, I would've smacked him.

FOUR

A SCREECHING NOISE penetrated my eardrums. I groaned and opened my eyes to stare at my alarm clock. That rooster had to die.

I staggered downstairs. Jerry, as usual, had been up long before me. He was sitting on the porch, eating a doughnut.

"What do you want for lunch?" he asked. "I thought I'd get a grill, maybe burn some steaks."

"Is it lunchtime already?"

"I'm planning ahead."

I shook my head. "I must still be asleep. I thought I heard you say something about planning ahead."

"Just a few hours."

"Steaks sound good for supper, but I'm having lunch with Ted Stacy, remember?"

He didn't seem at all concerned. "Oh, yeah. Well, have a good time."

"What household repair job are you going to muck up today?"

"Gee, I don't know. How about if I clean the chimney?"

"If I come back and find you stranded on the roof, I'm leaving you there."

"Fair enough."

SHANA MET ME at the door of her home. "Let's sit out on the porch. The house still smells charred."

We took seats in two rocking chairs. She gazed out at the front yard. Birds chirped at the feeder hung in the nearest tree. The scene was calm, but her eyes were filled with concern. "I've been thinking about what you said. I really don't have any enemies, and neither does Hayden. Everyone at Burlson and Rawls was sorry to see him go, and his main rival was delighted."

"That's where he worked in Parkland?"

"Yes, but selling just wasn't his thing. The hours and the competition got to be too much."

"Has he seen things before?"

"Lots of times. He has a very active imagination. But he's taking all this so seriously."

"You wouldn't mind if I had a look around the grounds, would you?" If someone was playing a trick, he or she may have left footprints or some other clue behind.

"Not at all."

I looked around Shana's house. I didn't find any footprints, human or dinosaur. The bushes were all intact except for a large boxwood near the back. It had split down the middle, whether from age or someone trying to climb on it, I couldn't tell. But the ground glittered with a few tiny round objects I recognized immediately. Sequins.

There were more sequins near the edge of the forest. I followed them along a trail that wandered through huge trees shaggy with moss surrounded by velvety green grass. Birds sang. Butterflies danced over the wildflowers. I stopped when I discovered a log cabin. There were no cars in the driveway, and no one answered when I knocked on the door. All the curtains were closed. I circled the cabin, but failed to find any more sequins. Beyond the cabin, the woods thinned, and I could see a meadow. It was hard to tell, but I was pretty sure it was the same meadow that bordered the Eberlin house.

When I got back to Shana's house, Gregory Prill waved to me from the porch.

"Good morning, Madeline. Out communing with nature, were you?"

"Just for a little while. I can't take too much nature."

His laugh was deep and full, not the high-pitched giggle I expected.

"Sounds like you need a drink."

I sat down in a rocking chair and accepted a glass of tea. "Thank you."

"I am so sorry I missed the events of last evening. You must tell all."

"Well, Hayden's friend Bummer thought he'd save us from the ghosts and nearly blew up the house."

"What an imbecile." He rolled his bulging eyes toward Shana and grinned a sly grin. "Everyone knows you need a qualified exorcist, like Cynthia Riley."

Shana bristled. "Don't mention that woman's name in my house."

He laughed again. "My dear Shana! If you think a scrawny Afghan hound of a woman like Cynthia Riley could possibly tempt Hayden away from you, you must be demented."

"Oh, I'm not worried about Hayden. I'm worried about how that harpy looks at him. She wants him, Prill, you know she does."

"And who could blame her? I want him, too. Don't you, Madeline?"

"Absolutely."

Shana had to smile. "This comedy act will never make it to the stage."

Prill readjusted his cape. "So, Madeline, what does your great detecting brain tell you about this case?"

"I don't have enough information yet," I said, "but I suspect it's someone playing a pretty elaborate trick."

"Shall I tell you what I think?"

"By all means."

He took a sip of his tea. "This ghost of his, Portia, the one he says is out to get him, is a symbol for all this emotion he says he's not carrying around inside, all the worry and frustration and jealousy. Portia is simply a symbol for Shana, a Shana he loves and hates."

"He doesn't hate me," Shana said.

"Didn't he tell you his dream? She was kissing him, so at first, he thought it was you. She's taking the success he feels should be his, so, in a sense, she's killing him."

"Prill—"

"And this Theo figure is simply his more reasonable side coming to the rescue, knocking him away from the confrontation. It's amazing what the mind can do. You could even call it suppressed desires. What a splendid title for a book."

I could tell Shana had had enough. "I think you need to leave the analyzing to the experts."

Prill bowed. "Actually, I need to just leave. Monthly meeting of FLUF. Tell Hayden he's way behind in his dues."

He left in his pearl-gray Mercedes. Shana offered me some more tea. "I've been thinking, Madeline. Maybe the dedication poem isn't what's bothering Hayden. We've had some other disagreements."

I figured she meant her successful career versus his stalled career. "Career problems?"

"Oh, no. About children."

There is no escape. "Children?"

"Hayden wants children, and I haven't the slightest interest."

I couldn't believe it. "Shana, am I speaking to the only other woman in this part of the country besides myself who is not interested in having children?"

She smiled. "Hayden's the only child I want, and if I'm reading all the signals right, you feel the same way about Jerry."

I felt my face grow hot. Before I could say anything, Shana apologized.

"It's none of my business, really, but I couldn't help noticing. I do write romance novels, you know. I'm used to those meaningful glances and heartfelt sighs."

"I'd hoped it wasn't that obvious."

"No. Don't mind me. Sometimes I have an overactive imagination, too."

"It's a recent development."

"Does he know?"

I shook my head. "He has a girlfriend. They seemed to have split up, which got me hoping. But it looks like they're back together."

"People can change their minds."

But I wanted Jerry to be happy, and if that meant Olivia Decker, who was I to get in the way?

She smiled. "Madeline, you're going to have to spell it out for him."

"Right now, the only word he can spell is *f-r-i-e-n-d*."

"Well, that's better than nothing."

I didn't want to discuss my problems. "So you and Hayden quarrel about children?"

"Not the way we blew up last night. It's more like sad, wounded looks from him and defiant glares from me. I grew up with three brothers and two sisters. I love all this peace and quiet, and I want to keep it as long as I can. Hayden's an only child. He wants to be a father. I can't quite decide why, but I think it has something to do with his own father running off. Maybe he has to prove he's a better man."

"Would this make him see ghostly women and dinosaurs in the woods?"

"In a word: yes. You should read some of his poems. I think he's channeling Edgar Allan Poe. Let me show you a sample."

She went into the house. I gazed at the quiet sun-filled woods. One by one, I'd lost my best girlfriends to Motherhood. Candy Sims, whose darkly comic observations on life used to have me holding my sides with laughter, now spoke only in bizarre baby talk. No conversation was spared; I always had to hear what Nunaw and Poopah thought of their little Tinky Boo. Alison Farmore did nothing but recite what Taylor and Tyler, the world's most gifted twin girls, had accomplished, while I wanted to scream, "Taylor and Tyler are boy's names!" Even B.J. O'Hara, my college roommate, once an aspiring architect, could talk of nothing but the virtues of Powder Pink over Lullaby Blue for Madison's nursery. Madison. Honestly. If I ever had a little girl, I'd name her something that sounded like a girl's name, something pretty and feminine.

Not that I'd ever have a little girl.

Shana returned, carrying a slim blue book. "You look so serious."

I grinned. "You don't want to know."

"This is Hayden's first collection, *Glass Plums.* Don't ask me what it means."

I thumbed through the pages. "That's okay. One of my girlfriends in college wrote strange poetry. We'd just read and nod and say, 'That's deep.'"

Hayden's poems were dark but somehow intriguing. I found lots of references to loss and pain and shadowy figures. The title poem had nothing to do with glass or plums.

> Your touch, cold with regret
> Your longing glance slow as the last drop of rain
> dreaming its way down the glass.
> I will destroy what harms you.

Hmm, kind of spooky. "Is he working on a second collection?"

"Yes. It takes him days to polish a single line, while I can easily write thousands of words a day when a story is rolling out."

I handed her the book. "He's a bit intense."

She looked worried. "Madeline, I'm really concerned. There has to be an explanation for these things he's seeing."

"I might camp out in your woods."

"Please do."

"Who lives in the log cabin?"

"Oh, that belongs to the Laytons. They aren't home. They spend their summers in the mountains." She checked her watch. "It's almost eleven. Care for some lunch?"

"No, thank you. I have plans."

"Well, don't worry about Jerry. He'll figure it out."

"Not now," I said. "It's too late. He and Olivia have kissed and made up."

Shana smiled. "Take it from me, the expert in romance. It's never too late."

JERRY WASN'T STUCK up the chimney or on the roof. He was sitting on the porch looking through the yellow pages. I didn't see smoke or water running down the steps.

"What did you break?"

"I'm going to hire someone to help me," he said. "I need time to concentrate on the spirit world."

"That's a good idea—the hiring part, I mean."

I went upstairs, took a shower, and purposely put on the best black dress I had and my go-to-hell high heels. Jerry's reaction wasn't quite what I'd hoped.

"Is he flying you to New York?"

"I felt like dressing up."

"You look ready for the Met."

The Met. Our senior year, we'd taken a road trip to New York City to see an opera at the Met. It was some Spanish thing, probably *Carmen*. I'd spent most of the opera either asleep, or watching Jerry enjoy the show. It was one of my favorite memories.

I paused at the porch steps, hoping Jerry would say something else about my ensemble, but all he said was, "Have a good time."

Ted Stacy's reaction to my finery was more satisfying. "You look sensational, Madeline. Way too glorious for the Atlas Café."

"I felt the need to be fancy today."

"Dixley will never be the same."

We took Ted's black BMW to Dixley, Celosia's arch rival. The Atlas Café was a shiny silver diner with a full parking lot.

Ted explained the café's popularity. "Best salad bar in the county, and the best iced tea."

I can do without the rabbit food, but there was plenty to choose from on the salad bar, including fried chicken, ham, and fish fillets. After we were seated and ordered drinks, we headed for the long buffet tables for load number one.

Ted grinned at my all-meat platter. "Next time, we'll go to Big Sid's House of Ribs."

"I'll take you up on that."

"Thought you women liked to watch the calories."

"Not when there's fried chicken on the menu."

"Then you'll be real happy with the desserts."

The waitress brought two large glasses of iced tea to our table. Ted thanked her.

"Who's your friend?" she asked.

"Kelly, meet Madeline Maclin. Madeline, Kelly Torrue."

"Nice to meet you," Kelly said. "First time at the Atlas?"

"Yes. You have a great selection."

"Special dessert today is fresh strawberry shortcake."

My eyes must have gleamed because Ted said, "We'll have two."

Kelly made a check on her order pad. "Bring 'em when you're done."

The fried chicken was deliciously crispy; the ham tasted

as if it had been cooked in honey. "Everything's very good," I said.

Ted's plate was heaped with salad. "Glad you like it. How are things going at the house? Your friend's decided to stay, I hear."

"He gets these ideas."

"Known him long?"

"We met at the University of North Carolina at Greensboro."

"Oh, yeah? I went to UNC Charlotte." Ted shook a generous dusting of Parmesan cheese onto his salad. "His last name's Fairweather, right? I thought all those folks went to Harvard or Yale."

"I'm not sure why he chose the university."

"What did you study?"

"History and English."

"And what made you decide to be an investigator?"

"Because it feels like a real accomplishment, not a fantasy one. And it doesn't involve a tiara."

"I know you told me about your pageant career and how you entered Miss Parkland for the money. I hope you'll talk to the Miss Celosia contestants about that. Young girls need positive role models. They need to know their options."

"I have been talking to the contestants, Juliet Lovelace in particular."

He grimaced. "Now, there's a young lady who needs some direction. Her aunt doesn't seem to care a bit what she does. It's a real shame, because she's a smart girl. She was the most talented intern I've had."

Randi Peterson's accusations about Juliet came to my mind. Ted certainly qualified as "good-looking." "Did you have any problems with her? Personal problems, I mean?"

"I like to give people opportunities, but I'm afraid Juliet took advantage of the situation."

"How so?"

"Let's just say it didn't work out." His smile returned. "But I don't want to talk about Juliet."

He was definitely uncomfortable discussing Juliet. "All right. Let's talk about you. Are you from Celosia?"

"I grew up in Charlotte, and when I had enough of the big city, I moved here. My grandparents were from Celosia. My best memories are of playing in the fields and woods all summer."

"Any family here?"

"I'm divorced."

"I am, too."

"Any kids?"

"No."

"Me, either. Erica and I never got around to it. We were too busy fighting. Now I'm glad, because I wouldn't have wanted to drag any children through all that. I'd still like to have children, though."

Why did everyone in the world feel the need to procreate? Ted looked at me with unmistakable hope. It was way too soon in this relationship to disappoint him, but what could I say that wouldn't sound too harsh?

I was saved by the arrival of our strawberry shortcakes.

We spent the rest of our lunch date enjoying the food and talking about Celosia. I asked Ted about Val Eberlin, but he hadn't known him very well.

"He'd come to town on occasion to buy groceries or go to the post office. That's where I'd see him. I had no idea he was related to the Fairweathers."

"How did he make a living?"

"I don't know. I always thought he was retired."

Kelly stopped at our table. She held a pitcher of iced tea. "Refills?"

"No, thanks," I said.

Ted pulled out his billfold. "We're ready for the check."

Kelly set the pitcher down and tore off a page from her pad. She handed the paper to Ted. "Ya'll come back."

Ted put some bills on the table. "Madeline, this has been a pleasure. I hope you'll let me treat you again."

"My treat next time," I said.

"If there's anything I can do to help with your case, let me know."

"Do you plan to stand outside the theater Saturday night, daring people to cross the picket line?"

He grinned. "We won't take things that far."

We drove back to Celosia. Ted walked me to my car and opened the door. "There's just one condition to our next date, Madeline."

"What's that?"

"You have to wear the same dress and shoes."

"That can be arranged."

"Till next time, then."

I liked Ted Stacy. He wasn't pushy. He didn't talk too much or sit like a log without attempting any conversation. He'd left a big tip. Bill had always stiffed the waitresses.

I didn't want to think about Bill. I found myself wanting to think about Ted.

WHEN I GOT BACK to the Eberlin house, I saw a dirty white van parked under a tree. The van's back doors were open, revealing rows of paint cans, stacks of wood, coils of extension cord, and various power tools. Inside, I found Jerry and a large, square-shaped woman painting the living room. The woman's short blond ponytail stuck out the back of a dirty white baseball cap. White paint-splattered overalls, a grubby tee shirt, and ancient sneakers completed her ensemble. Her small features gathered in the middle of a face tanned so dark, her blue eyes gleamed.

"You 'bout the clumsiest little guy I ever seen," she said as Jerry stepped in the paint tray. From the looks of his sneakers, this wasn't the first time. "Why don't you get out of here and let me work?"

"I can do it," he said.

"No, you can't. Go in the kitchen."

"Mac, tell Nell I know how to paint a wall."

The woman scowled at me.

"Nell," I said, "I'll get him out of your way."

She gave an amused snort. "Thank you."

"Come on, Jerry."

We went into the kitchen. He sat down at the table to sulk. "Banished. In my own home."

"She can finish a lot quicker without you. Who is she?"

"I didn't realize I was hiring a Viking. I thought, oh, a woman. That'll be nice. This is Celosia. She'll be gorgeous. Nell's father must have been a tank."

"Nell who?"

"Nell Brenner."

"Brenner as in chief of police Brenner?"

"I didn't ask."

"Stay here."

I returned to the living room to introduce myself.

"I'm Madeline Maclin."

She gave me a brief nod. "Nell Brenner. Been wanting to get my hands on this house for a long time. Looks like I'm not too late." She took a screwdriver from her overall pocket and pried open another can of paint. "You're the detective, right?"

"Yes. I'm investigating the goings-on at the local pageant. Are you any relation to the chief?"

"That's my dad."

Her father? She looked to be about sixty.

She set the lid onto a piece of newspaper on the floor. "He says it's just some teenagers cutting up."

"I'm also trying to find out who's playing ghost with Hayden Amry."

She shook her head. "That boy's had a hard time."

"How do you mean?"

She took a stick and stirred the paint. "First of all, the daddy runs off, leaves the mother to raise Hayden all on her own. Then he finally gets to being a success and had to leave his job in Parkland. Worked for some big company."

"Was he fired?"

"Nah. Had a breakdown. They were real nice about it. Hayden's not the salesman type, that's all. Too sensitive."

"A serious breakdown?" This would explain seeing ghosts and phantom dinosaurs.

"Stayed about a week in some hospital, resting mostly. Shana thought Autumn Fields would be a good place for peace and quiet, and now the boy's seeing things all over it."

"What about Shana? Do you know if she has any enemies?"

"A woman that pretty? You probably know how that is."

"Well, thanks, but I'm not in her league."

"Nobody is. But I don't know of an enemy, not here in town." She poured the paint into a tray. "So what's the story with you and Mr. Fix-It?"

"We're just friends."

She paused to give me a long, considering look. "Uh-huh."

"Known each other since college."

"Have you now?"

I needed to change the subject. "What can you tell me about Ted Stacy?"

"He's all right. Plays fair."

"Benjy Goins?"

"Class clown. Never got over it."

"Kimberly Dawn Williams?"

"Never seen so much hair on a human head." She pushed a paint roller into the tray. "Loved being Miss Celosia. Won't let anybody forget it, neither. Same little squirt she always was. We called her Kimmy D in school just to get her tail in a crack."

It was hard to imagine Nell Brenner and Kimberly Dawn Williams being in school together. "Juliet Lovelace?"

Nell smoothed the roller over the wall. "Now there's a wild one. Got one of the coaches fired. 'Course, he couldn't keep his hands where they belonged."

"Donna Sanchez and Randi Peterson said some disparaging things about her."

"Jealous bunch of little hellcats. That Sanchez was caught at a club in Far Corners. Story goes she was dancing on tables naked. And the other one's just as bad. Lost her driver's license almost before she got it."

Nell Brenner was turning out to be the best source I'd ever used. She kept painting, her smooth, even strokes sliding fresh blue paint over the dingy gray walls.

"What about Gregory Prill?"

She gave a snort. "Fussy old queen. Harmless, though."

"Would he have any reason to play tricks on the Amrys?"

"Lord, no. They're good friends." She dipped the roller back into the tray. She called into the kitchen, "Hey, shorty. Come see if this suits you." She winked at me. "I'm just picking at him."

"He can take it."

Jerry entered, trying to look dignified. "Am I allowed back in my own living room?"

"Just in the doorway," Nell said. "How's it look?"

"Looks great."

"Well, don't mess with it. It'll be dry in a couple of hours. I'll be back tomorrow to see about the plumbing."

"Okay, thanks."

Jerry waved good-bye as Nell's van lumbered down the drive.

I joined him on the porch. "So, aren't you going to ask me what I had for lunch?"

"Oh, yeah. How did that go?"

"We had a great time. We have a lot in common."

"Skip that part. What did you have to eat?"

I sat down in one of the rocking chairs and pulled off my high heels. "Everything. Full barn buffet at the Atlas Café. Strawberry shortcake for dessert."

"Well, while you were stuffing yourself, I had an important phone call."

"From the Acme Toy Company. They want their Magic Eight Ball back."

Jerry's grin was full of mischief. "No, from Geoff and Sean's aunt Flossie Mae."

"Oh, brother."

He could hardly contain himself. "She's coming here at 8:00 for a séance. She's bringing two friends with her."

"Jerry."

"I've been in town only a few days, and the word is out. The Snyder boys will pop."

I finally got his attention. "The only thing they'll pop is your nose."

"Oh, they won't be a problem. Aunt Flossie Mae sounded like a gal who gets her way. Come take a look at the séance room."

I followed him to the front parlor. He had pulled one of the tables to the center of the room and placed chairs around it. "When you turn off the lights, the room looks really spooky. The musty smell is good, too. I told Nell to leave this room as is."

"Couldn't you forget the séance stuff? It's so stupid."

"It brings in good money. Once Flossie Mae and her friends get the deluxe reading, I won't be able to keep up with the demand." He put his hands on the back of one chair. "This is my chair here, facing the window. I don't have time to set up the flying trumpets, but this will be a great place to see the reflection of the ectoplasm."

I sighed and left the room. There's no talking to him when he gets like this.

He came after me. "What? You don't like ectoplasm? I'll admit it's a little messy, but it's very effective."

"I need to change clothes."

"Can I borrow your car? I need to buy a few things before they get here."

"Sure. The keys are in it."

Jerry had been gone about ten minutes when I heard another car drive up. I looked out and saw something I didn't want to see: Olivia Decker. She got out of her car, looking trim and tiny in black jeans and a black tee shirt. Her cell phone was clipped to her belt. She came in and looked around the living room.

"Don't tell me Jerry did all this."

"He's paying someone to do it."

"With what? Where does he get the money?"

"I don't know."

"You could find out." She inspected the room. "This is what he does all day while you're out detecting?"

"Actually, we stay home and screw like weasels."

Her smile was patronizingly sweet. "Of course you do. Where is Jerry, by the way?"

"He had some errands to run in town. Why are you here, Olivia?"

"Jerry won't come to Parkland."

That wasn't much of an answer. "Haven't you given up yet?"

She flicked some imaginary dust from one of the chairs and sat down. "Here's the thing, Madeline. The more I thought about Jerry, the more I missed him. I know you think all I care about is his money, but I make plenty of money, myself. I don't really need any more. Of course, it would be nice, but it's not necessary. What I really want is to see if this relationship can work."

The scary part about this speech was that I almost believed her.

She readjusted one of her earrings. Her eyes narrowed. "And why are you still here?"

"I have a case. The local pageant director's having some trouble."

"Oh, a pageant. Must bring back memories."

"Not really."

"Why did you quit, anyway? Weren't you doing pretty well?"

"Ran out of sequins."

"I was always too short."

This surprised me. Olivia rarely revealed anything about herself. "That's not an issue these days."

"You had a shot at Miss North Carolina, didn't you?"

"I did Miss Parkland for the money."

She gave me a look. "And you think *I'm* desperate for money?" Her cell phone rang. "Excuse me." She unclipped it to answer. "Hello? Just a second." She went out to the porch. "Okay, that's better. What's up?"

I eavesdropped half-heartedly as Olivia tore into somebody named Barry for not having the proper paperwork done on a case. Ordinarily, I'd be tickled by her problems, but the hard cold fact she was here and scheming to get Jerry back depressed me more than I would've believed.

I was further depressed by the greeting Jerry gave her when he returned from town. He bounded up the porch steps, tossed his packages on the nearest chair, and swung her around.

"I'm so glad you're here! What do you think of the living room?"

Olivia caught her breath. "Well, it's a good start. Who's doing the work?"

"I found a really good handyman. Actually, she's a handy-woman. She's going to fix the plumbing and everything."

"You should've hired Elite Contractors and Service. They're the best."

"They're also the most expensive."

"Is this handywoman doing it for nothing?"

"No."

"What are you paying her with, beads?"

He took her hand. "Come see what I'm planning for the kitchen."

She sighed and gave me a look as if to say, this is non-sense. Any other time, I would've agreed, but now I wanted to be on Jerry's side.

She looked around the kitchen and shook her head. "Jerry, having plans is all well and good if the plans actually amount to something. What are you going to do with this house?"

"What do you mean? It's perfect for séances."

"Be serious."

"I am. I can have séances here, palm readings, Tarot card readings, Ouija board, whatever. Let me show you my séance room."

"Jerry, honestly."

He pulled her back to the front parlor. "See? It's perfect."

"Well, it's dark. You need to have this room painted, too. Maybe a nice bright yellow."

He made a face. "The entire Fairweather Mansion is yel-low."

"All right, then, a nice beige."

"Nope. Did you see all the rooms upstairs? Come on."

Olivia protested as he tugged her up the stairs. "Jerry, you have to think this through. Is this what you want to do the rest of your life?"

He gave her the complete tour, with her complaining every step of the way. I sat on the porch and wondered about what I wanted to do the rest of my life. Wasn't it the height of absurdity to be in love with someone who hadn't a clue? Someone who had the attention span of a puppy and whose idea of a good time was to pretend to talk to the dead?

As they came back downstairs, Olivia's phone beeped and she answered it.

"What? No, no, that's not what I meant at all. Of all the stupid—" She put the phone down. "Jerry, I've got to go take care of this."

He looked disappointed. "You'll miss the séance."

"I've seen you do that. Once is enough." She spoke into the phone. "Don't do anything until I get there." She hung up and gave him a quick peck on the cheek. "See you later."

AT TWILIGHT, three older women arrived in a huge Buick sedan and boldly came up the porch steps.

"Good evening," one said. "Is this where we can communicate with our loved ones from beyond the grave?"

Something about the set of this woman's jaw told me she was Flossie Mae Snyder, Geoff and Sean's aunt.

"Yes, ma'am," Jerry said. For the occasion, he'd put on his dark brown suit and a tie with flaming skulls outlined in gold thread. "Please come in."

The other women introduced themselves as Anna Lee Mosley and Winnifred Parks. Jerry escorted them to the front parlor and held their chairs as they sat down around the table. I watched from the doorway.

I've seen Jerry do this dozens of times, and it always amazes me how people believe something so goofy. Everyone holds hands. Jerry tells the people to concentrate on whatever questions they have for someone on the Other Side. Then he closes his eyes, sits really still, and starts talking in a faraway voice. The stuff he says is so general, you could easily apply it to your own life. Your mother is well and happy. She misses you. She's watching over you. Nothing specific.

This evening, things went a little differently.

Jerry placed a large candle in the center of the table. He lit the candle and sat down. He asked the women to hold hands. "Now I want each of you to think of a specific question you'd like to ask your loved one. I'll get in touch with my guide in the spirit realm and ask him to relay your questions and concerns. Don't be alarmed if I sound different. The guide will speak through me."

And why can't people see through you? That's the question.

Jerry closed his eyes. "Everyone concentrate. You may hear strange noises or see some unexplainable phenomena. Just remain calm and don't break the circle."

By this he meant, don't move your hands under the table where I'm pulling tricks with my toes.

There was a thump from somewhere underneath, but it sounded as if it were underneath the house, not the table. Jerry opened his eyes, clearly surprised by the noise. Then he closed his eyes again.

"I call to the spirit realm. I request your guidance. Come to me. Show me the way." He opened his eyes, giving them a glazed expression. When he spoke, his voice was distant and rough. "I am here."

Ooh, the great and powerful Wizard of Oz.

The women looked at each other, shivering with delight.

"Who has a request of me?"

Mrs. Mosley said, "I wish to speak to my grandmother, Eunice Tubbs."

Jerry took a moment to make some rattling sounds in his throat. "Eunice is well and happy and watching over you, Anna Lee."

She gave a little gasp. "Ask her if Grandpa Willie is all right."

"William is also well and happy. He spends many days doing his favorite things."

He can usually get people to tell him what he needs to

know. Mrs. Mosley was agog. "Fishing? There's fishing in the afterlife?"

I could've sworn Jerry winked at me. "Yes, and he always catches the big ones."

Mrs. Mosley beamed at her friends. "Did you hear that? How wonderful!"

There was another thump from below and a rustling noise. That couldn't possibly be rats, could it? They'd have to be awfully big. I didn't believe for a moment Jerry was making that noise.

He looked uneasy. "Who else has a request?"

"I do," Flossie Mae Snyder said. "I need to speak to my uncle Henry. He was supposed to leave me the grape platter, and my cousin Louella swiped it. I want him to tell me I'm the rightful owner of that platter."

"Henry. Henry, are you there?"

A sudden draft of cold air made the candle flame flicker and the women gasp. Jerry gave a start and sat up straight in his chair. His eyes opened even wider. The women stared, open-mouthed, waiting for some grand pronouncement from Beyond.

Flossie Mae Snyder glanced over her shoulder. "Is it Henry?"

A second gust of air blew out the candle. How did Jerry do that? He'd probably rigged the back door to open. I expected Uncle Henry's platter to land on the table next.

But Jerry jumped up, knocking over his chair. He was breathing hard. "Oh, my God."

This wasn't part of the usual performance. I followed his gaze to the hallway. Nothing was there. "What's going on? What do you see?"

He stared a few more minutes and abruptly came back. "I—I'm sorry. A little glitch in the universe. Sorry. Mac, if you wouldn't mind—the lights."

I switched on the lights. He was pale and trembling. The women were awe-struck.

"That was remarkable," Mrs. Mosley said. "You must have truly crossed over."

"Yes, I think I did. I mean, I know I did."

"Well, I for one am most impressed," Flossie Mae said. "Should we try again, or wait until another time?"

"Another time would be great," Jerry said. "The spirits are restless tonight. I'm not sure they'll cooperate. It's one of those Other World things. You know how it is. Sorry about your platter, Mrs. Snyder."

"Oh, don't worry about that," she said. "Henry always was a stubborn old cuss. We'll get him next time."

The women nodded. Still talking excitedly about Jerry's performance, they gathered their pocketbooks. Jerry escorted them to their car and came back to the house.

I met him at the door. "Okay, now what the hell was all that about?"

He hesitated as if he didn't want to come inside. "Nothing. I'm sure it was nothing."

I'd never seen him so rattled. "Jerry, I'm not one of your pigeons. What did you see?"

He looked around as if expecting something to jump out and say, "Boo!" "I had a vision, an honest to God vision. And it wasn't pretty."

"Okay."

"Hayden's ghostly woman. Portia. I saw her again."

"And you saw her where?"

He rubbed his forehead. "Right here. Inside the house. I thought I was going to have a heart attack."

"Did you ask Nell to come back tonight?" Nell's overalls, as I recalled, were white.

"No, it was the same woman I saw before. It was Portia. I recognized her from Hayden's description. She had black hair and a long white dress."

"There has to be an explanation."

"Oh, there's an explanation, all right. I really am psychic."

"No, Jerry. A reasonable explanation. She must have gone out the back door. I'll go have a look."

"I'd better come with you."

"I can take care of myself."

"I'm sure you can, but I don't want to be in the house by myself just now."

He followed me out the front door and around the house. The fields stretched in all directions, calm and dark.

"Jerry, there's no way anyone could sneak into the house."

"I know. That's why I'm sure it was Portia. A ghost wouldn't have any trouble going wherever she wanted."

We went in the back door and into the kitchen. "You fell and hit your head yesterday," I said. "You could be seeing all sorts of things."

I shouldn't have said that. His eyes widened.

"Oh, my gosh, Mac. Do you suppose that released my psychic potential and made me more receptive to the forces around here?"

"No, I think it made you even goofier than usual."

He shuddered. "Man, call the Snyders and give them the good news. No more séances for me."

"That's probably a good idea. Come on, let's get a snack." After some chips and soda, Jerry felt better.

"I've got to get to the theater by 8:30," I said. "You want to come with me? The sight of pretty girls trying to dance ought to cheer you up."

"Yeah," he said. "I think I'd like to get out of the house for a while."

"Okay. Suit up and let's go."

He took his jacket from the hat rack, left lights on all over the house, and locked the door behind us. We got in the car. As we drove down the winding driveway, he glanced back at the house.

"Is she waving good-bye?" I asked.

"All clear."

AS USUAL, another crisis had hit the Baker Auditorium. Benjy's friend had lasted exactly one rehearsal before leaving in tears.

Evan's handkerchief was in tatters. "We're back to square one. The girls have completely forgotten their dance. The pageant is tomorrow night! I don't know what we're going to do."

"What kind of dance does it have to be?" Jerry asked.

"At this point, I don't care."

"I know a real simple dance." He hopped up on the stage. "Try this, ladies."

The girls gave him their best smiles and all their attention. In about ten minutes, he'd taught them a very basic waltz step.

Evan stared. "They're all together!"

"Percy was trying too hard," I said.

"Put on some music."

It took the girls a minute or two to adjust, but following Jerry's lead, they were soon swaying nicely to the beat.

"When they have on their gowns, this will look wonderful," Evan said. He motioned Jerry over. "Thank you so much!"

"I never knew you were a choreographer," I said.

"There were lots of dances at the house," Jerry said.

I knew he meant the Fairweather Mansion, but he'd never mentioned any sort of festivities before. "Fancy balls? Cotillions?"

"Something like that."

The girls were delighted with their new number. Evan James couldn't stop beaming. Even dour Cindy cracked a smile.

"Now if we could just find a piano player," she said.

I nudged Jerry.

"Well, uh, I play a little," he said.

Evan was thrilled. "My goodness, of course you do! You're the concert pianist, aren't you?"

"That's my brother. I'm nowhere near as good."

"It doesn't matter. We need someone, anyone. Please. We're desperate."

"Please," all the girls said.

Jerry couldn't hold out against a pack of beauty queens. "I'll give it a try."

I knew Jerry could play because occasionally in college he'd sit down at the old piano in the student lounge and knock out some variation of "Chopsticks" or "Maple Leaf Rag." I didn't realize he was such a good sight reader. He didn't have any trouble playing the numbers Evan needed. Afterward, he sat in the front row with me and watched as the girls practiced standing and turning.

"You sounded pretty good at the keyboard," I said. "Why don't you take up music again? It's a lot safer and more legitimate than holding séances."

"But there's no money in it."

"But you don't care about money."

"But I like to eat."

"Seriously, why didn't you go on?"

He shrugged. "No need to. Besides, Des was always hogging the piano."

"I think you could play just as well as Des."

"Nah."

"Then next thing I know, you'll be growing Royal Sunset roses in the backyard."

"That's completely Tucker's department."

"Middle child."

"Overachiever."

Evan James clapped his hands for attention. "All right, girls. If you'll put on your evening gowns, please, and we'll go over the dance once more. Please wear the shoes you'll be wearing tomorrow night. I don't want anyone to trip and fall."

The contestants left the stage. Evan wiped his face with the remains of his handkerchief. "Thank goodness this is the last rehearsal. Jerry, you're a lifesaver. When this is all over, I want to talk to you about a possible job here at the theater."

I gave Jerry another nudge in the ribs. "A job."

"I heard him."

Everyone returned in evening gowns. The color of choice was white, although Donna looked stunning in a red beaded number, and Karen Mitman had chosen a light blue that did nothing for her dark complexion. I started to tell Jerry she'd look wonderful in yellow or gold, realized I was slipping into pageant-speak, and shut up.

"All right, everyone. Places, please." Evan looked around. "Where is Juliet?"

Donna made a face. "Making everyone wait, as usual."

Randi muttered, "Probably trying to steal someone else's shoes."

"Cindy, will you hurry her along?"

Cindy disappeared behind the curtains. Evan rearranged the contestants. "Now, ladies, I hope you remember your new dance. It looks absolutely perfect."

Cindy ran back, her eyes enormous behind her glasses. "Mister James, there's been some sort of accident. I think—" She had to stop and gulp for air before she could speak again. "I think Juliet's dead."

The girls gasped, and I thought Evan might faint. I hopped up on stage. "Show me."

Cindy led me backstage. Juliet Lovelace lay in a clump of white gown, her black hair in a tangle, her neck bent at an unnatural angle. I leaned down and felt for a pulse in her limp wrist. An extension cord was coiled near her body. I glanced up at the row of cords and ropes.

"Did you touch anything, Cindy?"

She shook her head. "Should I call nine-one-one?"

"Yes. And keep everyone away from this area."

Jerry looked over my shoulder. "Oh, my God. What happened?"

"It looks like someone used an extension cord to strangle her. Don't let anyone leave."

He hurried back to the auditorium. I heard him ask the girls and Evan to please sit down, there'd been an accident, and the police would want to talk to them. Their horrified murmurs mingled with the rustle of their gowns as they left the stage. I heard Evan sobbing.

I looked around, but the dark backstage area gave me no clues. The floor had been swept and the other curtains pulled aside for lights and the backdrop. The smell of perfume and hair spray led me to a backstage corner. It looked as if Juliet had made her own little dressing room, complete with makeup and mirror, so she wouldn't have to share. Her street clothes were on a hanger draped over a chair.

Juliet's privacy had cost her. If she'd been in the dressing room with the others, her assailant wouldn't have had the chance to sneak up in the dark and kill her. Then again, one of the others might be the killer.

As I walked back, something crunched under my shoe. I bent down to pick up the small pink object. The floor was sprinkled with Juliet's special silvery one-of-a-kind sequins, but what I'd stepped on looked like a piece of plastic fingernail. I checked Juliet's hands and saw several broken nails. She must have tried to fight off her attacker. But her fingernails were clear, and the piece I'd found was bright pink. I found another piece of pink fingernail near her arm. I put both pieces in my pocket. I also noticed that the hem of her gown was dirty.

By the time I returned to the auditorium, the police had arrived. I would've recognized Chief Brenner even out of uniform. Nell's father was big and broad with small features and blond hair exactly like hers, only his hair was a buzz cut of blond fuzz. When he found out the victim was Juliet Lovelace, his small features drew in further.

"Who found her?"

Cindy raised her hand. "I went backstage to see what was taking her so long. Then Ms. Maclin came and said she was dead and to call the police."

"Ms. Maclin?"

"I'm Madeline Maclin," I said. "I touched her only to check for a pulse. Nothing's been moved."

He nodded. "All right. I'll need to talk to everyone, one at a time, in the foyer."

The contestants all had the same alibi. They'd been together in the girls' dressing room. They hadn't seen Juliet. Evan had been on stage, talking with me and Jerry. Cindy had been sitting in the auditorium, taking notes. Now she sat by Evan as he wept into his handkerchief.

"This is horrible. Nothing like this has ever happened. We can't have the pageant now. It would be too dreadful. We'll have to cancel."

"It's all right," Cindy kept saying. "No one's blaming you."

"I know I make a fuss, but I enjoy putting on this program. Who would be cruel enough to murder Juliet just because she was likely to win?"

That might not have been the reason she was killed, I thought.

After Chief Brenner talked with Jerry, it was my turn.

"Nell tells me you're a private investigator," he said. "She also tells me Evan hired you to find out who's behind all the trouble here at the pageant. I don't think you figured on a murder."

"No, sir, and with your permission, I'd like to help."

He tapped his pen on his notepad. "Well, as you can imagine, we don't get many murders in Celosia. We have our share of drug problems and domestic disputes, but this is the first murder in about five years. It's a damn shame Miss Lovelace got herself killed, but she had plenty of enemies. We just need to figure out which one of them got mad enough to attack her." He rubbed the back of his neck. "And by 'we,' I mean the police, Ms. Maclin. You need to stay out of harm's way. Don't interfere with official police business, and anything you might accidentally find pertinent to the case, you bring right to me."

"Sir, I really think I could be useful."

"Real murder cases aren't like the ones you see on TV. You need to let us handle it."

He put his pen and notepad in his jacket pocket. He gave me a long, considering look, and I knew he was seeing only an ex-beauty queen who thought she'd play detective. That's when I made my decision. I handed him one of the pieces of pink plastic. The other I kept in my pocket. "I found this backstage. It may have come off the attacker's fingers."

He turned it in his large, worn fingers. "One of those fake nails?"

"Yes, sir. Most of the contestants wear them."

He nodded. "Thank you."

After Chief Brenner had spoken with Donna and Randi, I asked them to sit down with me in a corner of the auditorium. Both young women were pale and shaken. Donna twisted the edge of her gown.

"What do they think happened, Ms. Maclin? Did someone attack her?"

"That's what it looks like. Exactly where were you before you came out on stage?"

She took a steadying breath. "I was in the dressing room with all the other girls, except Juliet. She had to have her own special place backstage to change clothes."

"Did anyone object to this?"

"No, we were glad she was out of the dressing room."

"Randi, where were you?"

"In the dressing room with everyone else." She bit her lower lip as if trying not to cry. "We just put on our gowns and came out."

"Did you hear or see anything unusual backstage?" Both girls shook their heads. Evan and Cindy had been out front with me and Jerry. "Was anyone else backstage? A stage manager? Someone to pull the curtains and give you your cues?"

"Cindy will do all that during the real pageant." Donna began to cry. "Only now there's not going to be a pageant, is there?"

"I'm really scared," Randi said. "When can we go home?"

It took about an hour for the coroner to arrive and finish examining Juliet's body. The paramedics put her in an ambulance. Brenner allowed everyone back to the dressing room to change clothes and go home. The only contestant I didn't get to speak with was Karen Mitman, who looked more relieved than upset.

She'd be first on my list tomorrow morning.

Jerry didn't look shaken, only apprehensive.

"What's up?" I asked. "You're not a suspect."

"Mac, I'm beginning to believe this town is cursed. First my uncle and now Juliet. These things come in threes, you know."

"What things?"

"Deaths. Haven't you noticed? Whenever somebody famous dies, a few days later, two more famous people die."

"Okay, then, according to that theory, you're next."

"I'm not famous."

"Neither were Val and Juliet. Get a grip."

"There are evil forces at work here. By coming to Celosia, I may have set them in motion. I should never have held that séance. I must have let something loose."

"No, you have something loose—in your brain. There are

plenty of people who hated Juliet, real, live people, and I'm going to find out who killed her."

Chief Brenner had finished with us and said we could leave. Evan, supported by Cindy, came up to me. His face was gray.

"Madeline, I know Brenner will do all he can, but please say you'll continue your investigation. We must find out who did this."

"Of course I will."

"Juliet may have been spoiled and a practical joker, but, my God, she was only seventeen." His voice quit.

"Don't worry," I said. "I have no intention of stopping now."

"Something will have to be done. The girls need to know the pageant is over. We can't possibly go on."

Cindy patted his arm. "I told you I'd call everyone. Let's get you home." She guided him out.

Jerry and I were halfway up the aisle of the auditorium when Jerry stopped. "Oh, my God," he said.

"What?"

"That's who I saw!"

"What are you talking about?"

His eyes were huge. "During my séance! That wasn't Hayden's ghost. It was Juliet's. White dress, dark hair—it must have been her. She was trying to tell me she was going to be murdered."

Even for Jerry, this was over the top. "Jerry—"

"If only I hadn't been so surprised, she might have told me who killed her."

I was very glad that Evan James and Cindy were talking with Chief Brenner and not listening to this. "Suppose I believe you, just for a second. Why would Juliet Lovelace come to you?"

"Because she knows I'm receptive to spirits. I must have been sending out a powerful signal."

"And why come to your house? Wouldn't she be haunting the theater?"

He looked around. "She probably is now. I should try and get in touch with her."

I took him by the arm. "You should try and get in touch with reality. Come on."

FIVE

JERRY HESITATED BEFORE entering the house, but nothing jumped out at him. We weren't haunted by anything else that night except the vision of Juliet sprawled on the stage floor in her beautiful pageant gown. Unable to sleep, we sat on the porch for a long time, talking.

Jerry passed me one of the last two sodas he'd found in the fridge. "Did you learn anything useful from the contestants?"

"No one saw or heard anything unusual backstage. I'm going to talk with Karen Mitman tomorrow. Of all the girls, she wasn't crying or looking very upset. I guess she could've been in shock. And I have something to show the contestants. I didn't want to show them at the theater." I took the plastic fingernail out of my pocket.

"What's that?"

"A fingernail. I found it by Juliet's body. There were a lot of sequins, too. I'm not sure, but I think they're the same kind I found near Shana's house."

"Which means?"

"I'm a little closer to solving Hayden's ghost story." I put the fingernail back in my pocket. "But I never expected to have to solve a murder."

"Which you will solve, and then it's 'In your face, Reid Kent.'"

"That's part of it, I have to admit. But I really want to find out who killed Juliet. I want to put them away. Nobody has the right to do that to another human being. Sure, she wasn't everybody's favorite, but she didn't deserve to be choked to death. She didn't deserve to die before she had a chance to—"

I must have sounded seriously worked up. Jerry put his hand on my shoulder. "Hey, take it easy. We're both a little shaken by this."

"Did you ever think, a few days ago, when we were having lunch at Baxter's and talking about your house, that this sort of thing would happen?"

"You're not sorry you came, are you?"

"Oh, no. No." I took a deep breath to steady myself. I thought of everything I would've missed—Gregory Prill's dramatics, the exploding ghost dinner at Hayden and Shana's, Nell's wry observations, Ted's flattering interest. And being here with Jerry, doing what I knew I wanted to do. "No, this is what I want."

He held up his soda can and touched mine in salute. "Okay."

Okay. I took courage from his calm gray gaze. This is what I want.

SATURDAY MORNING, I found Karen Mitman at her parents' home on Main Street.

"I figured you'd come by," she said. "Let's sit on the porch. I really don't want my mom to hear us. Want some tea?"

I accepted a glass of tea and a seat on her front porch. Today, Karen was wearing a yellow tee shirt and shorts. A yellow headband held back her black curls. She could easily have been the winner of the Miss Celosia crown, except for the frown that creased her smooth forehead.

"Last night you didn't seem as upset as the other girls."

She glanced toward the door as if concerned someone would overhear. "Of course I'm upset about Juliet, but I'm really relieved we won't have the pageant. Entering the pageant was all my mother's idea. I didn't want to parade around in front of the whole town in my bathing suit. I didn't want to try to play that Chopin étude by memory. It's impossible."

I could certainly sympathize with Karen. "What did you think of Juliet?"

Karen sighed. "Well, I hate to talk about her when she's dead, but she was so mean to all of us. She bragged about herself all the time, especially in front of me. I guess, in her white world, I didn't exist."

"Did she make racist remarks?"

"Oh, she was real careful about that. She made sure no one ever heard her. But I heard her, 'cause she'd say them to me, like when I couldn't get the dance steps, she'd say, 'I thought all you people had rhythm' or 'Have you heard about the Miss Watermelon Pageant in Far Corners?' Things like that."

"You should have told someone."

Karen shrugged. "She said equally mean things about Donna Sanchez being Mexican and Randi Peterson having a drunk for a father. Mama said Juliet was just common, just showing her ignorance. Then Juliet said she'd win because she'd slept with all the men judges, even Mr. Hofsteder, and he's really old. She said she'd slept with Mr. Stacy, which I knew was a big fat lie."

I almost rocked back in my chair. "Ted Stacy?"

"Yes, the insurance man."

I hoped I didn't look as surprised as I felt. "Why didn't you believe her?"

"She tried to bring a sexual-harassment suit against him." Karen set her tea glass on the porch railing. "See, she was one of his summer interns. She complained to Mason and Freer, but they just laughed it off. And when she complained to the police, they didn't do anything, either."

No, not good at all, I thought.

Karen had a lot more to say. "She thought she was such hot stuff. She wasn't happy with just the guys our age. She chased after all the men. She tried to get her claws into Mr. Amry, too."

"How do you know that?"

"Because Shana blessed her out on Main Street, that's why."

"Tell me about that."

"I was in the drug store getting a Coke, and I heard them. Shana and Juliet were across the street in front of Georgia's. Shana said, 'You'd better leave him alone.' And Juliet said, 'You can't tell me what to do.' Things like that."

Karen's eyes gleamed. I could tell she enjoyed relating anything that showed Juliet in a bad light.

"Then Juliet said, 'It's a free country,' and Shana said, 'You can't go around treating people like that. One day you're going to be very sorry.' She's got a horrible temper, Shana does. I think they would've gotten into a fight except Officer Johns came by and told them to stop."

Karen picked up her tea glass and stirred the ice. I noticed her fingernails were cut short and painted with clear shiny polish.

I reached in my pocket for the fingernail. "Do you recognize this?"

Karen frowned at the fingernail. "I'm not sure. Is it Juliet's?"

"Did she wear this color?"

"I guess. I didn't really pay much attention to what she wore, to tell you the truth. I just tried to keep out of her way." She gave the door another worried glance. "If that's all, do you mind if I say good-bye? If my mother sees me talking to you, she'll think I'm interested in being in another pageant, and that's the last thing I want to do."

"It's okay, Karen." I got up. "Believe me, I understand."

As I WALKED BACK to my car, my cell phone beeped. Ted Stacy's name and number appeared on my caller ID. Ted's voice was strained.

"Madeline, are you still investigating the pageant?"

"Yes."

"Could you come over to my office right away?"

Ted's office was in shambles.

I paused in the doorway and stared. Everything that had been on Ted's desk was on the floor. The desk drawers hung open, their contents mangled. The bookshelves had been stripped, books tossed in untidy piles, their covers torn and bent. All the pictures and the mounted fish hung askew. I stepped over a pile of twisted folders. "Are you okay? What happened?"

Ted paused in his cleanup efforts to run his hand through his hair. "I'm fine. I surprised someone rooting around in my office." He pointed to the shattered window. "He got away."

"What was he after?"

"I have no idea."

"Did you get a look at him?"

"He bolted right out the window. I saw a blur of black, that's all. I don't usually come in on Saturday mornings, but I had some work I wanted to finish." He looked around at the mess. "If I can find it."

I picked up his pencil holder and set it back on the desk. The pencils had rolled under the desk and across the carpet. I stooped to gather them. "You keep any money here? Important papers someone would want?"

"No, nothing like that." His hands were unsteady as he straightened the mounted fish. "I wanted to talk to you. This happening right after Juliet's murder makes me worry the police might think I had something to do with it."

I found his stapler and desk calendar by the wall. "Why would they think that, Ted?"

He paused a moment. "When Juliet worked for me, she made some very inappropriate remarks of a—sexual nature."

"She made a pass at you?"

Again he ran his hand through his hair. "I probably should

have known better than to hire her, but I thought I'd give her a chance. I told her that sort of behavior would get her no-where, that she was better than that, she had brains and abil-ity. I also told her if she did anything like that again, she'd be fired. I wanted her to understand about consequences. Well, she got upset, and later she went to the police and claimed I was the one making advances. It was certainly embarrass-ing, but I'd never do anything to harm her."

"Do you have an alibi for ten o'clock last night?"

His smile was wry. "You don't waste any time, do you? Last night, at ten, I was here in the office, catching up on some paperwork. Missy went home at five, so I was alone."

"Have you called the police?"

"They've already been here. They got what they needed, so I'm cleaning up the rest."

"When was this?"

"I came in around eight this morning, saw the mess, called them. They were here a couple of hours. Which reminds me, do you see my clock anywhere?"

I found his desk clock beside the trashcan. "Did you get the impression they suspected you?"

"I hope not."

We gathered the remaining folders and stacked them in a chair. Ted swept the broken glass into a dustpan and tossed the pieces into the trashcan. He set his swivel chair upright and sagged into it. "Do you think we could leave the scene of the crime? I could use a drink."

"Ever since you mentioned Big Sid's House of Ribs, my mouth has been watering."

This finally made him smile. "We can fix that."

BIG SID'S WAS EVERYTHING a rib house should be—bright, noisy, and full of meat. Ignoring Ted's chuckle, I piled my plate with juicy ribs. He had a salad and a drink. We sat down at one of the picnic tables outside.

"If you like barbecue, I know a great place," I said. "Baxter's Barbecue in Parkland. Have you ever been there?"

"No. I'm not as carnivorous as you are."

"That'll be my treat next time."

"I'm glad to hear there's going to be a next time." Ted took a couple of bites of salad and put his fork down.

"Are you sure you're okay?" I asked.

"There's something else I need to tell you."

The tone of his voice made me stop eating.

"Juliet called me yesterday. She was upset. She said she'd done something foolish, and was in over her head. She said I was one person who'd understand. She wanted us to meet. I admit I hesitated, and she picked up on my hesitation. She said she had to go and hung up." He pushed his salad plate away. "I feel awful about this. Maybe if I'd met with her, she wouldn't have been killed."

"You have no idea what she meant?"

"Everything Juliet did was foolish. She had no direction. I tried to help her, and I almost lost my reputation."

What would Juliet have considered foolish? Burning the curtains? Pushing over the set? Taunting the other contestants? If she did those things, she probably enjoyed it. "The point is you tried, Ted. Maybe you're the only person who cared enough to try, and that's why Juliet called you."

"I don't know." He smiled a wry smile.

"What?" I asked. "Do I have sauce all over my face?"

"Just thinking. You're trying to solve the mystery, right? You'll be like that woman on TV who comes to town and immediately someone is murdered."

I laughed. "Oh, I know the one you mean. I always thought she was probably the killer, going from town to town, knocking off the most unpleasant citizen. It would be a great disguise."

"You won't be going from town to town, though."

"I won't?"

"You're going to stay in Celosia, aren't you?"

"I'm thinking about it."

Ted wiped his mouth with his napkin. "Well, I have a suggestion for you. There's an empty office in my building. Why not rent it and set up your own agency here in town?"

Instead of envisioning a new office in Ted's building, I had a sudden picture of the upstairs parlor of the Eberlin house. The perfect place for an office.

Is that what I really wanted?

I must have looked stunned. Ted held up a hand. "Just a suggestion."

I came back to reality. "It's a terrific suggestion, thank you."

"So you'll do it?"

"Let me see if I can solve this case first."

He smiled. "I know you can."

Ted's smile was genuine and warm. Big Sid's ribs were tasty and juicy. But my mind wandered from both delicious sights. The upstairs parlor of the Eberlin house! What was I thinking? This was an even bigger mystery.

THE SANCHEZ HOME was on Peacock Lane near the Walmart. Donna Sanchez was still upset about Juliet's murder, but for a different reason today.

"I hate her! Selfish, evil bitch!"

I thought for a moment she was going to slam the door in my face. "It's probably not a good idea to talk like that."

"I don't care. You realize, don't you, that she got her wish? *Nobody* won the pageant. There's not even going to be a pageant, and all the attention's on *her*. Even when she's dead, she's screwing me over."

I'd been through this kind of temper tantrum before. Backstage at pageants, sometimes all it took was a stuck zipper. "I realize you're upset. Could I ask you just a few questions?"

"Are you going to find the guy that killed her?"

"That's what I'm trying to do."

She opened the door wider. "Good. 'Cause when you find him, I want to thank him."

The Sanchez family living room was decorated in Early American. Pictures of Donna sat on every available surface. Donna in her cheerleading outfit. Donna in her prom dress. Little Donna holding a kitten.

She flopped down on the sofa. I chose one of the recliner chairs facing the wide-screen TV. Donna in a Christmas dress beamed from the top of the TV.

"I can't believe this." She was back to her rant. "I've waited my whole life to be in the Miss Celosia Pageant, and that stupid Juliet has to go and get herself killed and ruin everything. Why couldn't we have the pageant next month? That's plenty of time before Miss North Carolina."

I took out the piece of pink plastic. "Recognize this?"

She looked. "Looks like a fingernail."

"Juliet's?"

"Probably. She always liked that garish shade of pink." She handed it back to me and rubbed her hands on her shorts. "That's kind of gross. Did you take it off her hand?"

"Did anyone else have nails this color?"

"Don't look at me. I only use shades of magenta. That shade of pink would be too bright on me. There are probably hundreds of these things backstage. I guess you noticed they hardly ever clean up or sweep. That could be a relic from last year's pageant."

I put the fingernail in my pocket. "So no one else was wearing this color?"

"If Juliet was wearing it, we wouldn't touch it."

RANDI PETERSON wasn't angry. She was scared. In fact, she was too scared to open the door. She spoke through a crack.

"I don't want to talk about it. Oh, my God, I could be next. What if this is a serial killer who targets beauty-pageant contestants? What if he's making some sort of weird statement about women? It had to be one of those protesters. You know, they're not attractive women, and they're bound to be jealous."

I held the fingernail at her eye level. "Randi, would you please take a look at this and see if you recognize it?"

"What is it? Is it part of her *tongue?* Oh, my God, take it away! Go away!"

"No, no, it's a piece of plastic fingernail."

"That's horrible! Did you take it off her body?"

"Do you recognize it? Could it belong to someone else?"

She began to sob. "Just go away. I never want to see anything about a pageant ever again."

"I'm sorry you're so upset, but we're going to find out who killed Juliet. You shouldn't feel threatened in any way."

"This is Celosia. Things like this don't happen in Celosia."

"Things like this happen everywhere. You have to learn to deal with life, Randi."

She shut the door with a firm click.

Okay. That's one way to deal with life.

On my way home, I passed the TV and radio station. Three police cars were parked in the lot. I parked across the street and got out. The station had also had a break-in.

"Good afternoon, Ms. Maclin," Chief Brenner said.

"What happened here?" I asked.

Benjy Goins looked with disgust at the piles of videotapes on the floor. "Can you believe this? If somebody wanted something, why didn't they just ask?"

"What's missing?"

"Nothing! That's what's so screwy. The guys and I counted, and all the tapes are here, they were just pulled out of the shelves and scrambled. It's taken us all morning just to get them back in alphabetical order."

"When did this happen?"

"Must have been early this morning. We're not on all night like some stations. We sign off at midnight. Elwood locks up. I come back at five for our 6:00 AM sign-on."

Had the burglar been looking for a videotape? A videotape of what? I wondered.

Benjy smacked one fist in his hand. "I swear, if I find out who did this, I'm going to have their head."

Chief Brenner said, "We're going to talk to several people today, Benjy. Don't be making accusations over the airwaves."

"I won't, but I'd really like to."

"Thank you." Chief Brenner gestured to me. "Ms. Maclin, if I could have a word with you outside?"

I followed the chief to his patrol car. He folded his arms and leaned against the car. "Ms. Maclin, I've just had a call from Mrs. Peterson. Seems her daughter is very upset about Juliet Lovelace's murder, and you are not helping the situation. Now, I asked you not to get involved in this. A murder and two break-ins in Celosia constitute a serious crime wave. I'd rather not have to worry about your safety, as well."

"I just wanted to talk to Randi about the pageant. She's let her imagination run wild about this murder."

"And I believe you went to Ted Stacy's office?"

"Ted called me to come over. Your men had already finished."

Chief Brenner's little eyes narrowed even further. "Please listen carefully, Ms. Maclin. Anyone involved in this case and any crime scene is now officially off-limits. You see the yellow tape, you stay on your side."

"Yes, sir."

After warning me off, he couldn't resist asking me about my investigation. "Understand you talked with the Mitman girl this morning. Did she have anything useful to say?"

Since he wanted me to back off, I didn't see the need to

share my information with him. "Just that Juliet wasn't the most popular girl in the pageant."

"The other contestants have all been cleared. There wouldn't be any reason for you to talk to them about this."

"May I ask one thing? Did the piece of fingernail I found belong to Juliet?"

"That has yet to be determined."

As I started for my car, Chief Brenner said, "And where would you be heading now, Ms. Maclin?"

"To the Eberlin house."

"Thank you," he said. "Good day."

WHEN I STEPPED INSIDE the Eberlin house, I didn't recognize the living room. Gone was a trace of anything gray, from the light blue walls with white molding to the shiny wood floors. The old draperies had been taken down, so clean windows let in air and sunlight. Curved invitingly in the center of the room was a white sectional sofa with a scattering of blue cushions. Elegant lamps sat on end tables. A glass coffee table shaped like a large square was parked in front of the sofa. A new entertainment center gleamed from the corner by the fireplace. Over the mantel hung a modern-art painting of multicolored flowers.

Jerry grinned. "What do you think?"

"It's gorgeous."

He picked up a remote control from the coffee table and aimed it at the entertainment center. A dramatic bass voice began singing something operatic. "We've got cable, too."

"And who's paying for all this?"

He flopped down on the sofa. "Mr. Credit Card."

"Eventually, you have to pay him back, too."

"Once the Eberlin house gets going, that won't be a problem."

I joined him on the sofa. "Come on, Jerry. Tell me what's going on."

"Nothing. I just wanted to fix things up."

"I thought this was supposed to be a haunted mansion, not the cover of *House Beautiful*."

"Now I'm thinking this will be perfect for a New Age retreat center." He pointed to the painting. "Recognize that?"

I'd been too dazzled by the transformation to pay much attention to the painting. I took a closer look and shook my head in disbelief. "You kept it."

"It's my favorite."

I approached the painting, now remembering each brush stroke, each layer of color. As a last touch, I'd added a blue crescent moon in the corner. *Blue Moon Garden* I'd called it. Yes, there was the title, written very small in the bottom right-hand corner, along with my name and the date. I remembered the day I'd finished the painting and proudly documented my achievement. It had been a hot sunny day like today. The art-room windows had been open, adding smells of fresh paint and wet clay to the breeze. Jerry had leaned in one window. He'd been playing softball, his hair damp under his cap. I remembered how the sun on his face made his eyes almost transparent.

"That's the best one yet, Mac," he'd said.

I was going to be an artist.

"Fine," my mother had said, "throw away a perfectly good pageant career."

I let my hair and my clothes go wild, but even then people would approach with offers. Miss Collegiate Queen. Miss All-Campus Cutie. I politely refused, wanting to scream. Was "Beauty Queen" tattooed somewhere on my forehead?

My first art show was that fall. I had to do what I vowed I'd never do again. I needed money for canvases and frames and money to rent the exhibition hall. The only way to make real money real fast was to enter and win the Miss Parkland Pageant. The pageant was a huge success; my art show a complete critical disaster. My mother didn't say anything. Her satisfied smirk said it all.

"Come on," Jerry had said. "Let's go to Bermuda."

We had the Fairweather beach house to ourselves. Jerry went fishing and practiced bending spoons. I took long, soul-searching walks on the beach. I picked up shells and admired the shades of the water. No one asked me to be Miss Bermuda.

Then someone asked me if I'd seen a diamond watch. By listening and asking the right questions, I found that watch and a new purpose. Maybe I didn't know what I wanted, but I could help other people find what they wanted.

At night, Jerry and I sat on the deck and talked about life. He was very supportive of my new direction.

Why didn't I see it then? Jerry was always there. A safety net. An airbag against the crashes of life. I'd taken him for granted so long, no wonder a woman like Olivia could flirt and charm him. She saw the man. I saw a pal.

I thought of all this now as *Blue Moon Garden* bloomed in front of me.

Jerry had been watching me. "You know, the light's pretty good in the upstairs parlor."

The upstairs parlor. My office.

No. My studio.

I felt a thrill of excitement. For an instant, my fingers ached to hold a paintbrush, to spread color and catch light. I shrugged. "It was just a phase. I'm over it."

He looked as if he wanted to say something else. Then he said, "Come check out the kitchen."

I followed him into the kitchen. The old linoleum had been peeled off, and Nell was putting down new white tiles with a faint pattern of blue leaves.

"Nice, huh?" Jerry said. "I'm going to get a new stove and refrigerator, but we're leaving the table and chairs. Nell says they're in good shape."

Nell agreed. "Won't find nothing better."

"Then we'll start on the upstairs."

She chuckled. "What's this 'we' business? You'll stay down here."

I had to know what was going on. "It looks wonderful, Nell. Would you excuse us for a minute?" I took Jerry by the arm and led him back into the living room. "A New Age retreat center? You're going to charge people a couple hundred a week to gaze at their crystals and go 'om'?"

"Why not? They have to do it somewhere. Why not at the Eberlin house, which is known for its special vibes?"

"There are so many reasons why not, I don't know where to start."

And I might have started listing the reasons, but Olivia chose this moment to arrive. She stood in the front door and stared. She had her cell phone to her ear, but she put it away. I thought she'd be critical of the new décor, but she surprised me.

"Jerry, this is beautiful! I love it!"

"Does it look New Age?"

"I don't know about that, but it looks fantastic. Did you do this yourself? You couldn't have."

"Nell helped me."

"Well, it's such an improvement." She paused. "Why does it have to look New Age?"

"Because I'm planning to turn this house into a retreat center."

Olivia said what I would've said. "Oh, no, you are not. These mindless schemes of yours go nowhere." Then she seemed to catch herself. She paused and frowned as if she'd just thought of something. "You'd be much better off running a bed and breakfast."

"A New Age bed and breakfast?"

"Well, it doesn't have to be New Age, but people enjoy staying in old country homes. It might be very nice."

Wait a minute. Was she encouraging him? Didn't she want Jerry back in Parkland?

Jerry hugged her. "That's it! That's perfect! People will love it."

"Speaking of breakfast," I said, "who's going to cook?"

Jerry was off and running with this new plan. "I can cook breakfast. It's just scrambled eggs and bacon and toast. It's easy."

"You have to clean up, too."

"And plan ahead," Olivia said.

He was too excited to notice our sarcasm. "You could help me, Olivia. You could keep up with the business end. I'll provide the entertainment. Mac can refer all her clients to Celosia for their country vacations. Nell can put in another bathroom. Maybe we can remodel the attic rooms, if we could ever get in there."

Now there was a definite craftiness in Olivia's smile. "I have to admit, it sounds like a good investment. Let me check it out for you. There are all kinds of zoning laws and requirements. A bed and breakfast sounds more reasonable than your other ideas."

Hang on. This is Olivia's idea.

She checked her watch. "In fact, I'll get started right away. I'll be back after a while. Then maybe we can go do something special, all right?"

She gave Jerry a kiss and went to her car, where she waved and smiled before driving away. What a performance!

Oblivious to any subterfuge, Jerry said, "This is going to be great. Now that Olivia has a mission, she'll love it here. Once the Eberlin House B&B gets going, she'll want to be around to take charge. We'll be able to work things out."

He looked so pleased by this plan, I didn't have the heart to discourage him, or mention anything about Olivia's agenda. She had one, or she wouldn't have agreed to this scheme. Did she love him enough to move in permanently? Isn't that what I wanted to do?

"Okay," Jerry said, "if this B&B is going to work, we need to know what sort of space we're talking about. Time to explore the attic. I'm hoping for a few good ghosts."

Getting in was no problem with Nell and a crowbar. She wedged the attic door open. We stepped inside.

I expected cobwebs, battered trunks, boxes of Christmas decorations, and a rat or two. I imagined a laboratory with bubbling flasks and a body laid out on a slab. What I saw was far more fantastic.

A computer. Three video cameras mounted on tripods. Lights hung from the rafters. State-of-the-art taping and editing equipment and microphones I knew cost well into the thousands of dollars. A valentine-shaped bed with pink satin sheets.

Nell's small features wrinkled in confusion. "Is this some kind of TV studio?"

Jerry stood with his mouth open.

"Jerry," I said, "looks like your uncle Val was making very special movies."

He continued to stare. "I don't believe it."

Nell took a few steps closer and examined the light pole. "Well, I'll be. So this is how come people saw strange lights in the attic. What's all this?"

I turned on the nearest computer. "Let's find out."

The computer had nothing but the usual programs. We didn't find any CDs. We couldn't find any videotapes, either, but we found several empty cases.

Jerry checked the cameras. "What else could he have been doing up here?"

"And who else knew about it?"

"I can tell you that," Nell said. "Nobody. This kinda news would've been clear to Raleigh by now."

I drummed my fingers on the mousepad. "And who did he videotape?"

"Doing what with whom," Jerry said. "*If* it's X-rated. We don't know that."

I pointed to the pink satin bed. "That doesn't look like a set for a birthday party."

Nell sat on the bed. "Right comfy. Maybe he had a girlfriend." She bounced twice, and the bed popped like a huge party balloon. Jerry and I jumped as Nell landed with a thump.

"What the hell?" Jerry took her hand and tugged her to her feet. "An inflatable bed?"

Nell rubbed her rear. "Sorry about that. I think my screwdriver musta popped it."

"That's okay," he said. "Add it to the mystery list."

"It's getting to be a long list," I said. "Both Ted's office and the TV station have been trashed. Somebody's looking for something."

Nell looked around the attic room. "Well, ain't this a kick in the head."

"Nell," I said, "I'm going to ask you a big favor."

"Don't need to spell it out to me. Best to keep quiet about this."

I inspected some of the equipment. "The camera has the radio-station call letters on it."

"Maybe Benjy Goins knows what was going on," said Nell. "Wouldn't put it past him. Always had to be the funny man in school."

I didn't see anything funny about this, and I could tell Jerry didn't, either.

"We'll figure this out, won't we, Mac?"

"Call Des and see if he knows anything about your uncle."

"If I can track him down."

While Nell went back to her painting, Jerry checked with his older brother. A call to Des's townhouse apartment in

Parkland reached the answering machine, which informed us that Desmond Fairweather was on tour, and emergency calls could be placed with Sylvia Banner of the Arts Council.

Jerry hung up. "I'll try again later."

"What about Tucker?" I asked.

"I guess it's worth a shot."

I noticed he didn't have any trouble remembering his old phone number. After a few rings, someone answered. It must have been his younger brother because Jerry's face relaxed.

"Hiya, squirt. Still pulling weeds?"

I'm sure Tucker made an equally rude reply. Jerry laughed. "Yeah, still on the run. I'm calling from a pay phone and have only a few seconds before the Feds get here." He paused and laughed again. "No, seriously. Got a question for you. Do you remember anything about an uncle of ours named Val Eberlin? Eberlin. Yeah, I remember Uncle Oberon and Aunt Titania." He covered the phone for a moment and spoke to me. "Can you believe those names? Somebody had some fairy-tale issues." He listened to Tucker for a while and then said, "Okay. Yeah, I'm going to be in Celosia for a while. Yes, really. At this number." He gave him the phone number of the Eberlin house. "Thanks, pal. Go easy on the fertilizer." Jerry hung up and shook his head. "He doesn't remember an uncle Val."

"Well, then, there's always Harriet."

He shook his head. "You know I'm not going to talk to her."

I knew. Harriet, as the oldest of the four Fairweather children, had brought up her three brothers after their parents had died. She had been a strict disciplinarian, and Jerry had left as soon as he could. "I'll talk to her."

"Good luck."

"Does she still live in Parkland?"

"Yes, and don't tell her where I am."

"I wouldn't do that." I looked through the phone book. "Is she still Harriet Fairweather?"

"As far as I know."

There was a Harriet Fairweather listed. I punched in the number. After two rings, a woman's sharp voice said, "Hello?"

I'd met Harriet only once, and that was enough. She was the opposite of Jerry, dark and withdrawn. "Harriet, this is Madeline Maclin, Jerry's friend. How are you?"

Harriet was her usual friendly self. "What do you want?"

"I needed to ask you about your uncle, Val Eberlin."

"What about him? He's dead."

"Did you ever meet him?"

"He came to the house one time, as I recall. He didn't like my father, and my father didn't like him. What is this all about? Is Jeremyn there?"

"I'm working on a case, and Val Eberlin's name came up. It's nothing serious."

I could hear the bitterness in Harriet's voice. "Well, I wouldn't be surprised. Our whole family's cursed, you know, cursed with way too much curiosity."

She hung up without another word.

"Well, thanks, anyway," I said to the phone.

"Cheerful as ever, I'll bet," Jerry said.

"Yep. She met your uncle Val only once."

Our whole family's cursed.

I've been in the Fairweather Mansion. It's a huge yellow brick house with white trim and white columns. The gardens out back include fantastic mazes of shrubbery and stone fountains decorated with leaping dolphins. The rooms, decorated in shades of yellow and gold, are serene and full of light. Antique sofas and chairs share space with Asian hand-painted screens and ivory vases.

But the oddest thing in the house is the huge portrait of the Fairweather children that hangs over the mantel in the living room. Des, age eight, stands behind Jerry, age six, who is seated with two-year-old Tucker in his lap. The boys are smiling. Des has a protective hand on Jerry's shoulder. Jerry has his arms around Tucker.

Harriet's not in the picture.

"Now what?" Jerry asked.

"Maybe Benjy Goins will be more forthcoming. Ride with me?"

"I think I'll stay here and see what other secret porn studios I can find."

GOINS DIDN'T SEEM surprised by my questions. He checked to make sure he had the right tape running and then turned his attention to me. "Yeah, Val bought some used machines, editing equipment, a couple of used cameras."

"Did he tell you what he wanted all that for?"

"I didn't pay that much attention. He was an odd duck. He had all kinds of plans and schemes, and none of them ever worked out. He said something about filming Chiroptera. Now you tell me what that means."

"Chiroptera? Sounds like some kind of animal."

"What else would he film? Probably means mice or spiders."

Spiders would not need a heart-shaped bed.

"Benjy, how long was Eberlin dead before he was found?"

"I don't know. You'd have to ask the police."

Chief Brenner would not appreciate my questions. "Do you know the name of the mailman who found the body?"

"I think it was Dennis Padgett. He carries mail out to the farms."

Before checking with the post office, I stopped in Georgia's Books and looked up "Chiroptera" in one of the dictionaries. Chiroptera was the scientific name for the order of bats in the class Mammalia, phylum Chordata.

Bats in the attic. Perfect.

As I put the dictionary back in its place, Hayden called, "Madeline, could I ask you something?"

"Yes, of course." I came to the counter. "What's up?"

"Do you suppose Jerry would be willing to come check my house for evil spirits?"

He looked so serious and so worried I hated to disillusion him. "Hayden, most of what Jerry does is just for show."

"Oh, I'm sure it's more than that. Mrs. Mosley was in here earlier today, and she told me about the remarkable results he had with their séance. She said she'd never seen anything like it."

What could I say? "Well, that really wasn't a typical séance."

"She said he crossed over."

"That's probably what it looked like. Jerry's a very good actor."

Hayden didn't appear to hear me. "And now with this horrible thing that's happened to Juliet I'm afraid the spiritual energy around town is getting worse. If it's centered anywhere near my house, I need to know. Please. If Jerry can do anything to help, I'd appreciate it."

The entreaty in his blue-green eyes was impossible to resist. "I'll ask him."

Hayden relaxed. "Thanks."

"I guess anyone's better than Cynthia Riley."

"As much as I'd like to hire Cynthia, I don't think my marriage would stand the strain—which reminds me. How much does Jerry charge for a session?"

"I'll let you two figure that out," I said.

"Madeline, do you have any idea who killed Juliet? I can't stop thinking about it."

"Did you know her?"

"Not really. The only time I ever spoke to her was when I gave a talk to her English class about poetry."

"I don't know who did it," I said, "but I'm going to do my best to find out." You don't deserve to worry like this, I thought. If Jerry's little act can give you some peace of mind, then I say let him do it. "As soon as I get home, I'll have Jerry call you."

He thanked me again, and I set out for the post office.

THE WOMAN at the post office said I could find Dennis Padgett on Oak Street off of Main.

"He should be near Newsome Cleaners right now."

Dennis Padgett was a thin man with a few pale hairs waving above his head like the tendrils of a sea anemone. He was willing to talk to me if I was willing to trail him as he filled mailboxes along Oak Street.

"Can't slow down the delivery of the mail, miss."

"That's all right," I said. "I don't want to keep you from your duty. I just have a few questions."

"Fire away."

"I'd like to ask you about the day you found Val Eberlin."

Padgett rolled up a magazine and tucked it into the mailbox of a shoe store. "Sure sorry to find him like that. He was a right spry old bird."

"Where did you find him?"

"I wouldn't have even come up to the house that day except I had a package for him. Now, sometimes when he was in town, he'd pick up his mail, but I hadn't seen him for a while, and I didn't like to leave packages in that old bent mailbox of his. So I went up on the porch, figuring I'd just knock and leave the box if he was busy, but the front door was wide open, and he was lying there. Saw his feet first. Gave me a start."

"Just inside the front door?"

"Yes, ma'am, like he'd opened the door to go out and couldn't get no further."

"Do you have any idea how long Mr. Eberlin had been dead?"

"Could've been a couple of days. Could've been late as a week. That's something the police would know."

Padgett took a key from the ring at his belt to open the back of a metal mailbox. I was going to press for more details when something occurred to me. "What happened to the package?"

"I don't know, miss. Left it there."

"In the house?"

"I guess so. I set everything down right inside the door and ran inside to call the ambulance."

"Could this package have been a videotape?"

"Might have been. It was the right size, as I recall."

Padgett finished filling the slots in the metal mailbox. We walked to the next house. "Would someone else have stopped by to check on him?"

Padgett took a packet of letters from his bag. He slid them through the mail slot. "That's doubtful, miss. Everybody knew he liked to be left alone."

"Did he have anyone in town who was a best friend?"

"Everybody knows everybody here, but I can't say as he had any particular friends."

"Any visitors? Relatives stopping by?"

"Nope. The Fairweather boy's the first I ever seen."

I thanked him for his help. "If you happen to think of anything else, Mr. Padgett, I'd appreciate you calling me."

"Yes, ma'am. You'll be staying at the Eberlin house, then?"

"For a while."

He squinted at me with his pale eyes. "Thinking of moving to Celosia?"

"Probably not."

"But the Fairweather boy's here to stay?"

"I don't know."

"Like his uncle? Kind of a loner?"

"No, quite the opposite. Jerry likes having people around."

IT'S A GOOD THING Jerry likes having people around because that's how I found him when I returned to the house.

He was sitting at the kitchen table, holding his arm as if
it hurt. Attending him were a boy and a girl, both about ten
years old. The boy had on an overlarge tee shirt and baggy
shorts. Blond streaks striped his brown hair. The girl was a
beautiful black girl the color of caramel with neat cornrows
and gold earrings. Her shorts and tee shirt were pink. Both
glanced up, eyes wide.

"We didn't do it!" the boy said.

"We thought you were gone," the girl said.

The boy immediately forgot me and rounded on his com-
panion. "No, Denisha, you thought they were gone. You
wanted to come in."

The girl put her hands on her hips. "Austin Terrell, you
are the biggest liar."

"I told you to hold the cover."

"And I told you it was your turn to hold the cover."

"Guys," Jerry said, "it's okay."

I checked Jerry's arm. "What happened? Is it broken?"

"Ow! It is now."

"The cover fell on it," Austin said.

What were they talking about? "What cover?"

Austin exchanged a glance with Denisha, who said, "You
might as well show her. It's all spoiled now."

Austin sighed. "I'll show you." He went into the pantry.
"Come on."

In the very back of the pantry, he lifted a section of the
floor and showed me a neat set of steps leading down into a
passageway. A cool breeze from below brought the scent of
stone and earth. "It's a secret way in."

Good grief, I thought. What else are we going to find in
this house?

Austin was watching me carefully, as if trying to judge
my reaction. "Val used to let us use it. Miz Brenner drove
off and we thought you were gone, but then we saw Jerry and
got scared, and then the cover fell on his arm."

"I see."

"It's not broken, is it?"

"No, he just likes to make a fuss."

"I heard that," Jerry said.

We came back and sat down at the table. "Our breakfast ghosts," I said. "If you guys wanted some snacks, all you had to do was ask."

Denisha looked down. "We weren't sure how things would be now that Val's dead."

Austin said, "You aren't going to call the police, are you?"

I thought about it. "Well, you were already in the passageway. You could've run off, but you stayed to help. The next time you want to visit, come to the door." They nodded. "Your name is Austin Terrell?"

"Yes, and this is Denisha Simpson. She lives with her aunt Averall Mercer."

"Is your mother Samantha Terrell?"

He nodded.

"It's nice to meet you. I'm Madeline Maclin, and you've already met Jerry Fairweather."

"That's a neat name, Fairweather," Denisha said. "Was you born when it was nice outside?"

"My birthday's in May, so it probably was," he said.

"My birthday's in May, too. May twenty-sixth. I'm ten. Austin won't be ten till the end of July."

Austin immediately fired up. "Oh, like he cares, Denisha."

"You do, 'cause I'm older than you."

"By two months. That hardly counts."

"Does so."

"Okay, okay," I said. "How did you two get here? Did you walk all the way from town?"

"We know lots of shortcuts," Austin said. "It's not that far if you cut through the woods."

"And Val let you sneak in whenever you wanted to?"

Denisha shook her head. "We didn't come every day. We

have lots of other places we—" She stopped and clapped her hands over her mouth.

"Denisha!" Austin said.

I finished her sentence. "You have lots of other places you sneak into."

Austin came to the defense. "We don't ever take anything."

"Except cornflakes."

"Val said we could have those."

"All right," I said, "let me get this straight. You spend your summers hiding in other people's houses."

Denisha sighed heavily as if she couldn't believe how thick I was. "Noooo. We just go in for fun. It's a game, like *Super Spy*."

I glanced at Jerry. "I guess there's not a lot to do in Celosia."

"*Super Spy* is a great show," he said.

Austin and Denisha sat up. "You watch *Super Spy?*"

"'No secret is safe, no code unbreakable.'"

They began to rattle off their favorite episodes.

"Did you see the one where he had to get out of that castle and all he had was ten seconds before the bomb went off?"

"Or the one where the code was all in music notes but you had to play it on this certain organ in that spooky old church?"

"Or the one where he used this real, live electric eel and smacked the bad guy right in the face? Pow! 'Lights out!' I love that one."

"It might be on now," Jerry said. "It's almost five."

This announcement made Austin and Denisha leap up.

"Five! We gotta go. My mom'll be home in about twenty minutes. Come on, Denisha."

We followed them as they hurried to the front door.

"I really like what you've done with the place," Denisha said as she hopped down the porch steps.

"Thanks," Jerry said.

"Are you going to fix up the rest of the house, too?"

"Yes."

"But not the attic, right?"

Jerry glanced at me. "Why not?"

"That's the one place Val wouldn't let us go. He said it was super private business."

"It still is," I said. "Did any of Val's visitors go up there?"

They shook their heads. "What's up there?" Austin asked.

"Just a lot of very expensive stuff."

This explanation was enough. "Okay, well, see you later."

They waved good-bye and ran across the meadow to the dark edge of forest.

"Cute kids," Jerry said.

I couldn't help thinking what a great father he'd make. Lord, where did that idea come from?

"They're a whole lot more adventurous than I was at that age," I said.

"Let's see, at age ten, you were walking the runway, and I was playing with little cars, I guess. I wasn't much for exploring." He rubbed his arm.

"Are you going to live?"

"It's okay. I was a lot more surprised to see two little faces looking up at me from underground. Let's check out the passageway."

"First, you need to call Hayden. He wants you to exorcise his house."

"Be glad to."

Jerry called Hayden and set up a time to come sweep the Amry house for unwelcome ghosts. Then we went into the pantry. I lifted the trap door. There was a rush of cool air.

"Kind of dark down there. Do you have a flashlight?"

Jerry didn't have one, but I kept one in the car. I retrieved it, and we went down the steps and into a tunnel. I had to stoop a little bit. The walls were smooth and smelled of wet cement.

"This is great," Jerry said. "No wonder the kids like sneaking in."

The tunnel led to another set of steps. We climbed up and found ourselves next to the garage. A large bush covered this end of the passageway.

"Wow," Jerry said. "I wonder why he needed a secret entrance like this. Did you find out anything from Goins?"

"He says Val bought a lot of used equipment from the station. Here's the good news: your uncle was filming bats."

"Bats? That's all?"

"I didn't think it wise to mention the Valentine bed to Benjy Goins. I also spoke to the mailman who found Val. He came up to the house to deliver a package. He's pretty sure it was a videotape, and he left it here when he went for help."

Jerry frowned. "But we didn't find a tape. Could someone else have taken it?"

"And why would someone want it?"

A voice called, "Jerry!"

He brightened at the sound of Olivia's voice. "We're back here!"

She came around the corner of the house. "What are you doing?"

"There's a secret way into the house. Come on. I'll show you. It's really neat."

"Jerry, I'm not going to go down into a dirty hole. Come inside. We have a lot to discuss."

In the kitchen, Olivia put her briefcase on the table, opened it and pulled out a large stack of folders. She opened the first folder. "Okay, there's quite a lot involved. Let's start with the basics. I'll check with the local zoning laws and make sure we're not breaking any. As to insurance—do you even have insurance on this house?"

"I don't know," Jerry said.

"I'll check on that, too." She set that folder aside and opened another one. "Here's a list of all the health and safety regulations you have to meet before we can open for business. Is there another way of accessing the upstairs bedrooms? Do we have smoke detectors? Things like that." She passed that folder to Jerry and opened folder number three. "It's absolutely vital that you keep good records for tax purposes. You'll need a cash-receipts journal, and a cash-disbursements journal, plus you might do well to join the SBA and BBB."

"SBA?"

"Small Business Association and Better Business Bureau." She handed him a piece of paper. "Here's a sample income-projection sheet. If you have four rooms and charge sixty dollars per night and you're open one hundred days a year, that's a possible twenty-four thousand a year. Of course, you could always charge more or less than sixty dollars, depending on how many people you think will want to sleep here."

Jerry glanced at the paper and put it on top of the folders. He made a face at me as if to say, this is more than I bargained for.

Olivia moved on to the next item on her checklist. "Okay, here are some other things to consider. You're going to have to keep this place spotless. Have you thought about laundry service? What about your guests who smoke or drink? Will you let guests use the telephone? What if they want to bring their children or pets? And what will you do in case of a medical emergency? This house is pretty far from a hospital. Have you thought about any of these things, Jerry?"

"Well, no."

"We just need to sit down and hash out all the details."

He looked even more uncomfortable with this suggestion. Olivia, however, looked very self-satisfied. She gave me a little smile. She knew as well as I that Jerry resisted being pushed into situations that required too much work.

"All right, now, let's see. What's next? All the books say the main thing you need for a successful B&B is a good location. You have that, but what would your guests do?"

"Well, I was going to show them how to cleanse their auras and the best way to feel walls, but—wait a second."

As he paused, I saw Olivia's face tighten. Jerry, I thought, now's the time to be creative.

"I've got it! Not a New Age bed and breakfast. A haunted bed and breakfast!"

Olivia rolled her eyes in exasperation. "Why does it have to be haunted?"

"It fits in so much better with my original plans." His hands sketched an imaginary headline. "The Eberlin House Bed and Breakfast. Three ghosts, no naiting. That's what'll sell it, Olivia."

She pursed her lips. "No one wants to stay in a haunted house!"

"Are you kidding?"

"Well, I wouldn't. Would you, Madeline?"

It was my turn to give her a little smile. "I think it sounds fabulous."

I was rewarded with Jerry's pleased grin. "See? Mac has the right spirit of adventure. 'Spirit'—get it?"

"Jerry, we are talking about a reasonable business venture."

"A haunted house would be a lot more fun."

"I'm not talking about fun!"

"I am."

She put both hands flat on top of the stack of folders. "Are you telling me if you advertise this place as a haunted bed and breakfast, you'd be willing to take care of all the details, fill out all the forms, and turn this—this overgrown shack into a place people would actually pay to stay in?"

"Isn't that what you wanted?"

"Not if you're not going to take this seriously."

He was puzzled. "Let me see if I've got this straight. You want a bed and breakfast, but you don't want a haunted bed and breakfast."

She gathered up the folders and stuffed them back into her briefcase. "Tell you what. Let's just forget the whole thing." She stalked out.

He followed her. "Wait a minute. I don't understand why you're so angry. I want the same thing you want. I'm just adding a few ghosts."

Olivia stopped so suddenly, he almost ran into her. "You are not taking this seriously, Jerry. You need to decide which is more important, your ghosts or me."

Jerry watched forlornly as she drove away. I did a little victory dance and went to be consoling.

"Wow," he said. "What just happened?"

"She didn't like your idea."

"No joke." He watched until her car disappeared around the curve of the driveway. He didn't seem as upset as I thought he'd be. Maybe he believed she'd come back. "You like the idea, don't you, Mac?"

"Yes, I do." Especially since it drove Olivia away. "Best idea you've ever had."

"You usually have something to say about these ideas of mine."

"This time, I'm on your side."

He gave me a long, considering look. "You're always on my side, aren't you, Mac?"

"Yes, I am." And this was the perfect time to tell him why. He'd just had a great example of Olivia as Worst Possible Choice.

"Thanks." He took a deep breath. "Guess I'll give her time to cool off and give her a call."

SIX

SUNDAY MORNING, I lay for a while in bed. I was getting used to the sound of that rooster. I hadn't found Hayden's ghost, and I hadn't found Juliet's murderer, but I felt confident and full of energy. Maybe it was because I was doing something useful. Maybe it was because I had a purpose. Maybe it was because Olivia was gone. I could only hope she'd finally pushed too hard and would not return.

A cheerful chorus greeted me from the front porch. "Hello, Mac!"

Jerry, Austin, and Denisha were sitting in the rocking chairs, their bare feet propped up on the railing. They were sharing a box of cornflakes.

"Why aren't you guys in Sunday school?" I asked.

"Already been," Denisha said.

"You have?"

"Well, I have. Don't know about these other two."

I couldn't believe I'd slept so late. "What time is it?"

"It's snack time," Jerry said.

"Let me get my coffee and I'll join you."

The kitchen clock said 10:35 AM. I got my coffee, came back to the porch, and sat down in the one remaining rocker. "Well, give me some cornflakes."

Austin passed the box of cereal. I took out a handful and crunched.

Denisha informed me of their proper behavior. "We came in the front door."

"Thank you. Guys, did you come over to the house after Mr. Eberlin died?"

They looked at each other and didn't answer.

"It's okay if you did," I said. "Jerry and I are looking for something that's missing. It could be important."

Austin immediately went on the defensive. "We didn't take anything except that food. And Val didn't mind about that."

Denisha looked embarrassed. "Val used to give my aunt some things. But she only took the stuff he said she could have."

"That's okay. We're looking for a videotape."

She frowned in thought. "I don't remember that. Do you, Austin?"

Austin's eyes gleamed. "We could help you look for it, Mac. It'll be like a treasure hunt."

"That would be great, thanks."

"We'll finish our snack first."

"Of course."

Denisha took another handful of cereal and her big brown eyes suddenly filled with tears. "Val really liked cornflakes. We'd have them every time we came over."

"This is a memorial snack," Jerry said.

I took a sip of my coffee. "I'm sure Val would've appreciated that."

Denisha nodded. "He always bought Girl Scout cookies from me, even though he didn't really like them."

"Did he ever tell you what he was filming?" I asked.

"Something about bats. I wasn't going to go up there and find out. I don't like bats. They eat your hair."

As usual, her remarks made Austin furious. "Denisha, they do not eat hair! That's some old wise tale."

"Wives' tale, Austin. And they do so. They get all tangled up and then they have to eat their way out."

"Well, how could they get tangled in your hair? You've got it braided down, plus they'd choke on all those beads."

"Don't be making fun of my hair, Austin Terrell. You look like some kind of pineporky with all them spikes."

Austin doubled over laughing. "Porcupine! Not pineporky!"

"Whatever!"

"Come on, let's go look for treasure. Come on, Jerry."

Jerry and Austin raced down the porch steps and around the corner of the house.

Denisha closed the cornflakes box and gave me an appraising stare. "Seen you out with Ted Stacy. He's a mighty handsome man."

"I think so, too."

"How come Jerry's going with that bossy blonde lady?"

"I don't know. Must be love."

She gave me a sideways glance. "You like him, don't you?"

"Of course I do. He's my best friend."

"Austin's my boyfriend."

"Good."

"Only he don't know it."

I wanted to say, I know the feeling.

AFTER TWO HOURS of searching, we found several old keys, thirty-five cents, faded envelopes, and a dead, fossilized rat Austin claimed for his collection. No videotape.

We flopped back on the porch and had a restorative cornflakes break.

"When were you going to Hayden's?" I asked Jerry.

"He said to stop by anytime today."

"We could go now. I need to talk to Shana. Anybody else want a ride?"

"No, thanks," Austin said. "We're going to ride bikes for a while, right, Denisha?"

She carefully folded the inside wrapper of the cornflakes box. "Unless you want us to keep looking for the tape."

"Maybe later," Jerry said.

Austin nodded. "Sure."

I thanked the kids again for helping Jerry. "It's a good thing you two are around. I think you've noticed Jerry's slightly accident-prone."

Denisha gave me a sympathetic look. "My aunt's the same way. I wouldn't call her clumsy, but she keeps running into things."

"Things keep running into Jerry."

"One time, she tripped over this cord and knocked the TV down. It split right down the middle."

"Jerry can trip over sidewalk cracks."

Jerry looked exasperated. "Hey, I'm standing right here."

"All in one piece, which is how I expect to find you."

Austin and Denisha hopped on their bikes and rode over the meadow to the woods.

"You need any special exorcism tools?" I asked.

"Just my sunny nature and natural charm."

As we got out of the car, Hayden came down the steps of his front porch to greet us.

"I told Shana you might stop by for a visit. Don't say anything about the exorcism."

"Gotcha," Jerry said.

Shana waved from her chair. She had a thick spiral notebook balanced in her lap. "Hello! Come in."

"We don't want to interrupt your work," I said.

She put her pen in the notebook to hold her place and closed the book. "I'm at a chapter break. Sit down."

Hayden said, "Honey, I want to show Jerry the den. We'll be right back."

"Take your time."

Hayden and Jerry went into the house. Shana gave me a knowing smile.

"He wants Jerry to check for evil spirits, doesn't he?"

I sat down in the chair next to her. "Yes, but it's supposed to be a secret."

"Well, if it'll make him feel better."

"Has he had any more nightmares about Portia?"

She nodded. "Juliet's murder has really upset him, but any murder would've upset him. The whole point of living in Celosia is to be in a safe little town." She set her notebook on the floor. "I hear I'm a suspect. I don't know whether to be flattered or dismayed."

"As long as you have an alibi for ten o'clock Friday night, you're safe."

"I'm afraid I don't. I was all alone in my living room writing. Oh, no, wait. Hayden called me around ten to tell me he'd be working late."

I'd have to check on that. Of course, Shana and Hayden were both writers and could easily make up an alibi, but my instincts weren't going in that direction.

Shana's graceful brows drew together. "It's my temper, isn't it? After that flaming display the other night, you can't help but see me as Prime Suspect."

"That and your quarrel with Juliet."

She sighed. "I knew you'd hear about that, eventually."

"What was the problem?"

"My youngest brother was so in love with her. I didn't say anything at first, but I was afraid she was just playing with him, and she was. She let him date her for about a month, and then dropped him. No explanation. It broke his heart."

"Sounds like you had every right to be angry."

"Oh, that's not the worst part. About the time he got over her, here she comes, sashaying back, like, 'I'm so beautiful, I know you'll want me, no matter how cruelly I treated you.' I just blew up. I tried to tell her how dangerous it was to use her beauty like a weapon. I know what that's like, and I think you do, too. It's very easy to use your looks to get what you want. Of course, she didn't listen to me."

"Did your brother listen to you?"

"Fortunately, he learned his lesson, but it made me furious to see him so upset. But I'm an adult. I should be able to control myself better." She pushed back her red-gold hair as she stood up. "What I can't understand is how someone so attractive could be so evil."

She disappeared inside for a moment and returned with iced tea and sugar cookies. I hoped with all my heart I wasn't dealing with another attractive yet evil person.

She set the refreshments on a little wicker table. "I heard about Ted's office and the break-in at Benjy's station. Do you think the incidents are related?"

"It could be."

"Does it have anything to do with Juliet's murder?"

"I don't know." I checked her fingernails. They were short and unpainted. "There are lots of things I don't know right now."

Shana took a cookie. "Anything new to report on the Fairweather case?"

"Olivia thinks the Eberlin house would make a great bed and breakfast."

"Well, it might. I never thought of that. Looks a little spooky, though."

"That's why Jerry thinks the house would be a perfect haunted bed and breakfast."

Shana laughed. "Well, Hayden wouldn't stay there."

"I was hoping Olivia wouldn't, either, but Jerry's still trying to win her over."

"You've never said anything to Jerry about the way you feel? Not even at college?"

I shook my head. "At the time, Jerry was dating a woman named Patsy Bell Beaumont. The latest in a series of cute, brainless coeds. He was also interested in one of the French exchange students, but after one semester, she went back to France."

"So he was never seriously involved with anyone?"

"No, not really."

"What about after college?"

"After graduation, I pursued my art career and Jerry went traveling. He sent me ridiculous postcards and ugly souvenirs. He went to Egypt and Stonehenge and Bali, 'acquiring vibes,' as he said."

"You didn't want to go with him?"

"You know, looking back on it now, the timing was all wrong. He was ready to go forward with our relationship, but I didn't see it. I was all wrapped up in my plans. I said nothing was more important than my career. I even gave him the Big Speech."

Shana reached for another cookie. "Uh-oh. 'Big Speech'? Capital letters?"

"Yes, that one. 'Nothing is going to stop me this time. I've been thwarted before. Never again.'"

"I always liked the word 'thwarted.' Thounds like thomthing Thyvester the cat would thay. Tell me more about this Big Speech."

"I think, for the first time in his life, Jerry took something seriously. He honored my request and kept out of my way. Of course, the art career never panned out, and here I am."

Shana looked at me thoughtfully. "Yes, here you are, and you know what? If you really want him, you're going to have to revise that Big Speech."

"Revise?"

"I'm the writer. Let me. 'Nothing is more important than my relationship with Jerry Fairweather. I've been thwarted before, but nothing is going to stop me this time.'" She grinned. "What do you think?"

I had to smile. "I think you just like saying 'thwarted.'"

Shana started to say something else when a beige Lincoln town car drove up. She crushed the cookie in her hand. "I don't believe it."

The woman who got out of the car was long and lean with a prominent nose. She tossed her head, her shoulder-length blond hair swinging. I figured this was the infamous Cynthia Riley. I was right.

"Hello, Shana," the woman said. "I hope you don't mind, but I heard that Hayden might need my services."

Shana stood up and blocked the way up the porch steps. "Hello, Cynthia," she answered. "Yes, I mind."

Cynthia Riley tossed her head again and trilled a laugh. "Now, really. I just want to assess the house for conflicting auras. It won't take a minute. But I see you have company. Is this a bad time?" Without waiting for a reply, she came up the first few steps and reached past Shana to offer me a thin hand. "Cynthia Riley, Exorcist and Spiritual Adviser."

"I'm Madeline Maclin," I said, "private investigator."

"Yes, I've heard of you. You're staying at the Eberlin house, aren't you? I understand the place positively reeks of spiritual energy."

"Something reeks, all right," Shana said. "I think it's your perfume."

Cynthia Riley stepped back and gave another laugh. "Dear Shana, let's not fight. If your dear husband is concerned about the spirits in your house, don't you owe it to him to try any and all resources?"

Shana's lips were set in a thin line. "There are no spirits in my house."

"Hayden thinks there are."

"Hayden also thinks the pyramids were built by aliens. Go home, Cynthia."

Cynthia Riley swung her long-nosed face to me. I couldn't help but recall Prill's description of her as an Afghan hound. There was a definite resemblance.

"Ms. Maclin, your charming friend Jerry is attuned to the spirit world, isn't that so? What did he believe was going on here?" Again, she didn't wait for an answer. "Oh, and this horrible news about Juliet Lovelace. Some very bad vibes at the theater."

Shana was trying to keep her temper. "Why don't you go over there, then?" she said to Cynthia. "I'm sure the police could use your help tracking down the killer. Maybe you could zoom in on his brain waves or whatever it is you do."

Cynthia didn't seem offended. "I've already offered my services to the police department. I'd really like to hear what a professional like Ms. Maclin has to say about all this."

"The jury's still out," I said.

"Well, if I were you, I'd do a background check on Evan James."

"Why is that?"

"It has been my experience that men who suppress their inner female—their lunar child, if you will—and sublimate these feelings by becoming deeply involved with beauty pageants have serious issues regarding women."

"I'll do that, thank you." No need to explain to Cynthia Riley that Evan James had been out in the auditorium with everyone else when Juliet was killed.

Cynthia Riley glanced at Shana and apparently decided she wasn't going to be allowed into the house. "Hayden will be disappointed if I don't inspect the house."

Shana's voice was grim. "He'll just have to live with his disappointment."

Cynthia tossed her head. "I'll just be going, then. A pleasure to meet you, Ms. Maclin. Perhaps we can work together to solve this case."

She got into her car and drove away. Shana slowly unclenched her fists and brushed cookie crumbs away. "I cannot believe Hayden has anything to do with that woman."

"She seems ready to pin the murder on Evan."

"Oh, she's been mad at him for years. According to local gossip, she was in a Miss Celosia Pageant and lost, and she blamed Evan. Something about her microphone going out in the middle of her song. From what I understand, it was a blessing. I think the crowd gave Evan a medal. More cookies? There are a few here I didn't destroy."

When Hayden and Jerry came back to the porch, Hayden looked relieved. Jerry's eyes were sparkling.

"Mac, you should see the upstairs. I want Nell to paint my bedroom like that."

Shana stood. "Let me give you the tour, Madeline."

I could tell Shana had chosen the décor, for the rest of the Amrys' house was decorated in bold colors. The bedroom walls gleamed bright shades of yellow and red; Hayden's office was a calm green; Shana's office shone with yellow and gold.

"But I never work here," she said. "I like the porch best."

I had noticed a stack of paper on Hayden's desk. "How's your work coming along?" I asked him. Then I wished I hadn't asked, because the relief in his eyes faded.

"Could be better."

Shana gave him a hug. "Don't worry about it. Come sit outside with me and keep me company."

He checked his wristwatch. "I need to get to the bookstore. I promised Georgia I'd finish the magazine order today."

"And leave our guests? Madeline, why don't you and Jerry stay for lunch?"

Jerry was about to agree when I snagged his arm. "Thanks, but we've got plans. Maybe some other time."

"Okay," she said.

"Yes, thanks so much," Hayden said.

"We could've stayed," Jerry said as we got into my car.

"Did you rid the house of evil?"

"Sure."

"Then our work here is done."

We'd gotten to the end of the drive when Jerry said, "There weren't any evil spirits in that house."

"Is this your professional opinion?"

"No vibes of any kind."

"That's good, then, isn't it? Why are you looking so grim? Were you ready for an epic battle?"

"It's Hayden. I'm worried about the guy. I mean, at one point, his hands were shaking. I think he's headed for another meltdown."

"Shana will take care of him."

"She's great, isn't she?"

Oh, no. Did I have more competition? Of course Jerry would be attracted to such a beautiful woman. "She's certainly gorgeous."

"Yes, but she's so loyal to Hayden. You can tell she really cares about him. That's what marriage is all about. Stand by your man."

I could breathe again. "I'm glad you feel that way," I said, and I meant it on several levels.

I WANTED TO SPEAK with the rest of the Miss Celosia contestants.

Jerry wanted to paint the kitchen cabinets, so I took him home and continued my investigation.

Mary Lee Winston told me how Juliet had stolen her boyfriend.

"She knew I loved Kevin, and she just charmed him away and then dumped him! He was so upset, he didn't come running back to me like he should have!"

Amy Britt informed me of Juliet's habit of cheating on English tests.

"She'd use the Internet at the library to find a paper on whatever subject the teacher wanted, and then she'd change it just enough so that it looked like her own work. I was the best writer in the class, but Mrs. Bowers never knew that. She thought Juliet was the next Danielle Steele."

I wasn't quite sure how to interpret that.

Joan Jessup gave me all the details on Juliet's behavior at parties.

"And she was never invited! She'd just show up, and nobody had the nerve to tell her to leave, especially not the boys. They'd just stand and gawk at her. She always wore really tight short dresses and no bra. She'd drink too much and start dancing around. It was awful!"

Everyone I spoke to had a Juliet horror story. Everyone I spoke to was glad she was gone—not particularly glad she was dead, but glad she was out of their lives, out of Celosia.

I'd heard enough for one day and decided to grab a burger and go home. I walked down Main Street past Georgia's Books, narrowly avoiding Prill, who was crossing at the post office, a small elderly woman clutching his cape.

"Inside, quick," Hayden said. He pulled me into the bookstore.

I laughed at his sudden move. "What's going on?"

"You know how he's been trying to sell me some woman's poetry. I'll bet any amount of money that is Emily Nesp with him right now. If he comes in here, tell him I'm not working today. Tell him I've gone down the Amazon."

I peered out the door. "They went into the post office."

"Probably to mail her latest tome to the Smithsonian," Hayden said. "He's been driving me crazy with her ridiculous verses. She's the worst poet you could possibly imagine. Worse than me."

"Don't talk like that. You're just having a little dry spell. It happens to everybody. I had to leave Parkland because I couldn't get work."

"I'd think Parkland would be a great place for crime."

I thought of Reid Kent and the look on his face when I caught him in my office. "All kinds. Unfortunately, no one was hiring me to solve them."

"How's this case coming along?" he asked.

"I want to talk to you about Shana."

His eyes widened. "Is she a suspect?"

"Was she with you Friday night at ten?"

He looked dismayed. "No. I was here, calling in some last-minute orders." His expression cleared. "But I called her, as well, to tell her I'd be late."

"When was this?"

"Sometime between nine-thirty and ten, I'm almost certain. Uh-oh. Too late."

I thought Hayden had remembered a damaging detail. Then I saw Prill enter the store. He waved a stack of paper at Hayden.

"Look here. Some of her latest."

"Spare me."

Prill glared. "I'm doing you a favor, you ignorant clod. Read this." He thrust one paper forward.

Hayden took the paper and scanned the words. "I've been reading small print all morning, so I know my eyes are tired, but not this tired. What is this? Gibberish, looks like."

"Don't you see? She's made up her own poetic language."

Hayden held the paper at arm's length. "I can't even read it. Is this supposed to be poetry?"

"It's the innermost thoughts of a flower. Read the title, you stupid thing."

"'My Pansy's Soul'?" Hayden began to chuckle. "I don't believe this."

Prill sighed in exasperation. "Of course you don't! Didn't I tell you you were mired in conventionality?"

"Just yesterday. Madeline, you have to read this."

I took the paper and read the flowery script. Hayden was right. It didn't make any sense.

Prill pulled another paper from the stack. "Look at this one. 'The Dust Speaks: A Mote's Eye View.' And this one. 'Reflections on a Fragment.' This is golden stuff, Hayden, a totally new art form. Stop laughing! I'm giving you first crack at these."

Hayden couldn't stop. He laughed until tears rolled down his cheeks. Then he put his head down on his arms on the desk and laughed some more.

Prill was furious. "Don't you understand what this means? Our entire concept of poetry will be altered, revitalized! What is wrong with you? This is obviously not the time to approach you with something of this magnitude."

Hayden sat up and wiped his eyes. "Bring back the spasmodic bells. At least that's in English. Sort of." He fluttered the copy of "My Pansy's Soul." "I can use this. The block is broken."

Prill snatched the paper out of his hand. "You are completely useless. I don't know why I bother with you. You'll be sorry you laughed at this opportunity of a lifetime."

Hayden couldn't stop chuckling. "Aren't you going to let me read the rest?"

Prill clutched the papers to his chest and folded his cape around them. "I called your house a thousand times last night. Where were you? There was a sale at Terrance's."

"I was working."

"Working on your own pitiful poems? Putting your socks in alphabetical order?"

"Working here at the store."

Prill gave a snort. "Brooding, most likely. When does the library committee meet again? Have you thought about what you're going to say about *Destinies?*"

Hayden's voice threatened to wobble. "Please let me take one of her latest efforts. It would be just the thing to sway the committee."

Prill drew himself up. "You are making sport of me, sir, and I will not have it. Good day!"

He sailed out. Georgia poked her head out from the children's section. "What was so funny?"

"We had a poetry reading," I said.

"Not Emily Nesp again."

"Thank God he didn't drag poor Ms. Nesp in here with him," Hayden said. "I couldn't stop laughing."

Georgia smiled. "Well, it's been a while since I heard you laugh like that. Maybe her poetry is good for something."

I had to agree. The tired lines were gone from Hayden's eyes. "I didn't understand a word of it. Prill worked himself into a real snit."

Hayden chuckled again. "'My Pansy's Soul.'"

"No comment," Georgia said.

WHEN I GOT BACK to the house, Jerry wasn't in the kitchen. He was on the front porch talking with Flossie Mae Snyder. She must have just arrived. Her huge car clicked as it cooled.

"My friends and I are still talking about your séance," she said. "That last one was certainly impressive. When can we schedule another?"

"Please have a seat, Mrs. Snyder," he said. She sat down in one of the rocking chairs. "Thanks, but I'm working on a new project. My girlfriend and I are planning on opening a haunted bed and breakfast."

"Yes, I'd heard something about that. It sounds most intriguing." She gave me a sharp glance. "Thought your girlfriend was a detective, though."

"Olivia Decker is my girlfriend. I don't believe you've met her."

There. He'd said it. That was it, then.

Flossie Mae gave him a look over the top of her glasses. "So you got two women living here?"

"Just about."

She laughed and reached over to pinch his cheek. "I knew you were a rascal first time I saw you. What did you do to the boys to get them so riled?"

Jerry perched on the porch rail. "I promise I've never done a thing to Sean or Geoff. They're just way too serious."

"Lord, yes. Just like their mother. But what about your folks? They from around here? Val never said a thing about relatives."

"My parents died when I was small. I have two brothers and a sister who live in Parkland."

Flossie Mae nodded. "Seems to me I recall something about that. Was it a fire? Tell me if I'm being too nosey."

"That's okay," Jerry said. "There was some sort of fire. I don't remember a lot about it."

"Have you been able to contact your parents during one of your séances?"

Jerry looked taken aback. "I never considered that."

Good heavens, I thought. Don't encourage him.

"Perhaps you should, before you give it up completely."

"Thank you, Mrs. Snyder. It might be worth a try."

She looked at her watch and got up. "Well, my sewing circle meets in about ten minutes. If you decide to get back in the séance business, you give me a call."

Jerry walked her out to her car and held the door. She drove off, and he came back to the porch.

"I see you have a groupie," I said.

"She's a real character."

"I guess we'll be hearing from Sean or Geoff pretty soon."

"Yep. I'll say ten minutes."

"I'll say fifteen."

In exactly ten minutes, Sean Snyder drove up in a cloud of dust, parked, and got out, fists clenched. He charged up the porch steps and shook a fist in Jerry's face.

"You may have fooled Aunt Flossie, but you don't fool me. This is just another scheme of yours to fleece unsuspecting widows."

Jerry just grinned. "And orphans."

Sean didn't get the joke. "What?"

"Widows and orphans. You're supposed to say unsuspecting widows and orphans."

I could see Sean's teeth grind together. "Be as flippant as you like. Geoff and I will find a way to stop you."

"You don't have to stop me, Sean. I've stopped myself. I'm going legit."

"Oh, ha, ha."

"Ask your aunt if you don't believe me."

"And what brought about this transformation?"

"I'm opening a bed and breakfast."

This stopped Sean cold for a few minutes. "A what?"

"A bed and breakfast. You know. People stay overnight, and you feed them in the morning."

Sean gave the house a horrified glance. "Good Lord. Who'd want to stay here?"

"You haven't seen the improvements. Come on in."

Sean didn't move. "I'm not going in there, and neither will anyone else. This house has a terrible reputation."

"Well, I'm going to change that."

"You don't fool me for an instant. You're going to lure innocent tourists in and then pick their pockets with your illegal and devious tricks."

"What tricks?"

"Geoff and I saw you and your partner—what was his name?"

Jerry sat back on the porch railing. "Jeff. Only he spells it the right way."

"We saw you and Jeff pull that phony mind-reading act. I'll bet you got over five hundred dollars that night before we exposed you to the authorities."

"Seven hundred and fifty. It would've been more, but Jeff's microphone kept picking up the local news."

I thought Sean was going to go through the roof.

"You even admit to fraudulent practices! Why aren't you in jail?"

"No jail can hold me, Sean. I just walk through the walls."

Sean stuck his nose so close to Jerry's, I thought for a moment he was going to attempt a head-butt. "Well, I promise you, Geoff and I will be watching closely, and if there's even the slightest hint of illegal activity up here, we'll have the law down on you."

Jerry didn't flinch. "This is going to be a legitimate business, Sean. You can ask Olivia."

"Don't think I won't!"

With this threat, Sean huffed back to his car, got in, and drove away.

Jerry waved good-bye. "One day, he's just going to pop like a balloon. There'll be little pieces of Snyder all over the yard."

I wondered what Jerry really had in mind. "You aren't planning anything illegal, are you?"

"Nothing I do is illegal. People want to believe. That's the great thing about them. Oh, here comes Olivia. Sean just missed her. Too bad."

I wish I'd missed her. Olivia. Damn. He must have called her.

Olivia parked her car beside mine and got out, carrying a shopping bag. Jerry bounded down the steps to her. I went upstairs to avoid seeing their happy meeting. I paused in the hallway and looked toward the parlor. Even from here, I could see the gleam of light; light that I knew would be perfect. I walked to the parlor and stood in the doorway, imagining how I'd rearrange things. The fancy Victorian furniture would have to go. I could put a desk and chair in one corner, some file cabinets and maybe a nice plant or two. The rest of the room would be filled with my artist supplies, paints and brushes and—

No. No, an office might be nice, but how could I hope

to create art here when Jerry and Olivia were lip-locked in their bedroom?

I could hear her. When was her incessant chatter going to get on his nerves? I went to the landing and listened. They were in the downstairs parlor, Olivia holding forth on her master plan for the bed and breakfast.

"Jerry, I found these candles at Candle De-Light. They'll go perfectly with your living-room colors. This is a special lighter, too. It's the latest thing. And I've been thinking an afternoon tea might be nice. Vegetables from your garden—if you ever have one. Tours, perhaps, of the area. We could get those little bottles of shampoo and lotion, like hotels have for their guests. Oh, you know what would look good? A grand piano right by those windows."

"And who would be playing this grand piano?" Jerry asked.

"Well, you certainly can."

"I think this room is a better séance room."

"Jerry, we are discussing a bed and breakfast, not a spook house at the fair. And why is Madeline still here?"

After all this time and despite all evidence to the contrary, she still perceives me as a threat.

"She's on a case," Jerry said.

"Do you honestly think she can solve a murder mystery?"

Getting personal here. I leaned over the railing to hear better.

Olivia said, "This is Madeline Maclin we're talking about. She can take pictures of cheating husbands and find watches and rings, but murder? Don't you think that's out of her league?"

Well, excuse me, missy.

"She can do it," Jerry said.

"I still don't see why she has to stay here."

"Mac's my best friend."

"You say that all the time, and it's impossible."

"Why?"

"Men and women can't be best friends. There's too much sexual tension involved."

Jerry laughed. "Mac and I don't have any sexual tension."

Ow. Jerry, you are as thick as two planks.

"You can't tell me you don't find her attractive," Olivia said.

"I think she's gorgeous."

Thanks for that much.

Olivia let out an exasperated sigh. "See?"

"Well, damn it, Olivia, I'm not blind."

"How do you think I feel with her in the house?"

"We've been through a lot together. I can't just throw that away."

"A few drunken brawls and you're blood brothers? We've been through a lot together, too, Jerry."

But Olivia hadn't jumped off the roof of the science building. Olivia hadn't traveled all night in the back of Sam Ferguson's Dodge pickup to see Ben Risky and the Fiery Mountain Boys' farewell performance in Charlotte. Olivia hadn't gone cross-country in a two-door Geo Metro looking for the tallest, scariest roller coasters, or been underground at Disney World, or seen *The Tales of Hoffmann* all sixteen times it was performed by the Houston Opera.

Nor would she want to.

She didn't even want to go into the secret passageway. If she married Jerry, his fun times would be over. Couldn't he see that?

I waited, hoping this would escalate into a first-class argument, but Olivia abruptly changed the subject.

"Can this Nell person do floors?"

"I'm sure she can," Jerry said.

"Because the bedroom floors are hardwood and should be refinished."

"I'll ask her."

"And have you decided what to do about the upstairs parlor?"

That's mine, I wanted to shout. My studio.

Wait a minute. What sort of mushrooms had I been chewing?

"I haven't decided," Jerry said.

"You could make it into a suite. It would triple your profits."

She went on about inventory and cash flow and turnover. I'm sure Jerry's eyes had glazed over long before she finished. I didn't want them to know I'd been listening, so I trotted down the stairs to the kitchen. Nell was getting a beer out of the refrigerator.

"Blondie still here?"

I nodded. She tossed me a beer. "Thanks."

She popped the top and took a swig. "You'd better make your move pretty soon."

"I'm not going to make a move."

"Then how's he gonna know how you feel?"

It was bad enough having Shana rewrite my life. I didn't want advice from Nell.

"Just paint, okay?"

JULIET'S FUNERAL SERVICE was held in a small gray stone church on Main Street. Evan James and Cindy were there, as well as the judges, Benjy Goins, Kimberly Dawn, and Chuck Hofsteder. Randi, Karen, and most of the Miss Celosia Pageant contestants were there, but Donna Sanchez was absent. The rest of the pews were filled with townspeople and teenagers. A slim woman in black sat by herself in the front pew. I guessed she was the relative Ted had mentioned. Ted came in and sat near the back. Chuck Hofsteder sat by himself, wiping his eyes.

I slid into the pew next to him. "My condolences, Chuck."

He blew his nose into a Kleenex. "She was a lovely girl. Such a waste. She could've gone all the way to the top. Celosia didn't know what it had. She would've made this town famous. Who've we got now? None of the other girls come close."

"Maybe next year."

He nodded and gave his eyes a final wipe. "Yes, you're right. I should be looking toward the future."

"How did you hear about Juliet?" I asked.

"I was at the country club having dinner, and the news went around like wildfire. I couldn't believe it. I called Benjy to see if he'd heard, and he was just as appalled as I was."

The service began. After the choir sang a hymn, we were asked to bow our heads in prayer. The minister had a short sermon about how tragic it was for a young life to be cut short. Another hymn, a parting prayer, and we were done.

Chuck Hofsteder shook my hand. His fingers were damp.

"Thank you for sitting with me, Madeline."

"I could tell you were upset."

"Juliet was our best hope since Kimberly Dawn." He sighed. "You know how it is. You're tall. The shorter girls just don't have that regal air. Juliet was the tallest girl in the competition. It makes a difference. Kimberly was the tallest in her pageant, too."

And being tall myself, I hadn't really noticed.

Chuck was still bemoaning the lack of talent in Celosia. "Donna and Karen are just too petite, and Randi lacks finesse." His gaze settled on the choir. "Now there's a possibility. That young lady on the front row. What do you think?"

Scouting for contestants at a funeral. Pageants must have fried his brain.

He went up the aisle. "I'm going to speak with her about next year."

Ted met me in the parking lot. "Madeline," he said. "The police won't tell me anything. Do you know anything?"

"Not much. I was hoping the killer would show up with a big lighted sign on his chest." I frowned. Ted was tall, but then, so were all the judges and Evan James. Whoever killed Juliet had to be tall enough to reach the cords hanging on the wall. I could reach them; Ted could, too.

I thought I recognized a woman standing by the church door talking with the pastor. "Is that one of your protesters?"

"Samantha Terrell."

Samantha Terrell saw me and came over, smiling. I remembered the small woman with her cloud of light brown hair from that first day I'd met the protesters. Her smile was a larger version of her son's smile.

"Austin can't stop talking about you and Jerry," she said. "He has the best time at your house. I hope he's not bothering you."

"Not at all," I said. "Jerry needs someone to play with."

The pastor moved on to another group of people. Samantha Terrell sighed and shook her head. "This is so sad about Juliet, isn't it? Did you speak with her aunt, Ted?"

"No, she slipped out before I could say anything to her."

"Did you know her family?" I asked Samantha.

"I knew her mother. Wild as a buck. She had Juliet when she was sixteen and never could control her."

"Madeline is investigating Juliet's murder," Ted said.

Samantha's dark eyes widened. "Really? Is that why you're in town? I thought you came to see about the Eberlin house."

"I seem to have fallen into this case."

"Do you have any suspects?"

Ted sighed. "Me."

Samantha frowned and for that moment looked exactly like Austin at the receiving end of one of Denisha's pronouncements. "Ted Stacy, your problems with Juliet are old news." She turned to me. "He told you about that ridiculous sexual harassment complaint, didn't he? Absolutely ridiculous."

"It doesn't look good for me, Sam," he said. "Some people have been giving me very dirty looks."

"They're crazy. The murderer could've been some nut off the streets, some escaped lunatic."

"That seems far-fetched for Celosia."

"So does murder."

Chuck Hofsteder came up to us, smiling a broad smile. "Good news, Madeline. Jennifer Sasser is very interested in the Miss Celosia Pageant. She says no one's ever asked her. Can you believe that? This is great. She'll be a terrific contestant."

Ted looked at him askance. "This hardly seems the time to be celebrating something so trivial."

Chuck waved him off. "Ted, everybody knows how you feel about pageants. You wouldn't understand."

"You're right. I don't."

"Madeline, you know what I'm talking about. If we want the pageant to have a future, we have to start building it back up now. Jennifer says she has a cousin who'd be interested, too. You wouldn't by any chance be available to do some coaching, would you? These girls are brand new to the pageant scene. They could use some of your expertise."

"No, thanks, Chuck," I said. "I'm retired."

He scanned the crowd. "You know, Augusta Freer has a niece about pageant age. I ought to ask her if Denise wants to try out."

He hurried off to speak to a woman standing in the parking lot. Ted and I exchanged a look of disbelief with Samantha.

"Speaking of escaped lunatics," she said. "Well, I've got to go pick up the girls at the movies. Ted, no more of this 'I'm the prime suspect' talk, you hear me? Nice to see you again, Madeline."

Ted waited until she had gone and then smiled wryly. "I was going to see if you'd like lunch, but my appetite's gone."

"Mine, too," I said.

"Call you later?"

"Sure."

I watched him cross the churchyard to his car. I felt uneasy. There wasn't any solid evidence that put Ted at the scene of the crime, but with his history of problems with Juliet, would the police, anxious to find the murderer, be inclined to believe Ted was in some way responsible for Juliet's death? I wanted to talk with Chief Brenner, but I knew he'd just warn me off again.

I walked over to Evan James and Cindy. In her usual forthright way, Cindy was trying to console Evan.

"You've got to stop blaming yourself. You couldn't have done anything. If you'd been backstage, you might have gotten killed, too."

Evan wiped his eyes with his handkerchief and blew his nose. "It's just so unsettling."

"You need to think about the future. Why don't you help with the next musical? That'll take your mind off pageants for a while."

"Pageants are my life. You know that."

Resisting the urge to roll my eyes, I offered my sympathies. "I'm sorry you're feeling so bad about this, Evan."

He gave his nose another blow. "Thank you, Madeline. I can't help thinking there could have been something I could've done to keep this awful thing from happening."

"There's no way you could've known."

"That's what I keep trying to tell him," Cindy said.

Evan sniffed. "How is your investigation coming along?"

"Well, every time I get a lead, it leads me to someone else. I wanted to ask you about Cynthia Riley."

Cindy made a disgusted sound. Evan looked puzzled.

"Cynthia Riley? She was in the pageant years ago."

"I heard there was a problem with her microphone and she blamed you."

"Oh, that." He frowned as if recalling the incident. "Yes,

she was quite incensed. The power failure was unintentional. At the time, we were working with some inferior mikes, and they had a bad habit of cutting out during performances. I didn't think she was ever going to forgive me."

"But she wouldn't have won, anyway," Cindy said. "She couldn't sing, and she looked like a clothes hanger in that gown."

"Cindy." Evan's voice sounded tired. "No more negativity, please."

"Well, she did. She was too thin and bony to be a queen. Besides, it was Kimberly Dawn's year."

"Oh, that's right."

"This is going to sound far-fetched," I said, "but do you think Cynthia Riley could still be holding a grudge?"

"Oh, my, no," Evan said. "We've spoken many times since that pageant, and she's always been perfectly civil. She's even laughed about the incident, saying I saved the world from hearing her sing."

"She's an exorcist, right?"

Cindy gave a snort. "She can certainly scare anything away."

"Cindy, please. Madeline, Cynthia is a buyer for Farrell's, a chain of ladies' dress shops, and very successful. She doesn't need pageants. As for the exorcist business, I think she dabbles every now and then."

"Do you know if she had any contact with Juliet?"

Evan looked to Cindy, who shrugged. "I'm sure she knew who Juliet was. Everyone knew."

I thanked them for the information. My next stop was the local Farrell's store.

The dress shop was in the Olympia Mall, Parkland's largest mall. Inquiries about Cynthia Riley led me to the bridal section where Cynthia was inspecting a shipment of bridesmaids' dresses. She had on another clingy beige outfit and lots of gold jewelry.

"Good afternoon," she said. "It's Madeline, I believe? How can I help you?"

"Do you have time to answer a few questions?"

"My pleasure." She indicated two pink-and-gold chairs usually reserved for brides and their mothers. "Shall we sit down?"

We sat. Cynthia crossed one slim leg over the other and smoothed her skirt. Her beige pumps and stockings matched her dress. She tossed back her hair.

"Now then, what do you need to know? Did Shana send you after me?" She seemed pleased by the idea.

"This visit is about something else. Did you know Juliet Lovelace?"

"Yes, of course." If Cynthia Riley had seemed pleased before, this question thrilled her. "Am I a suspect? How exciting! Oh, no, wait. She was killed Friday night. I was here at the store in a meeting with ten other people. Guess that lets me out."

I felt an overwhelming desire to pull her ever-swinging hair. "Sorry you're so disappointed."

"Well, really, why would I kill Juliet? I hardly knew her. We had nothing in common."

"You had a pageant career once."

"Oh, that." She waved a hand. "Nonsense. It was the thing to do in Celosia. All the girls tried out. I suppose you heard about what happened during my talent. I was hopping mad at the time, but now I look back and laugh. I can't sing. Whatever made me think I could?"

"Still, it must have been disappointing."

"If I'd kept up with my horoscope that day, I would've seen it wasn't in the stars. My talents lie elsewhere. If you think I've been harboring resentment all these years, you're wrong. There's nothing worse than an ex-beauty queen who can't get off the runway. We're not all Kimberly Dawns who have to be around the pageants every year, and pretend to have a modeling career when we're making sleazy lingerie 'commercials.'"

Sounded a little resentful to me. "She beat you out in your year, right?"

"What can I say? The planets were not aligned. But I managed to escape Celosia and find a real career." Another toss of her head. "The game's up. I know why you're really here. Go back and tell Shana I won't come to her house again. Of course, I can't promise I won't stop by the bookstore every now and then."

"That wouldn't be very smart."

"Hayden is simply too much of a temptation."

I tried to keep my tone light. "Why don't you just leave him alone?"

She gave me a long, considering stare. "I might just do that. After all, there's another man in town."

Good lord. Was she going after Jerry?

The shock must have shown on my face. Cynthia Riley laughed.

"Well, you're not sleeping with him, are you? I've seen him with this tiny little blonde. She doesn't look like much of a threat."

As much as I would love to see Cynthia Riley and Olivia Decker duke it out, I was too appalled by Cynthia's nerve to think of a reply.

She continued, "Of course, if the two of you are an item, then it just makes life more of a challenge."

I stood. I managed to keep my voice in control. "Thank you for your time."

"You're welcome." She tossed her head and smiled a superior smile. "I'm sure we'll be seeing each other again."

I WAS GLAD I had the drive from Parkland to Celosia to clear my mind. It would make me very happy to pin Juliet's murder on Cynthia Riley. Unfortunately, before I left Farrell's, I checked with the manager. There had been a meeting Friday night, and Cynthia had been present.

I gripped the steering wheel and had a serious talk with myself. Settle down. She's not the first woman to want Jerry, and she won't be the last. You have to do something to make sure you are the last. And what have you done lately? Nothing.

Jerry hadn't gone to the funeral. He told me long ago the only other funeral he'd be attending would be his own. Still, the gloomy event of the day must have had some impact on him. When I entered the house, I heard music, and it wasn't the sprightly "Doll Song" from *Hoffmann,* or *Paul Bunyan*'s cheerful chorus of lumberjacks. It was the aria Paul Bunyan's daughter, Tiny, sings, lamenting the death of her mother. The soprano's clear voice was filled with anguish.

I stood for a long while, listening. My mother was alive. Jerry's had vanished in flames. He rarely spoke about her or his father. I often sensed he was holding in an ocean's worth of emotion, and one little crack would result in a deluge of grief. I stepped inside. Jerry muted the sound, but not before I saw the look on his face.

The best way to be in these circumstances is casual. "What's up?"

He turned the volume down. "Just seeing how the CD sounds."

"Nothing like a little *Paul Bunyan* in the afternoon."

His attention was on the CD player. "This is a really great system."

"Are you to the part about the soup and beans?"

"Way past that."

"Damn. That's my favorite." I knew better than to say anything about his parents. I looked around the room for something else to talk about. There were two large square candles on the mantel. "Nice candles."

"Olivia brought them."

A peace offering?

"Check out the lighter."

The lighter was a long silver rod. One click and you had a nice flame. "Bet that set her back a little."

"She always has to have the best."

I was concerned that Olivia was already spending her own money on this venture. "Okay, so your guests have super deluxe candles. That's nice."

I sat down on the sofa and gazed at *Blue Moon Garden*. For a moment, I imagined myself in my upstairs studio putting the final touches on another picture of wildflowers, maybe the wildflowers that grew around the Eberlin house, the Queen Anne's lace and the buttercups, white and gold, like the Fairweather mansion. I really wished Jerry could talk a little about his family.

"You seem kind of down. Did you and Olivia have another disagreement?"

"I've been thinking about my family."

Whoa.

"About Uncle Val in particular. I should've stayed out of the attic."

"Jerry, your uncle might have been eccentric, but people in town have said lots of good things about him. Wouldn't Austin and Denisha be unable to talk about him or mourn him if he'd done anything improper?"

He looked at me. "You're right. They're his biggest fans. But he still could've been running a little porn business on the side."

"I don't think so."

He put the CD in its case and slid it into the shelf under the player. "Well, gee, Mac, I guess you know my mysterious uncle better than I do."

"The kids are perceptive. They would've known if something was wrong."

"Maybe."

"They crack me up the way they talk to each other. That Austin's so smart, and Denisha's beautiful and perceptive, too. She— Oh, lord."

"What?"

"I'm doing it."

"Doing what?"

"Talking about the kids. Please stop me."

"They aren't your kids."

"I came dangerously close to sounding like a proud parent."

"That's okay. I like them, too. They're neat kids." He joined me on the sofa. "Kinda reminds me of how Des and Tucker and I were before—" He stopped. "Before we grew up."

He and I both knew he meant to say something else. I tried to change the subject. "I think we need to find that videotape."

He sighed. "Which brings us back to Uncle Val as porn producer."

I ignored that. "If the mailman left the package with the videotape here, then somebody must have taken it."

"And we still have no idea why."

"I won't know that until I find out who got in the house."

"Well, when we first got here, the house was locked. The place looked like Val had just stepped out for a minute. Nothing else was missing."

"But we don't know that nothing else was missing. We don't know what was in the house to begin with. There might have been something of value a thief was after, and he or she picked up the package, too."

"So somebody broke in."

"Or had a key. Or knew about the secret passageway."

Jerry slumped back on the sofa. "All I can think about is Uncle Val's Valentine bed."

"No need to worry about that. Nell popped it." I wished he would cheer up. "Is Nell going to redo the attic?"

"That's something Olivia and I need to discuss. She's supposed to be here in a little while to talk some more B&B business."

Olivia, the Thing That Would Not Leave. "How's that coming along?"

"She still doesn't like the idea of a haunted house."

I don't think I'll ever understand his fascination with this silly stuff, but right now, I was glad he was standing firm. "So you're not going to give up?"

"Nope."

"You're choosing ghosts over Olivia?"

"Not exactly. She doesn't have to believe in ghosts for the haunted B&B to work."

Not the answer I wanted to hear. "Is there any leftover pizza?"

We took our cold slices of pizza and sodas to the porch and sat down. Jerry was still in an abstracted mood, and so was I. I thought about what Olivia had said and how I'd almost shouted the parlor was my studio. For a moment, I fantasized living in this house, waking up next to Jerry, having breakfast on the porch, and then strolling upstairs to a large room filled with light and canvases. I imagined spending my days creating wildly colored views of the fields and sunsets and my nights curled in Jerry's arms. This was about as perfect a fantasy as I could imagine.

And that's just what it was: a fantasy.

"You're thinking deep," Jerry said.

I'm thinking how I'd like to paint you. I'm wondering if I could get just the right light in your eyes.

"Trying to sort out all the facts in this case."

"You'll solve it. I know you will."

His confidence in the face of Olivia's criticism brought a lump of emotion to my throat. No matter what I attempted, he always believed in me.

I managed to swallow the lump and my last bite of pizza.

"Thanks." This was a perfect time to say so many of the things I'd wanted to say.

I'm not sure what I would've said. With the rotten timing that seemed to be standard in Celosia, a little red Escort came up the drive and parked by the trees. Twenty got out. She reached into the back seat and pulled out some suits on hangers.

"Is this a bad time? I want to see if these fit."

"Come on in," Jerry said. "Have you had lunch? There's some pizza left."

"Oh, no, thanks. I'm kind of in a rush. So many things to do. Try these on."

Jerry took the suits into the house. Twenty sat down in one of the rocking chairs. She had on red leather shorts and an orange tube top. She tugged the tube top up and the shorts down and fanned herself with her hand.

"I tell you, it's been one thing after another getting this show together. I stopped by and left Hayden's suits. He looks amazingly good in black."

"I saw him at the store this morning. He seems to be doing better."

Today Twenty's earrings looked like little gold lightning bolts. They caught the light and made odd jittery patterns as she turned her head. "All this about Juliet Lovelace is so upsetting. I mean, her killer is still out there. Have you found out anything, Madeline?"

"I'm still gathering information."

"I don't know what to think. Nothing like this has ever happened in Celosia." She gave her shorts another tug. "Then there's all that with Ted Stacy's office being burgled and the TV station. It makes me very nervous." She spread her hands on her legs and drummed her fingers. Her fingernails were alternating red and orange. "And I have to admit this the first time I've ever been to the Eberlin house. I'm so curious."

"You'll have to see all the improvements."

"Okay," Jerry called from inside. "Are you ready for this?"

He strolled out in the dark blue suit and gave us the full model treatment. He turned around, he opened the jacket to show the lining, he removed the jacket and slung it over one shoulder.

Twenty laughed and clapped her hands. The little lightning bolts flashed. "That's perfect! That's exactly what you should do in the show."

He smoothed the sleeves of the jacket. "This is a great suit. I know just the tie to go with it."

"Not the flamingoes," I said.

"I was thinking of the light bulbs."

"Go try on the gray," Twenty said. She waited until he'd gone and turned to me. "He knows just how to pose, doesn't he? He's a natural."

"A natural ham." No need to tell Twenty Jerry had been posing for most of his adult life.

She focused her attention on the door. "I know the gray is going to be absolutely fantastic."

I thought Jerry looked good in the dark blue suit until I saw him in the gray. He came out, smiling, and did the same routine. The gray suit made his eyes shine. I felt the heat rise in my face. He looked every inch the successful executive. A young lawyer, maybe, or head of his own company. All the things he could be if he put as much time and energy into a real career as he did in his psychic schemes.

Good Lord, I thought. I'm thinking like Olivia.

He put the jacket back on and straightened the lapels. "What do you think?"

Twenty clasped her hands together. "It's perfect."

My throat had clogged again. Yes, it is.

"Mac, this suit is just right for the hula-girl tie."

"No, no," Twenty said. "I have ties and shirts and everything. You don't have to bring a thing, just yourself. The show is in two weeks, Saturday night at Myers in Parkland. You need to be there by six-thirty."

"Okay."

"And you might need to encourage Hayden. He's not as comfortable as you with the idea of being in a fashion show."

"No problem."

I had to do something before I grabbed Jerry and took him right there on the porch. "Jerry, while you're changing, I'll show Twenty the house."

Twenty was amazed by the living room. "This looks like something out of a magazine! It's gorgeous!" She admired all the furnishings. "And this painting—" She squinted at the signature. "Madeline, did you do this?"

"Back in my college days."

"Well, it's very good. Have you ever considered a career as an artist?"

"Briefly."

"Pardon me for saying this, but it might be better than being a detective. It might be safer, I mean."

I knew exactly what she meant. "Would you like to see the kitchen?"

"Just for a moment. I really have to dash."

After Twenty dashed, Jerry and I finished the pizza.

I was still trying to recover. "You looked pretty snazzy in those suits. Perhaps you should consider a career as a fashion model."

"A psychic fashion model. I could predict all the trends. I'll need an entourage, though. Care to drive the limo?"

"You probably need to think about getting your own car."

"It's too bad Val didn't leave me one." Jerry frowned. "Wait a minute. How did Val get to town? Did he have a car?"

I thought this over. "Jerry, remember when we first came to Celosia, and the guy at the gas station mentioned how he admired Val's old car?"

"Yes."

"Well, where is it? There isn't a car in the garage." I could feel ideas trying to come together. "It's an old car. It could be valuable. And now we've got two things missing."

"You think whoever took the car might have taken the video?"

"It's worth a shot. We have to find that car."

"Maybe the gas-station guy would know."

We drove into town and stopped at the service station to speak to the lanky man in the John Deere cap.

"Oh, hi," he said. "You two all settled in? Not been carried off by ghosts yet?"

"Not yet," Jerry said. "Any idea what happened to Val Eberlin's old car?"

The man turned his head aside to spit a short stream of tobacco juice. "I kept asking him to sell it to me, but he never would. Averall Mercer got it."

"Did he leave it to her?"

"Beats me. You'll have to ask her about that. She lives on Piney Lane. Go left and after about three blocks, look for the street sign. Go down five houses on your left. That's the Mercer place."

We got back into the car. "Isn't Averall Mercer Denisha's aunt?" I asked.

"I think so."

We found Piney Lane. Averall Mercer's house was a small yellow house covered with flowering vines. All kinds of potted plants and hanging baskets decorated the porch.

Jerry peered around the house. "I don't see a car of any kind."

"Let's find out."

A thin black woman met us on the porch. She wiped her hands on her apron. "Can I help you?"

"I'm Madeline Maclin and this is Jerry Fairweather, Val Eberlin' nephew," I said. "We're looking for Val's car, and the fellows down at the gas station said you might know where it is."

"That old Chevy? I sold it to a man up the highway."

"Did my uncle leave it to you?" Jerry asked.

She nodded. "But I didn't have no use for it. The money came in mighty handy, though. I expect that's why Val said I could have it. See, I used to do some ironing for him. He didn't like sending his shirts to the cleaners, so he'd wash them himself, and I'd iron them." She smiled at Jerry. "Son, your uncle was a mighty generous man. He was always real polite to me and always bought cookies from my little niece, and if he had something extra, he'd share with my family. Last time I went up there, he had left quite a few nice things. After he passed, I brought them all back in the car. Got your extra house key around here somewhere. I'll find it for you."

So Mrs. Mercer had been in the house. "Did you happen to find a package?" I held my hands several inches apart. "It would've been about this size. There was a videotape inside."

She thought a moment. "No, sorry. Don't recall anything like that."

I'd been so sure she'd picked it up.

Then Jerry said, "Could it have fallen out in the car?"

"Might have. It was pretty loaded up that last trip. I'll get you the address of the man that bought it off me. You wait right here."

She went into the house. Immediately, Denisha popped out, eyes wide. "Don't tell my aunt I know you! It's supposed to be a secret."

This didn't surprise me. "Your aunt didn't know you and Austin were sneaking into Val's house?"

"No, and don't tell her I still am! It'll ruin everything." Her eyes narrowed. "Why are you here? You're not here to tell on me, are you?"

"We're looking for Val's car," I said.

"I coulda told you where it was. Shh! She's coming. Play like we don't know each other."

Mrs. Mercer returned with a slip of paper. "This is my niece, Denisha. Denisha, this is Ms. Maclin and Mr. Fairweather from up at Mr. Eberlin's house."

Denisha looked as serene as an angel. "How do you do?"

"Nice to meet you, Denisha," Jerry said.

"Thank you, Mr. Fairweather. Ain't that a nice name, Auntie?"

"Very nice."

"Are they living in Mr. Eberlin's house now?"

"I believe so." Mrs. Mercer handed the paper to Jerry. "Here's the name and address. Tully Springfield, two twenty-one Old Highway Twelve. I hope that helps you out."

Jerry thanked her. We went back to the car. Denisha waved good-bye from the porch.

"That girl has a career in the theater just waiting for her," I said.

Old Highway Twelve wound out among the cornfields and meadows. We stopped and checked several mailboxes, trying to find 221.

"We're halfway to Virginia," Jerry said as we drove around another series of curves.

I saw a split-rail fence up ahead. Each rail had been painted a different color. "Do you suppose Mr. Springfield is the owner of that rainbow fence?"

The mailbox at the corner of the fence was shaped like a fish, only this fish had on stars and stripes and an Uncle Sam top hat.

Jerry checked the number. "This is it."

"This is it, all right."

Scattered on the sprawling front yard was an amazing collection of yard art: a donkey pulling a cart, frogs in a love seat, plastic deer, wagon wheels, squirrels, chickens, giant mushrooms, and birdbaths. Adorning the house were climbing cats, seahorses, American eagles, and smiley faces. Each piece had been repainted. The donkey was purple with yellow stripes. The frogs were blue and red. The climbing cats were Day-Glo orange. Everything had stripes or polka dots.

"Jerry, I hate to think what he's done to the car."

"Well, there it is."

"Good grief."

It was impossible to tell what the old Chevy's original color had been. The car was now sky blue with paisley patterns of yellow and red.

Jerry laughed. "Looks like something you'd drive to an Indian wedding."

We parked beside a row of silver reflecting balls and got out. The house was a low structure with a panoramic view of the Blue Ridge. Without the garish zoo, it would have been a nice mountain retreat.

Jerry rubbed the head of a huge stone owl. "This is so neat, Mac. I'm having acid flashbacks."

"Do I dare ring the bell? The whole place might vanish."

"Hello," a voice said. "Come on around."

Jerry and I cautiously made our way through the menagerie to the backyard, which was surprisingly free of kitsch. A man stood at an easel, putting the finishing touches on a fantastically accurate landscape of the mountain scene.

"May I help you?" he asked.

I was still trying to clear my head of the front yard. "Are you Tully Springfield?"

"Yes."

Although Tully Springfield's hair was gray, his face was unlined. His eyes were a brilliant blue. He had on jeans and a faded blue shirt streaked with paint.

"I'm Madeline Maclin, and this is Jerry Fairweather, Val Eberlin's nephew. We were told you had Val's car."

He looked at Jerry, alarmed. "Was it supposed to come to you? It, uh, looks a little different now."

"No, we'd just like to have a look," Jerry said. "We're trying to find a package that may have been left in it."

Tully Springfield relaxed. "Oh, that. You know, I've been meaning to get that back to Averall. Is it something important?"

"It could be. Do you mind if we take it?"

"Not at all. Save me a trip."

I couldn't keep my eyes off his painting. "That's a wonderful landscape."

He shrugged. "Pays the bills. Let me show you my real masterpieces."

I couldn't imagine what he meant by real masterpieces. Jerry and I followed him into the house. The entire back room facing the mountains was a well-stocked artist's studio. Brushes filled jars of water and turpentine. Canvases were stacked in every corner. Tully Springfield led us past rows of remarkable landscapes. I kept expecting him to stop and point to them. Instead, he paused at a hideous collection of painted clowns and sad-eyed children surrounded by more of the lurid yard creatures.

He beamed. "Here."

"Oh," I said. "Um. These? They're very nice."

Behind Springfield's back, Jerry made a horrified face at me and mimed throwing up.

Oblivious to more than Jerry's opinion, Tully Springfield said, "The landscapes are okay, but this is what I really enjoy. I don't understand why they don't sell as well, though."

What could I say? "Well, critics, you know."

"Mac's an artist, too," Jerry said.

I could've kicked him. Tully Springfield's face brightened. "Then you know all about how difficult it is to be taken seriously. What was your name again? I'm sorry. I've forgotten."

"Madeline Maclin. Madeline is fine."

"Please call me Tully. What sort of things do you paint, Madeline? Do you like clowns?"

Now Jerry crossed his eyes at me. It was hard to keep a straight face. "I've never attempted one."

"Clowns are such a challenge. So many people get them wrong, which is why you see so many bad imitations. The colors, for one thing, and then there's the expression. No two can be alike, you know. Each clown has his own distinctive makeup. Let me show you."

He showed us about fifty different paintings of clowns. Clowns holding dinky little umbrellas, clowns spilling out of little cars, juggling clowns, pie-faced clowns, clowns in the rain. Jerry kept modifying his snorts of laughter into sneezes. Tully didn't notice.

"And over here is my Lost Carnival Series." He started through another stack of paintings and stopped. "My goodness, I'm a terrible host. You came for the package, didn't you? Not to see all this. I'm sorry. I rarely have visitors, especially fellow artists. I guess I got carried away."

"It's all right," I said. "I enjoyed it."

"Let me get the package for you. I think I know where it is."

He disappeared into the depths of the house.

I turned to Jerry and held up my finger. "Don't say one word."

He let out the laughter he'd been trying to suppress. "I'm going to buy one and hang it in my room. It'll scare the ghosts away."

I walked back to the lush mountain landscapes, surprised by the feelings that rose up in me. Since college, I hadn't wanted to even sketch, but now I wanted to grab a brush and fill in the green shadows of trees. I wanted to see if I could capture the blue haze that settled over the mountains and the way the sun's slanting rays sent searchlights of gold through the forest. Tully Springfield could do it. I could, too.

"These are gorgeous. Why can't he see that?"

Jerry had on his most innocent expression. "Oh, you know these artist types. They never think their work is any good."

I glared at him and didn't answer.

He picked up a paintbrush. "We'll never see him again. He's already forgotten we're here."

"Don't mess with his stuff. He's got some of the best materials I've seen. Top quality."

"I bet he'd share."

"You need to shut up now."

Jerry replaced the paintbrush and sat down in one of the wooden folding chairs by Tully's desk. "Seriously, if things don't work out with Ted, this guy's not bad. Sure, he's a little absentminded, but think what you could do with a studio like this."

Why did he feel the need to fix me up with everyone else? "I have to admit this studio's really nice."

"And Tully's looking at you like he thinks you're really nice, too."

"Will you quit playing Cupid?"

"Now that I've got Olivia, we've got to find somebody for you."

"So all four of us can live happily ever after in the Eberlin House?"

"Why not?"

Because I can't live in the Eberlin house with you and Olivia, you dope. Ted's offer of office space in his building was sounding better every day. Maybe I could live there, too, get a cot and a coffee pot. But I'd still be in Celosia. I'd still be near Jerry.

"I don't know," I said. "Maybe. We'll see what happens."

Jerry left the desk and inspected a family of plastic ducks. "I kind of like this shade of pink. Do you suppose he was going for the flamingo look?"

"I knew something was missing. No plastic flamingoes."

"Whoops."

"What did you do?"

"Nothing. Some of the paint came off. It's an improvement, really."

"I can't take you anywhere."

"Is it ruined beyond all reason?"

I checked the duck's head. "It's okay." We straightened just as Tully Springfield returned with the package.

"I didn't open it," he said. "I set it aside to take to town the next time I went, and with one thing and another, I never went. My apologies."

"That's all right," I said. "It was safer here with you."

He smiled. "Well, that's good news. Usually, I make things worse. Could I offer you some lemonade? Apple pie?"

I needed to know more about Tully Springfield. "Some lemonade would be nice."

"This way, please."

The rest of Tully's house was surprisingly bare and decorated in Mountain Cabin. The furniture in front of the fireplace in the den was made of logs and draped with striped Indian blankets. The lampshades had pictures of moose. A tree stump with a piece of glass on top served as a coffee table. The only thing out of place was the clown portrait hanging over the mantel, all sad eyes and turned-down mouth.

"One of my favorites," Tully said.

I could tell Jerry was trying not to laugh. He looked around the room and saw something in the window that caught his attention. "Great crystals."

"Ah, yes, they catch the morning sunlight. I believe quite strongly in crystal healing."

"I've done a little research into that, myself." Jerry reached for one of the crystals. "Do you mind?"

"No, go right ahead. The amethyst is my favorite."

"This is a nice chunk of rock."

Tully handed me a glass of lemonade.

"Did you know Val well?" I asked.

"I'm afraid not. I'd see him every now and then at the drug store." He tapped his chest. "We had the same heart condition, so we'd discuss how we were getting along, medications we were trying, things like that. I was a bit surprised to hear he'd died. I thought he was doing pretty well, but I didn't see him every time I went to Celosia. I'm usually in Virginia for the art shows."

"When's your next show?" I asked.

"I'd have to check my calendar."

"Would you mind checking?" I gave him my best smile. "I might like to go."

"One moment."

Jerry was still playing with the crystals. "That's more like it, Mac."

"More like what?"

"Ted Stacy better watch his back."

I shushed him. "I'm working."

He almost dropped a hunk of rose quartz. "You think Tully's a suspect?"

I kept my voice down. "Not if he can prove he was in Virginia Friday night."

"But he's a nut. He paints clowns."

"And maybe Juliet made disparaging remarks about his work. We artists are sensitive, remember?"

He set the rock back on the window ledge. "I think you just want to find something wrong with the guy so you don't have to date him."

"Here we are," Tully said. He brought in a large calendar with dates circled in red. "The Bayport Gallery had a showing last Friday, so the next show I'll attend is week after this at Steamboat Falls. I'd be very happy to have you come along. Perhaps it would inspire you to take up your work again."

If he was telling the truth, Tully was nowhere near the theater on Friday night.

"So you haven't heard about the trouble in town?"

He shook his head. "What trouble?"

"One of the Miss Celosia contestants was murdered."

I watched his eyes. He seemed genuinely puzzled. "Murdered? Who would want to kill a beauty queen?"

I found it odd he didn't ask who the victim was. "That's what has everyone talking."

"Do the police have any idea who did it?"

"I don't think so."

"You must wonder what sort of place you've moved to. I don't think there's been a murder in Celosia in years. More lemonade?"

Did he really not care, or was he just in his own little world out here? "No, thanks. The victim was Juliet Lovelace. Did you know her?"

He shook his head. "This was a young lady, I take it?"

"Seventeen."

"I wouldn't know anyone that young. It's been thirty years since I was in high school. A real tragedy, I'm sure."

I couldn't tell by his tone of voice if he meant the tragedy was Juliet's death or the fact he was no longer young enough to be a teenager.

He turned to Jerry. "Can I get you some more lemonade, Jerry?"

"No, thank you." Jerry picked up another piece of glittering rock. "Which of these crystals do you find the most receptive?"

"The amethyst is reliable, but I'd say for the best effects, I use the obsidian."

"Oh, yeah? I never thought of that."

"Although it isn't truly a crystal, obsidian is excellent for blocking and reversing harmful rays."

Jerry's likely to talk for hours about this kind of thing, but something had occurred to me. "Tully, you say Val's medicine was working for him."

"Yes, he often said so, and he was never without his nitroglycerin pills."

In searching the house for videotapes, Jerry, the kids, and I had found lots of things, but we hadn't found any pills, not even a bottle of aspirin.

Tully patted his shirt pocket. "Like me, he always had some in his pocket. And I remember him telling me he kept some in a little table by the door so he wouldn't have to run all the way to the bathroom or kitchen cabinets. Guess he was out."

Maybe. I wouldn't know anything more about this or about Tully Springfield until I asked Nell or Denisha. I set my glass on the tree-stump table and stood up.

"We appreciate your hospitality, but Jerry and I need to get back to town."

"Please come again soon. I'd love to see some of your work, Madeline."

"I'm out of practice."

He gestured to the studio. "I have more than enough here. If you want to get started again, you must feel free to use whatever you like."

I didn't dare look at Jerry. "That's very generous."

He insisted we take a birdbath, so Jerry chose one that didn't glow in the dark. Tully helped him put it in the trunk.

"I don't have a phone, Madeline, but I'm nearly always here. Please consider my offer."

"I will, thank you."

"Woo, woo," Jerry said as we drove away. "You've got this guy in your pocket."

"Don't be ridiculous."

"But I approve of him. Anyone who's that big into crystals is okay by me."

"I'm so glad."

"You don't really suspect him, do you? What's his motive? Did Juliet ridicule his clown pictures? If that's the case, there'd be bodies strewn everywhere."

"I don't know. I was more interested in what he had to say about Val's pills."

Jerry's eyes got large. "You think there's something suspicious about Val's death?"

"It just seems odd that if Val always had his pills with him, he couldn't get to them on time. I hope there's something useful on this tape."

"We can look at it as soon as we get home," Jerry said. "Olivia can handle things at the—argg!"

I almost ran off the road. "What?"

"Olivia! I totally forgot she was coming to talk about the house! Oh, man, if she's there waiting on me, she is going to be royally pissed."

Olivia was waiting, and "royally pissed" didn't begin to describe her expression. She stood on the porch, arms folded, eyes blazing.

"Jerry Fairweather, if you are not going to give the bed and breakfast your full and undivided attention, I am not going to spend one more minute of my valuable time on this project!"

"Sorry, honey." He tried to hug her, but she shrugged him off. "Mac and I were looking for something important, and we had to go way out in the country to this—"

"I don't want to hear about it. What could be more important than fixing this house and getting it ready for potential guests? Are you serious about wanting to open a bed and breakfast by September?"

"Yes, of course."

"Then you need to be more responsible! You need to do your part and not run off to play with Madeline. This isn't college. This isn't spring break. This is real life."

He took a step back. "Well, maybe I don't like real life."

"That's obvious."

"I said I was sorry. You're better at these things than I am, anyway."

"That's not the point. This is a partnership. You have to do your share whether you like it or not. You have to grow up."

Okay, Jerry, I thought. Now's your chance. You can choose real life with Olivia, or you can continue to play with me.

He didn't say anything. Olivia looked at her watch and made an exasperated sound. "I'm late for another appointment. We'll discuss this when I get back."

She strode down the steps to her car. She didn't look at me. When she'd gone, I wasn't really sure what to say to Jerry.

When he turned to me, his expression was determined. "Let's check out the videotape."

I opened the package and took out the tape. The label said *The Nocturnal Habits of* Centurio senex.

Jerry nodded. "Sounds pretty kinky to me."

"There's a letter." I unfolded the paper and read aloud, "'Dear Sir: While we are interested in the mating habits of *Centurio senex,* we do not need or appreciate suggestive material. We sincerely hope this tape was sent to us by mistake and look forward to the next in your series of documentaries.'"

Jerry and I looked at each other. Then we raced for the living room. I popped the tape in the VCR. Jerry hit the remote. As *The Nocturnal Habits of* Centurio senex unwound, our eyes grew wider and our mouths hung lower. Kimberly Dawn Williams, in all her nude and not-all-blond glory writhed upon the pink heart-shaped bed in the attic, panting and groaning in a ghastly parody of sexual excitement.

"Well," I said, "this is not what I expected."

Jerry cleared his throat. "She looks pretty good for an old bat."

I turned it off. We sat for a few moments, still slack-jawed. I was afraid the image was permanently burned into my brain.

Finally, Jerry said, "Okay, so while Val's away on a bat-hunting expedition, Kimberly Dawn decides to use his studio to jump start her second career."

"Or make a birthday surprise for that certain someone."

"What a great idea. Think Olivia will go for it?"

"The only thing Olivia wants to go for is your throat." I hit the eject button and slid the tape back into its cover. "If I were Kimberly Dawn, former Miss Celosia and reigning society queen, I wouldn't want anyone to see this."

"What are we going to do with it?" Jerry asked.

"We're going to keep it a secret." I pulled out my phone.

"In this town?"

"Exactly."

He understood. "Oh, that kind of secret."

"I'm going to start with Dennis the Mailman."

Dennis Padgett was glad to hear the mail had gone through. "I just wanted to let you know that Jerry and I found the package in Val's car out at Tully Springfield's."

"That's great. Was it a videotape?"

"A very special, one-of-a-kind videotape."

"Glad to be of assistance, miss."

"That's it?" Jerry said when I hung up. "'A very special, one-of-a-kind videotape'? Not 'Kimberly Dawn Starring in *Lust in the Attic*'?"

"Give it time," I said. "I have every faith in the small-town network."

SEVEN

THE NEXT MORNING, Jerry wanted to try a pancake recipe that he thought his B&B customers would like.

I sat down at the kitchen table. "Are these special haunted pancakes shaped like little ghosts?"

He turned from the stove to grin at me. "Regular round pancakes. The syrup is haunted."

Shana was right. I needed to step up my campaign, and now was the perfect time. Olivia hadn't put in an appearance since her big blow up the day before. Jerry and I had recovered from the sight of Kimberly Dawn as Porn Queen of Celosia. This was a pleasant little domestic scene, complete with the warm, sweet smell of pancakes.

I didn't get my chance. As I opened my mouth, Nell knocked on the back door. The first thing she said when she came in was, "What's all this about a videotape you found out at Tully Springfield's?"

I gave Jerry an I-told-you-so look, and he acknowledged my superiority with a wry grin. "I was hoping you'd stop by, Nell. I'd like to ask you a few questions about Juliet. Have you had breakfast? Jerry's making pancakes."

"Don't mind if I do."

Nell and I sat down at the kitchen table. Jerry went to the stove.

Nell grinned. "You mean Junior can cook?"

He pointed the spatula at her. "You want some pancakes or not?"

"Hell, yeah. I want a big stack."

Jerry cooked the pancakes, flipping them out of the pan and onto our plates like a circus act.

Nell covered her pancakes in syrup, took a big mouthful, chewed, and nodded her approval. "Pretty good for a short-order cook." She put the emphasis on "short."

"Nell," I asked, "where are Juliet's parents?"

"They split up and moved away two years ago. Can't say that they were very good role models. Always drinking and arguing like a pair of wildcats. The aunt took her in, but that's not much better. She's never home."

"Where does she live?"

"Nice little blue house on Grayson Street, just behind the Super Food. Juliet might as well have been living on her own. But lots of folks felt sorry for her, tried to help her. You see where it got Ted Stacy."

"Did anyone else try to help her? The judges liked her."

"Well, they wanted to beat Dixley, and she was their best chance."

It sounded to me as if the judges were using Juliet. She probably knew this. After all, she was using them and the pageant. Ted, however, had been genuinely concerned, and she pushed him away with accusations. Maybe Juliet resented help. Maybe she didn't feel she was worthy of help. Maybe she didn't recognize kindness when she saw it.

"Nell, did Hayden try to help her in any way?"

"Oh, I'm sure he didn't mean to embarrass the girl. He's not like that."

I couldn't imagine Juliet being embarrassed by anything. "What do you mean?"

Nell took another big bite, chewed, and swallowed. "See, him being a poet and all, he went to the school to give a talk and help the kids with their poetry. Then he read them out loud to the class."

"Let me guess. Juliet's poem was too hot and steamy for high school?"

"No, from what I hear, it was more like rainbows and puppy dogs."

"Juliet's poem?"

"She probably didn't like the other kids laughing at her."

Public ridicule. Never a nice experience.

Jerry brought his plate of pancakes to the table and sat down. "Kind of set her reputation back, didn't it?"

No, I thought. It revealed a side she didn't want anyone to see.

Nell reached for the syrup. "Just thought of somebody else who tried to help. Augusta Freer. She's the wife of Toby Freer of Freer and Mason. Teaches English. Never says anything bad about any of her students." Jerry flopped more pancakes on her plate, and she proceeded to drown them in syrup. "You go to the funeral?"

"I did," I said.

"Hoping to catch the killer skulking around, like they do on TV?"

"I can dream, can't I?"

"Heard there was quite a few people there."

"More than I expected. All the judges, Evan James, Cindy, and a lot of high-school students."

"Hear you found Val's car. I coulda told you where it was." Between Nell and Denisha, there were no secrets in Celosia.

Nell held up her coffee cup. "Oh, waiter."

Jerry filled her cup and turned to me. "Anything for you, ma'am?"

Just you. "No, thanks."

He went back to the stove. "More pancakes on the way."

"Keep 'em comin'," Nell said. She shoveled the last of her stack into her mouth and spoke around her food. "So you met Tully Springfield. He's a weird one."

"He was quite pleasant."

"Oh, yeah, well, it's all the medication."

"Yes, he told me about his heart condition."

"Yeah, he's bipolar, too, or whatever they call bad mood swings these days. Had a big blowout at the grocery store one day. That's why he don't come to town much."

I envisioned Tully with a semiautomatic, mowing down hapless shoppers and supermarket displays. "A blowout?"

"A breakdown, I guess I should say. Just totally lost it in the produce section. Maybe the melons weren't ripe enough."

"Yes, but he's not dangerous, is he?"

She shrugged.

"Did he know Juliet? Would she have crossed him in some way?"

"He probably knows who she is. Remember where you are, Madeline. Everybody knows everybody here."

"He said he didn't know her."

"Wouldn't matter to him if he did. All he cares about are those pictures of his."

Jerry brought another stack of pancakes to the table and sat down. "Those freaky clown pictures?"

Nell's eyes narrowed. "I happen to like those."

Jerry grinned at me in pure impish delight. "Excuse me. I meant to say those charming clown pictures."

"I'm trying to eliminate Tully as a suspect," I said. "Do you think his condition makes him violent?"

"No more than Hayden Amry's. See, these artistic guys can't handle the pressure." She took her fork and stole three pancakes from Jerry's stack. "It's a good thing you're not talented, peewee."

We ate until we were properly stuffed. Nell pushed her empty plate away. "This tape you found. Worth getting killed over?"

"It all depends on how desperate the person was to get it back."

Nell made a thoughtful "Hmm" noise and drank her coffee. "I'm going to see about those floors."

After she'd gone upstairs, Jerry offered me the last of the pancakes.

"No, thanks. Those were great, by the way."

He gathered the dirty dishes. "What did you mean about a desperate person wanting the tape back?"

"Here's how I see it, Jerry. We search the house for videotapes, and find none. Only empty cases in the attic. Ted's office and Benjy's station were ransacked. At the station, all the tapes were on the floor, as if someone had been pawing through them. All these odd incidents involving videotapes are too much of a coincidence to be ignored. I think somebody besides us has been looking for a videotape. A specific videotape. This person couldn't find it here in the attic, so he or she must have thought Ted or Benjy had it. Which means there's a connection between what was going on in the attic and with Juliet's murder."

"Then why did you broadcast the news that you'd found a tape?"

"I'm hoping the killer will come looking for it."

He stopped. "Whoa, hold on. You didn't tell me this part."

"This is the part where it gets serious," I said.

Jerry looked puzzled. "I don't get it. It's just a sleazy little film, right? Maybe Kimberly Dawn would be embarrassed if people saw it, but how does Juliet fit in?"

"There's one way to find out." I picked up my pocketbook and car keys. "I'm going to have a look in Juliet's house."

Jerry trailed me to the living room. "You're not leaving me in the House of Impending Doom."

"Impending Doom. Would that be the Return of Olivia?"

"Ha, ha. No, the House of the Phantom Videotape Murderer."

"Isn't that what you wanted the house to be?"

"Yes, but not really."

"Come on, then, and bring your special keys."

WE DROVE TO the Super Food and found Grayson Street. There was one blue house on the street. Jerry and I decided it must be Juliet's.

Jerry was concerned about being seen. "Chief Brenner mentioned he didn't want you to fool around with crime scenes, didn't he?"

"He said if I see yellow tape, don't cross it. Do you see any yellow tape?"

"No. How are you going to get in?"

"That's why I brought you and your special keys along."

"I haven't done this in a long time, Mac."

"Are you saying you can't do it?"

He glowered. "A simple front door, no dead bolt or anything? You must be kidding."

"Let's see if anyone's at home first."

We didn't see any cars parked in the driveway or out front. I knocked and rang the bell. Jerry peeked in the windows.

"All clear."

He didn't have any trouble picking the lock. We let ourselves in. The living room had a sofa and a TV and little else, as if Juliet and her aunt never used the room. Of the two bedrooms, it was easy to guess which one was Juliet's. That girl had more clothes and shoes than most department stores. She had six jewelry boxes loaded with costume jewelry, mostly fake pearls and rhinestones. Among the mass quantities of makeup, hair spray, and negligees, I found a folder marked "Poems." Inside the folder were pages and pages of Juliet's poetry. Many of the poems were about flying to fantasy worlds on unicorns and flowers turning into stars. Several were typical teenage expressions of being misunderstood. "I walk alone in the rain," "My life is a sunset that no one will see," that kind of thing. Also in the folder were addresses of poetry magazines and submissions guidelines.

"She was serious about her poetry, Jerry."

"Is it any good?"

"It's not bad."

I closed the folder. On the bookshelf next to the bed were books on collecting seashells, collections of poems by Emily Dickinson and Robert Frost, classics like *Little Women* and *Black Beauty,* and books on makeup tips and fashion design. Lying on top of these books was a slim fantasy novel with a black cover and silver spiderweb design. The book was titled *The Monsters of Spider's Rest.* I read page one and sat down. The first character mentioned was an evil young woman named Portia. She was described as having black hair and black eyes. She wore a long white gown and had a black heart-shaped mark on her forehead.

Jerry had been rooting in the closet. "Find something?"

"Jerry, you have to read this."

"What is it?"

"Just read a little and see if it reminds you of anything."

He took the book. I watched as he read. His eyes widened, and he made surprised noises.

"Mac, this is Hayden's story!"

"Exactly."

"A spooky woman named Portia is after this guy, and there's a monster named Theo—everything's the same."

"Yep." I took the book and read the end flap. "'Spider's Rest is the eyesore of Specter, a foreboding mansion owned by Tylin ValEndise. Young monster hunter Holly Dark is assigned to guard the mansion and to spy on its owner. Is Ty creating monsters of his own? Why does he feed the creatures at his door? Little does Holly realize she must rescue Ty from evil beings, as well as from his unfeeling family, the true monsters of Spider's Rest.'" I shut the book. "It's all here—Portia, Theo, the alternate universe—and my guess is Hayden is a stand-in for the hero, Tylin. At least, that's what she wants him to believe."

"What's Juliet doing with it?"

"Studying for her role as Portia."

"You mean, when he heard a ghostly voice and saw Portia, it was really Juliet dressed up?"

"Sure. She appears a few times as Portia, tells him this horror story, and Hayden's imagination runs screaming into the night."

Jerry looked troubled. "That's the meanest trick I ever heard of. She had to know it would scare him."

"Of course she did. She wanted to pay him back for exposing what she thought of as her weakness by exposing his. I have to admire her creativity, but it was focused in the wrong direction. She must have felt extremely insecure to tear everyone down. I wish someone had been able to reach her."

"Sounds like Hayden tried."

"His mistake was trying in front of her peers. I think if he'd talked to her by herself, she would've appreciated his advice."

"So all we have to do is show Hayden this book, and he'll be okay."

I took *The Monsters of Spider's Rest* and put it in my pocketbook. "It's probably not going to be that easy, but it's a start."

Jerry sat still for so long, I thought he'd really gone into a trance. "Jerry?"

"Then that's who I saw."

"When you fell?"

"And when I had the séance. It wasn't Juliet's ghost. It must have been Juliet dressed up as Portia."

"Why would she be at the Eberlin house? She'd have no reason to scare you."

"Maybe that's where she went to practice being scary, and to get into her ghost makeup."

That didn't make sense. "The Eberlin house is too far away from town. If she was running back and forth from Val's to Hayden's, she wouldn't want anyone to see her, so she wouldn't use her car. We're looking for a hideout, some-place between the Eberlin house and the Amrys' house."

Jerry snapped his fingers. "The kids will know. Aren't they always sneaking into places?"

"We don't need the kids," I said. "I know."

THE LAYTONS HAD a more elaborate lock that Jerry wasn't sure he could pick, but a locked door hadn't kept Juliet from sneaking in a back window, and it didn't stop me and Jerry, either. I hopped in easily, but Jerry fell over the woodbox.

"Ow! Damn, what's that doing under the window?"

The Laytons must have saved up all their pennies be-cause this was the snazziest cabin I'd ever seen. Unlike Tully Springfield's rustic décor, the living room had an elegant peach-and-maroon color scheme, huge artificial flower ar-rangements, and a selection of expensive-looking books about photography.

Jerry hobbled up, rubbing his knee. "What are we look-ing for?"

"I'm not sure. It doesn't look like anything's been dis-turbed."

The kitchen gleamed silver and white. The two bedrooms looked like sets for an upscale soap opera.

"I was hoping to step on another pink fingernail."

"How about a sequin?"

"You're kidding."

He held up the shiny disk on the tip of his finger. I took it. "Is it Juliet's?" he asked.

I couldn't tell for sure, but the sequin looked very much like the ones I'd seen around Hayden's house and scattered on the floor backstage, those special one-of-a-kind sequins that caused Randi so much grief. "Sure looks like it. Let's see if we can find anything else."

We checked the bathrooms and the closets.

Jerry shook his head. "Nothing."

"Did you straighten the woodbox? I want to leave every-thing the way we found it."

A few of the logs had rolled under a chair. Jerry stooped down to reach for them and came up with a pair of silky red panties. "Uh, is this a clue?"

We pushed the chair aside. Underneath was a box filled with all sorts of lacy underthings and a makeup kit.

Jerry took out a matching red bra. "I don't remember Portia being this sexy."

The makeup kit contained a large tube of white founda-tion and several black eyeliners, just what a ghost would need for that special dead look. "This was Juliet's hideout, all right. I don't know how the lingerie fits in." There were crotchless panties and fringed leather bras, a short rhinestone-studded vest, and metallic G-strings. "These look more like costumes."

"Maybe she was saving them for another story."

"Or another kind of pageant."

"Miss Sex Kitten? I wouldn't mind judging that."

I punched his arm. "Pick up the logs, please."

We took the box and let ourselves out the front door, which I closed and locked. The forest, as before, looked peaceful in the late morning light. As we walked back through the woods, I envisioned Juliet, dressed in her white gown, hur-rying down the pathway to the Amrys' house, slipping be-neath Hayden's window, and laughing inside as she gave her ghostly performance.

"I still don't know why she'd be at the Eberlin house," Jerry said.

"What if Juliet knew about the kids' secret passage? Wait a minute. That explains the spooky draft of cold air."

"The what?"

"The night of your séance, remember? Whenever the pas-sage doorway is open, cool air comes out. Juliet must have been in the passage that night, Jerry. What if she was look-ing for a certain videotape?"

"You think she knew about Kimberly Dawn's second career?"

"If she did, she might have thought it would give her a certain leverage in the pageant." Then I stopped. "But Ted's office and Benjy's station were searched after Juliet's death."

"And if Juliet found a tape, it was *Centurio senex* doing his thing."

"Right. That must have been a shock."

"Not as shocking as what we got to see."

"And unfortunately, I need to see it again."

He stared at me. "You've got to be kidding."

"Something just occurred to me, Jerry. We've been too grossed out to see the whole video. Who's running the cam-era?"

"Either Uncle Val, or Kimberly Dawn just set it herself. You can do that."

"Maybe. Let's see."

WE RETURNED to the house. Nell reported there had been no visitors and that she was going into town for more varnish. Jerry sat down on the sofa with his back to the TV. "I'll lis-ten for clues."

It was rough going, but I managed to watch the entire video. It lasted about twenty minutes. During the whole film, Kimberly Dawn's hair never moved. The rest of her did. At one point, I glanced at Jerry.

"You're not being much help."

"I can't look at it. Listening to it's bad enough. What's all that 'left, right' business, anyway? When I'm having a, uh, moment, I'm not usually concerned about direction."

"'Left, right'?"

"Just before the long grotesque 'aah' sound."

I stopped the tape and ran it back a few minutes.

"Are you going to watch it again?" Jerry said in disbelief.

"Just that part." I tried to concentrate on the sound and not the picture. Sure enough, right before Kimberly Dawn let out an unearthly moan of manufactured passion a distant voice in the background could be heard saying, "Left, no, right. Right. The other way."

I sat so still Jerry finally turned around. "What is it?"

I'd heard that voice before, a voice demanding, "No, no, Miss Peace Haven! To your left! The other way!"

"I know who that is."

"Who what is?"

"The cameraman. It's Percy, the choreographer who quit the pageant. The first day I met Evan James, Percy was videotaping the contestants to show them how badly they were screwing up his routine."

"Before or after he videotaped Kimberly Dawn trying to screw herself?"

I turned off the TV and VCR. "That's two people who know this tape exists."

"I thought Percy left town."

"Let's find out. Besides, I need a sequin."

WE DROVE to the theater and found Evan James in his office. He was looking through a stack of glossy head shots of the contestants. Juliet's picture was on top of the stack.

"Hello, Madeline," he said. "I'm so glad you came by. I feel I owe you an apology."

"For what?"

"When I hired you to find out who was doing all these things in the theater, I never imagined you'd have to be involved in such a terrible crime. Quite frankly, I'm worried for your safety."

"That's all right, Evan."

He put his hand protectively over the pictures. "Do you suppose this murderer is targeting pageant contestants? If anything happened to any of these other girls, I'd never forgive myself."

"I'm talking to everyone I can. Do you know how I can get in touch with Percy?"

He reached for his phone. "Cindy will know."

The ever-efficient Cindy provided me with Percy's address and phone number.

When I hung up with Cindy, Evan said, "What's this about a missing videotape? I heard something about it at Deely's this morning. Does it have anything to do with Juliet?"

The news was traveling faster than I'd hoped. "That's what I'm trying to find out."

"You don't think Percy was responsible?"

"I'm checking all possible angles."

Evan had a new handkerchief, which he used to wipe his brow. "Good Lord. I hired Percy on Chuck Hofsteder's recommendation. If it turns out he had anything to do with Juliet being killed—" His voice quit.

"I don't see how any of this could be your fault, Evan."

He took a deep breath. "No. You're right. I've got to stop blaming myself. Thank you. Madeline, on a brighter note, I'm thinking of coordinating the Miss Little River Pageant next month. I hope you'll stop by and give the girls some encouraging words."

Encouraging words like *Get out while you still can.*

"Oh, Jerry, are you available to play the piano? The music director at Little Falls has no sense of rhythm."

"I don't know," he said.

"The pay is very good."

"I'll think about it."

"Do you mind if I look around?" I asked.

"Not at all."

Jerry and I went backstage. "Damn," I said, "somebody's cleaned up."

"They can't have gotten all the sequins."

"You're right. Sequins are hard to kill."

"Here's one."

Jerry found three, and I found one more. I compared them to the one he'd found in the Laytons' cabin. "We have a match."

Back at the car, I punched in Percy's number. "Let's see what Percy has to say about *Barbie Does Celosia.*"

Percy's voice on his answering machine informed us that he was currently unavailable but would return our call as soon as possible. I left my cell-phone number and a message:

"Percy, this is Madeline Maclin. I've just seen an interesting independent film starring Kimberly Dawn Williams. The audio could stand a little tweaking. Any suggestions?"

"Now what about Chuck Hofsteder?" Jerry asked when I hung up. "How does he figure into all this?"

"We can pay Chuck a little visit and find out."

"This doesn't involve breaking into another house, does it?"

"I thought you liked living on the edge."

We didn't have to break into Chuck Hofsteder's house. He was out mowing his lawn and grateful for the opportunity to stop.

He waved us up to his front porch, where he took a swig of water from a container on the steps. "Come on up. I was just about ready for a drink. Get you folks anything?"

"No, thanks," I said. "I'm hoping you can answer some questions about Percy. How do you know him?"

"Oh, he does lots of pageants. I'd seen his work at the Miss Cornflower Pageant in South Pines and thought he'd be perfect for Miss Celosia. It's a shame things didn't work out." He took a big gulp of water. "Are you still investigating Juliet's murder? Do you think Percy's involved?"

"I'm just trying to figure a few things. You've known him awhile, then. Did he know any of the other judges?"

"They'd heard of him, of course, but this was the first time any of us had actually met him. I didn't really know him before."

"And what was your impression?"

"Oh, the man's immensely talented, too talented for our poor little pageant, I'm afraid. I don't blame him for getting frustrated with our girls."

"Is that all he does, choreograph pageants?"

"I believe he's involved with other talent shows, dinner theaters, things like that."

"Movies?"

"Oh, yes. Yes, he's a pro. It's too bad he wouldn't stay, not even for Juliet." He coughed, embarrassed. "Dear me, I can't say her name without choking up. Are you any closer to solving this, Madeline?"

"I may be," I said.

WE LEFT CHUCK still gulping water and sat down in the car.

"You ought to take the accompanist job," I said.

"Not if I'm busy with the B&B."

"You're going through with it?"

"Sure, why not?"

"There are lots of things you could do with music. One of the churches might need an organist. I think Celosia has a community band."

Jerry gave me a look I couldn't quite interpret. "I'll take up the piano again if you'll start painting again."

"I don't know about that."

"Tell me you haven't thought about it. I can read minds, you know."

"Okay. Maybe a little."

"You can be a detective and an artist, you know."

"It's just— I don't know how to explain it."

"You don't have to, Mac, not to me. Forget the ultimatum.

Take up your artwork if and when you want to. The upstairs parlor will wait for you."

But will you wait for me? A strain of song from *Paul Bunyan* suddenly came to mind. *Some meet early, some meet late, some like me have long to wait.* How much longer was I going to have to wait? I had to say something now. I had to let Jerry know how I felt, or I was going to lose him to Olivia and her damned bed and breakfast.

"Jerry."

He turned to me.

I can do this. It's easy. I just say, you are my best friend in the whole world, and I want our relationship to become something more. I think it will work. I know it will work.

My cell phone beeped.

It was Percy, full of gush. "My dear Madeline, how nice to hear from you. I was outside deadheading my roses and just missed your call. I'm wondering how in the world you managed to find Kimberly Dawn's audition tape."

"Audition tape?" I exchanged a baffled look with Jerry.

"Yes, yes," Percy said. "You realize, of course, this is a delicate situation and has to be handled just right."

I thought he was talking about Kimberly Dawn's reputation in town. He wasn't.

"If I submit the tape now without proper music and lighting, she'll never get one of the top spots, and you know Kimberly Dawn. She won't settle for second best."

"Percy, what are you talking about?" I asked.

"*The Naked Review.* Surely you've heard of it."

"*The Naked Review?* No."

He made a tsking sound. "I forget, you're out of the loop. *The Naked Review* is the next step in Kimberly Dawn's illustrious career. The series of videotapes is famous for its ex-beauty queens. She'll be a sensation. But we can't peak too soon. That tape is a rough draft, if you will, of the spectacle it will become."

"Did anyone else know about this tape?" I asked.

"No. We filmed the whole thing one weekend when Val was away."

"Is this the only copy of the tape?"

"Yes. So for heaven's sake, don't lose it. Have you called her? She'll want it back, I'm sure."

"I'm pretty sure she knows I have it."

"Good. Just have her call me, and I'll fix it up."

"One more thing," I said. "Did you suggest this to her, or was it her idea?"

"I mentioned I had connections with *The Naked Review* if she was interested, and she was. We had several talks about it. She was especially interested in directing, creating more exotic scenarios, looking for new talent. I told her I could help with that."

"Did you mention your 'connections' to any of the contestants?"

"Good heavens, no. I'm not interested in underage girls, no matter how mature they may act. I'm not going there. Now, if that's all, I have to go. Good-bye."

He hung up. I faced Jerry, who'd been wide-eyed since I'd mentioned *The Naked Review.* "Percy's a scout for a series of X-rated videos. Kimberly Dawn took him up on his offer. He had several talks with her. Maybe Juliet overheard—" I realized I, too, had overheard something, something I'd dismissed as a pageant problem. I would have to mention that at my next talk with Kimberly Dawn.

"What do we do now?"

"We should probably check the secret passageway for clues."

When we got back to the house, Austin and Denisha were sitting in the front-porch rockers.

Austin hopped up. "We came to watch *Super Spy,* if that's okay."

"We didn't go in the house," Denisha said.

"Okay," Jerry said. "Let's watch TV."

The clue hunt would have to wait. I didn't want the kids involved in any part of this mystery. I sat out on the porch and read more of *The Monsters of Spider's Rest.* Portia and her evil followers intended to sacrifice Tylin in a cult ritual. Juliet had underlined Portia's warning to Tylin. "You must wear black and come to the clearing by the river. There you will die. It's the only way you can save your loved ones." The story continued with brave young Holly Dark saving Tylin from the Star Worshippers who met in that clearing. She had the help of Tylin's pet monsters, who unfortunately died in the rescue attempt. I had just finished the climactic scene when my phone beeped.

Shana's worried voice said, "Madeline, I need your help. Hayden's disappeared. He locked Prill in the house and went into the woods."

I heard Prill's voice in the background. "Impudent young bounder!"

"Did he see Portia again?" I asked.

"I don't know. Prill, did he say anything about Portia?"

"He said she told him to wear black and come to the clearing," Prill answered.

"Shana," I said, "I think I know what's going on. I'll be right there."

I didn't want to leave Jerry, but I didn't want to leave the kids, either, or drag them along into the forest. "Jerry, Hayden's wandered off, and I've got to go help Shana find him. Just be careful."

"It's okay," he said. "You have to find Hayden before anything happens to him. If we see anyone, we'll run and hide in the passageway like super spies."

"I'll be back as soon as I can."

SHANA MET ME on her front-porch steps. "Prill's already looking. We think Hayden may have headed toward the Laytons' cabin. That's in a clearing."

"Is there a clearing by a river?"

"Well, there's one near the creek."

We hurried into the woods. "I'd hate to try to stumble around here in pitch darkness," she said.

"How far is this clearing?"

"Not far."

Shadows lengthened as we ran through the trees. In the fading light, I could easily see how Hayden's imagination put ghosts and creatures lurking around every turn.

Shana spoke over her shoulder. "Madeline, please tell me what's going on."

"I think Hayden's acting out a scene from a book, a horror story."

"But what's he going to do?"

"I don't know." In the story, the hero was almost killed by the evil cult. Could Juliet's killer be out here, waiting for victim number two? I didn't say this out loud. Unless Juliet had been a member of a secret cult, another attack didn't seem likely. Still, Hayden didn't need to be wandering in the woods, not in his confused state of mind.

We found Hayden standing in the middle of the clearing, looking around as if dazed.

Shana embraced her husband. "Hayden, are you all right? Answer me."

Hayden's eyes refocused. "Shana?"

"Yes, of course it's me."

Prill's voice sounded from a distance. "Where are you, you miserable little cur?"

"I thought you were—" He looked from me to Shana and then to Prill, who arrived on the scene, panting. "Wait. This can't be right. What am I doing out here?"

I took his arm. "We need to get you back to the house."

Prill took his other arm. "Allow me."

With me on one side and Prill on the other, Hayden could walk. "I'm all right," he said.

"You are not," Prill said. "What do you mean by locking me in the house and running off into the woods? I had to go all the way around through the dining-room windows! Do you see this hole in my cape? You'll pay for this. Idiot. What were you doing, gathering nuts?"

Shana's voice shook. "Don't ever do this again, do you hear me? You can have all the ghosts you want."

"No." He stopped and we had to stop with him. "You're all I want." He kissed her and would have gone on kissing her if Prill hadn't made loud annoyed snorts.

"Good heavens, man! Did anyone ask for an overt display of affection? You need help."

"He needs to see the book I brought him," I said.

BACK IN Shana's living room, we settled Hayden on the couch and let him read *The Monsters of Spider's Rest.* Halfway through, he began to tremble. Shana put her arms around him.

"It's all right. It's just a story."

"I know," he said. "I can't believe— This is such a relief." He wiped his eyes. "Thank you, Madeline."

"You're welcome."

"Where did you find this book?"

"Juliet Lovelace had it."

"Juliet?"

"Juliet was Portia. She took lines from this book and did her best to make your nightmares come true."

He shook his head in disbelief. "But why?"

"I think she was trying to get back at you for reading her poem to the class."

"What? But it was a beautiful poem."

"Do you remember how the class reacted?"

He frowned in thought. Then his expression changed. "Oh, my God. I remember now. I didn't understand why the whole class laughed. I tried to tell her it was a wonderful poem and she shouldn't be embarrassed."

"I hate to say it, but that probably made things worse."

"I can't believe I was so stupid."

Shana gave him another hug. "It's okay. You didn't know." There was the sound of someone clearing his throat, and Shana grinned. "Prill wants to speak to you. Are you ready?"

Hayden managed a weak smile. "Not particularly."

Prill glared. "I heard that! Stand aside, Madeline. I want to smack this impudent young bounder for putting us both through hell."

"Now how did I put you through hell?" Hayden asked.

"I was locked in your house! I was desperately trying to find my way out to come to your aid! And look at this hole in my cape! Do you know what it will cost to return it to its former glory?"

"Thanks for your help," Hayden said.

Prill shook his finger. "Kind words will not pacify me, sir! If we hear one more word about a ghost, any ghost, we will lock you up and throw away the key."

"All right."

This took most of Prill's steam. "Well," he said, "all right, then. What exactly did you see?"

He rubbed his eyes. "I'm not sure. I was in my office try-ing to write, and I must have fallen asleep. I could've sworn Portia came in. It must have been a dream."

Prill shook my hand. "Congratulations, Madeline. You have just successfully busted your first ghost."

Shana gave Hayden another hug. "You've got to stop try-ing so hard."

"I'll have a word with you later," Prill said as he exited.

"And I've got to get back home," I said. "I still have one more mystery to solve."

I DIDN'T RECOGNIZE the car in the driveway. I did recognize the woman who let me in the front door.

Kimberly Dawn Williams said, "I believe you have something that belongs to me."

The TV was still on, but there was no sign of Jerry, Austin, or Denisha. I prayed they were either hiding in the passageway or miles from the house by now. "I might."

"Let's be civilized about this, Madeline. I know you have my videotape. I'd like to have it back."

"You wouldn't mind answering a few questions first?"

She made a small gesture, inviting me to sit down on the sofa, every inch the gracious social hostess. "Not at all. In fact, I have a few questions for you. Shall I go first?"

"Please do."

"Where did you find it? I've been looking everywhere for it."

"Val mailed it off by mistake."

"My goodness."

"Why were you using his studio?"

"Benjy told me last year that Val had set up a studio. I asked Val if Percy and I could use it, and he said yes. But how did the tape get back here?"

"The company that makes bat documentaries returned it when they saw it wasn't exactly what they needed. Did Val know what kind of film this was?"

"Oh, you've seen it?"

"Yes."

"Well, you understand then why it must be kept secret. Even though she's dead, it wouldn't be right to let such a tape exist."

"'She'?"

"Juliet, of course. Didn't you recognize her?"

I had to keep myself from rocking back in surprise. Juliet. Good Lord. "The tape is of you."

She looked startled. Then she waved her hand as if this didn't matter. "Good heavens, don't tell me it's one of mine."

It was my turn to be startled. "There's more than one?"

"Well, it's not something I advertise here in town, but I have a little mail-order business. It's just a hobby, really."

I wasn't sure how many more of these revelations I wanted to hear, but there was something I had to know, no matter how queasy it made me feel. I realized now why Jerry and I had found fancy lingerie hidden at the Laytons' cabin. "So you introduced Juliet to the Wonderful World of Porn."

I saw that she wanted to deny it, but knew that it was too late. She patted her helmet of hair. "My goodness, Madeline. You make it sound so sordid. She wanted to get into the business. She knew she didn't have anything going for her except her looks, and she intended to use them any way she could." She tried a light little laugh that didn't work. "That girl thought she was hot stuff, but her first effort was actually a bit comical."

"Percy didn't know about Juliet and her tape, did he? You filmed Juliet, though you knew she wasn't eighteen."

For the first time, a flush of red darkened Kimberly Dawn's perfect cheeks. "Juliet lied to me about her age. She lied about everything. Does any of that matter now? The poor girl is dead, a sad ending to a sad story."

"She knew about Percy's other directing jobs, didn't she? She was probably planning to tell him about the tape. It was you who caused all the problems at the pageant, wasn't it, hoping Percy would quit before Juliet approached him, before he found out what you'd done."

"Are you accusing me of vandalism? You'd better watch what you say."

"What were you and Juliet quarreling about at the theater?"

"That? It was nothing. She was not supposed to be using her cell phone during rehearsal."

Her cell phone. Something clicked in my mind. Juliet's interrupted call to Ted.

She stood up. "This is nonsense. If you don't have Juliet's tape, then where is it?"

That's what Juliet was looking for the night of the séance. Her tape. The dirt on Juliet's dress wasn't from backstage. It must have come from the passageway, I realized. She must have just made it back to the rehearsal before Jerry and I arrived. And that's what Kimberly Dawn must have been looking for in Ted's office and at Benjy's station. If she caught Juliet talking to Ted, she could have assumed he knew about the tape. Maybe he even had it. Benjy knew about Val's studio, so it was possible Juliet had talked to him, as well.

Kimberly Dawn had recovered her poise, but there was an edge to her voice. "Where is Juliet's tape, Madeline?"

I had more questions. "How long had you been using Val's studio for your 'business'?"

"I paid him for it, if that's what's bothering you."

"No, what's bothering me is what you were using his studio for."

She shrugged. "He really didn't care what a grown woman did to earn a living."

"Maybe not. Everyone says he was a loner, real easy-going. But I think he would have cared if he'd found out who else was using his studio, if he'd found that particular tape. You know, the one nobody can find. The one you thought I had. Because one other thing I know about Val is that he loved kids."

She picked up her pocketbook. "I believe this conversation is over."

"He confronted you about it, didn't he? He knew Juliet was only seventeen, a loner, like himself. Her tape got mixed up with his bat tapes, and he saw it. I'm betting this upset him so much, he told you he was turning you in for corrupting a minor. Maybe you argued about it. So much that it brought on his angina. He went for his pills. But you got to them first. And you kept them from him."

"I don't have to listen to this. Val Eberlin died of a heart attack. I had nothing to do with it."

"But you had something to do with Juliet."

She looked at me, the plastic smile still in place.

"I'm guessing she suspected you were involved with Val's death. She probably acted strangely enough that you caught on. And then this girl, that so many people thought did not have a decent bone in her body, did a strange thing. She realized the porn business wasn't all dressing up and posing like being in a pageant. It had a dark and dangerous side. So she turned to the only person who had treated her with respect. She called Ted Stacy for help. She called the man who tried to teach her that there were consequences, who believed in her, for help. Unfortunately, you overheard her, and understood what she was talking about. So she had to go, too. But Juliet still existed on the tape you'd made. You had to find that tape, even if it meant looking all over Celosia, and destroy it before it destroyed you."

She tried to keep from looking bored. "Are you done?"

"Your fingernails. You left them backstage the night you murdered Juliet."

"That's absurd."

I took the fingernail out of my pocket. "I have one right here. The other one's at the police lab. I'm sure they'll find traces of Juliet's blood on it."

This was a complete lie, but it was the best I could think of at the moment. Unfortunately, Kimberly Dawn didn't buy it.

"You really are foolish, aren't you?"

"You're tall enough to reach the cords hanging backstage, and you bragged how you've kept in shape. I think you could strangle her, especially when she wasn't expecting anyone back in her little private dressing area."

Kimberly Dawn sneered. "That's nonsense."

I thought she was reaching into her pocketbook for her keys. Instead, she brought out a dainty little pistol. Even though my every nerve was immediately on standby, I couldn't help noticing the handle was pink.

She leveled the little gun at my heart. "You know, when he hears the shot, I hope your young man will come out from wherever he's hiding so I can shoot him, too."

"Oh, he's long gone," I said, hoping he was. "Nell Brenner's here, though. You know, the chief of police's daughter? She's upstairs refinishing the floors."

Kimberly Dawn smiled. "Nice try. Nell's van isn't parked outside."

"I don't really think you want to kill someone else," I said. "How are you going to explain it?"

"I came to talk to you about pageants, of course. What could be more natural than two beauty queens having a chat? People here don't really believe you're any sort of detective, anyway. You're just some snoopy, interfering woman who can get away with asking annoying questions because you're attractive. It's easy for people like us." She gave a little laugh. "We can get away with murder."

"And Jerry?"

"Everyone knows the Fairweathers are unstable. I believe the two of you had a lovers' quarrel. He shot you and then killed himself. It'll add to the unhealthy allure of this house."

"That would work, except we aren't lovers."

"Oh, come on."

Even the villains can see through me. This is getting ridiculous. "No one's going to believe Jerry used that sissy little gun."

It didn't take her long to come up with Plan B. "You're right. Maybe something a bit more dramatic." She looked around. "It really is a shame how these old houses burn so quickly. Maybe the Eberlin house should go out in a burst of glory. No one would miss it, that's for certain." She reached into her pocketbook again. "You know so much about fingernails, Madeline. Maybe you remember something about fingernail polish remover. Anything come to mind? It's flammable. Why don't we see how flammable it is."

"You carry fingernail polish remover in your pocketbook?"

"I carry everything. You never know when you'll have a fashion emergency."

I could not believe I was going to be done in by a beauty product.

She shook the bottle. "There's really not enough in here for the whole house, but it'll be a good start. Let me see if I have some matches." She took out a compact, a mirror, a comb, a brush, and a can of hair spray. "I could've sworn I had a pack in here. Oh, well, I believe I see a lighter."

Olivia's fancy useless candles and the lighter were on the mantel. As Kimberly Dawn reached for the lighter, I dove for the can of hair spray, popped the lid, and sprayed full force into her face. She shrieked and tried to bat the fumes away. I grabbed the lighter.

"Fingernail polish remover isn't the only thing flammable around here," I said. "You have enough hair spray on your hair to go up like the Hindenburg."

She blinked furiously, tears streaking her makeup. "Keep away from me!"

"Drop the gun."

She waved the gun in my direction. "Don't come any closer!"

She fired. It made a surprisingly loud noise for such a little pistol. Blinded by the hair spray, she missed me by a good three feet and hit one of the lamps. I didn't wait to find out how many bullets the gun held. I used the other lamp to knock the gun out of her hand.

Sobbing and cursing in a most unqueenly fashion, Kimberly Dawn sank to the sofa. I retrieved the little pistol.

Jerry ran in from the kitchen, wide-eyed. "Was that a gunshot?"

"It's okay," I said. "Where are the kids?"

"I told them to stay in the passageway. We were practicing our spy techniques."

"Go tell them everything's all right and to stay put for now. I'm calling the police."

"Are you all right?"

"I'm fine, but your new lamps made the ultimate sacrifice." I reached for my phone. Before I could call the police, a police car drove up in the yard.

Chief Brenner knocked on the door.

"That's what I call service," I said. "Come in."

"Service?" he said.

"I was just about to call you. This former Miss Celosia just tried to kill me." I handed the gun to Chief Brenner and directed his attention to the dead lamp. "I believe she also killed Juliet Lovelace. And Val Eberlin."

He stared at Kimberly Dawn. She was still gasping and weeping from the hair spray. "Miss Williams, do you have anything to say?"

Kimberly Dawn tried to glare at me, but her eyes were almost swollen shut. "Whatever she says, she's lying."

Chief Brenner took her by the arm. "Why don't you come along with me, Miss Williams? We'll discuss this down at the station. Ms. Maclin, I'm going to want to speak with you, too."

As he tucked her into the police car, I had to ask, "How did you know to come out here?"

He shut the door. "I didn't. I'm here in response to a complaint."

I started to laugh. "Oh, boy."

"Geoff and Sean Snyder have been pestering me to see what's going on at the house. They seem to think that Mr.

Fairweather is engaged in certain illegal activities. Got tired of listening to them, so I came over today."

I couldn't stop smiling. "They're going to be furious."

"How so?"

"They probably saved Jerry's life."

Chief Brenner looked understandably puzzled. "I'm not sure that's what they intended."

"I know it's not. But if I hadn't been able to disarm Kimberly Dawn, her plan was to kill me and Jerry, and set fire to the house. Tell the Snyders thanks, will you?"

"I will. Oh, and Ms. Maclin?"

"Yes, sir?"

"Next time, leave the confronting part of this business to the police. You could've gotten yourself killed."

JERRY WAS SO DELIGHTED by the Snyders coming to the rescue he was still grinning by dinnertime. Olivia, arriving just in time to spoil a perfect evening alone together, was not as thrilled by his escapade.

"So you not only let Mac put you in danger but the lives of two children, as well. That's just wonderful, Jerry."

"But it all worked out. Mac caught the killer. And we weren't in danger. We jumped down into the passageway the minute Kimberly Dawn drove up, and while we were down there, we found some sequins that prove Juliet Lovelace used the passageway."

"And why would Juliet Lovelace be sneaking around your uncle's house?"

"She was looking for a videotape."

"I thought you just told me she was running around pretending to be this book character."

"That, too."

"So where's this tape that caused all the fuss?" asked Olivia.

"We never found it." Jerry looked at me. "Should I get in touch with Uncle Val?"

Olivia rolled her eyes. "Oh, please."

"If you like," I said to Jerry. "But knowing how he felt about kids, I think you know what he would say."

Jerry closed his eyes as if tuning into the spirit world. "He'd say, I destroyed it before anyone else could see it." He opened his eyes. "That's what I'd do."

A line from Hayden's *Glass Plums* came to mind:
I will destroy what harms you.

"I think that's exactly what he did."

Olivia shook her head. "And you like this screwy little town and want to spend your days planning for a haunted B&B."

"Don't you?"

"No. I can't stand running back and forth like this anymore!" She sighed. "Why don't you come back to Parkland? You can stay with me until we get things straightened out."

"What about the B&B?"

She let her breath out in an exasperated huff.

"Your new lighter came in handy, Olivia, thanks," I said.

She eyed me. I could tell she was wondering if my remark was a joke. "You're welcome."

"You know," Jerry said, "now that the house is the site of an actual murder attempt, we could have some great mystery tours here. Don't fix the lamp or the bullet hole, and have a sign on the lighter saying, 'This lighter saved the day.'"

Olivia put up both hands. "No! No, that's it! I've had it!" She pushed herself away from the table. "I've had it with this stupid little town, I've had it with Madeline hanging around all the time, and I've definitely had it with you and your wild ideas. All you do is fantasize about what fun it will be. You can't see that this is beyond you, because you'd actually have to work." She grabbed her pocketbook and headed for the door, pausing for a final shot. "That's your problem, Jerry, you have too much imagination!"

I saw through her game. She never wanted to live in

Celosia or help with a bed and breakfast of any kind. She'd been hoping to scare him away by showing him how hard it would be.

I glanced at Jerry to see how he was taking her exit. He sat in his chair, a blank look on his face. He didn't look relieved or resigned or any one of several emotions I expected. It was as if he'd been handed a problem too big to solve.

Finally he turned to me. "Let's eat out on the porch."

We were on the porch eating cornflakes when Dennis Padgett drove up in his mail truck. He hopped out and handed me a letter.

"Special delivery, miss. Mr. Amry said to hand it to you personally." He drove back down the driveway.

I opened the letter, read it, and smiled.

"What is it?" Jerry asked.

I handed him the letter. "A poem from Hayden."

Jerry read it. "Hey, it makes sense."

"It's really nice."

Jerry read it aloud:

> "Along dark and twisting paths,
> Light glimmers.
> Truth revealed
> A heart released.
> This same heart thanks you."

I found a smaller piece of paper tucked inside the envelope. "Here's a note from Shana. She says he wrote this and then wrote the dedication poem for the new school in about twenty minutes."

"Great news."

We sat for a while in silence. Then I said, "Looks like I can't escape the pageant world."

Jerry took another handful of cornflakes. "Why do you say that?"

"Without my insider's knowledge of sequins and hair spray, I never would've solved this."

He shook his head. "I would've said it was your artist's way of looking at things that solved this mystery."

"Oh, really?"

"The color of a fingernail, the sparkle of a sequin."

I punched his arm. "Quit hogging all the cereal."

He passed me the box. "So, are you staying?"

"For now."

"Taking the office at Ted's?"

"I'm checking on that tomorrow."

"Here's hoping there's enough crime to keep you busy."

I thought of my revised Big Speech. Nothing is more important than my relationship with Jerry Fairweather. "Oh, I'm sure I'll find something to work on."

TUESDAY MORNING, Ted made all the arrangements for me to rent the office in his building. Afterward, I strolled over to Georgia's Books, just in time for Prill's steamroller entrance. He sailed in, his cape billowing behind. He pointed a long finger at Hayden.

"There you are! Thought you'd get away, did you? Impossible!"

Georgia and I moved aside to give Prill a clear path to Hayden at the counter.

"Hello, Prill," he said.

"Are you sufficiently recovered to bear the brunt of my outrage?" Prill asked.

"Oh, yes. Go ahead."

"Why should I bother?" Prill said with a dramatic gesture. "Why should I waste my breath? You know this speech as well as I do."

"Let's cut it short," Hayden said. "I bow to your superior knowledge." As Prill watched in astonishment, he went to the poetry section and took the copy of *Destinies* from the bottom shelf. "In the window today marked 'Special.' And I'll recommend her to the library committee when we meet next week."

Prill's eyes rolled. "You astound me, sir! Am I to understand that you give up? You concede? Victory is mine? I am speechless. Completely bereft of speech. This is beyond words."

Hayden motioned to the phone behind the counter. "Call her and give her the good news if you like."

Prill began to laugh. "I can't believe this. Wonderful! You've made my day."

"Quit gloating and call her."

Prill kept laughing. "I can't."

"Why not?" Hayden said. "Is she in seclusion somewhere, thinking up more world-shattering ideas?"

"No, no." Prill stopped laughing, but his eyes twinkled.

I had already figured this out. "Hayden, there is no Emily Nesp."

"No—?" he began, puzzled. "What is all this?"

Prill dusted his hands. "She's served her purpose, so now I dispose of her."

"That lady I saw you with the other day—"

"My great-aunt Tilly, in town to buy some toiletries."

Hayden still looked baffled, so I said, "He made her up."

Hayden's voice rose. "You made her up? All this bellowing about her work was an act? And her poems—"

"I wrote them."

Hayden stared at him. "But why? I didn't think you liked to play practical jokes."

"No jokes, sir. I was quite serious."

"Emily Nesp drove me crazy."

Prill leaned forward. "No, dear boy," he said in an entirely different tone. "She kept you sane."

Hayden opened his mouth as if to argue, then closed it.

"Am I right?" Prill said. "She was always good for a laugh, our Emily."

Hayden looked at him. "You're right."

"A bizarre, truly wacky old lady. I shall miss her."

"I will, too," he said.

"Never fear! I can always resurrect her, if need be."

"That won't be necessary," Hayden said.

"Good. Well, I must rush off and tell the other members of FLUF about your decision. No reneging now! I expect to see *Destinies* prominently displayed when I return."

"I'll take care of that right away," Hayden said. "Oh, and Miss Nesp."

Prill paused at the door, his cape swirling around him. "Yes?"

Hayden grinned. It was the first true smile I'd seen him smile. "Thanks."

Prill bowed. "Anything for poetry, sir! Good day."

ON MY WAY HOME, I stopped by the Freers' house to speak with Augusta Freer. She was a small, dark-haired woman with a pleasant little face.

"You're the detective, aren't you?" she said. "You know, I could not believe that Kimberly Dawn would do such a horrible thing. She was somewhat self-centered as a child, but to take that to such lengths. I can't imagine it."

"I understand you were Juliet Lovelace's English teacher," I said.

"Yes. What a horrible tragedy. She was a difficult young woman, but she had a bright future ahead of her, if she'd only been able to pursue it."

"She was going into English?"

"No, no. Her real love was art."

"Really?"

Augusta pointed to a framed picture on the wall. "She

gave me that as a thank-you present at the end of this school year."

The picture showed three irises—a dark purple, a light purple, and a yellow. The colors were expertly done; the shadowing subtle and effective. I found it difficult to associate this delicate painting with the arrogant young woman who'd tried to alienate everyone around her.

"It's beautiful. She was very talented."

Augusta Freer nodded. "She loved to paint and draw, but her mother never encouraged her. I think all this flashy pageant stuff was a way of getting back at her parents."

I couldn't take my gaze from the painting. My heart ached for the confused young woman who had such promise.

I WAS STILL in a gloomy mood when I got home. A large van was parked out front. For a moment, I thought Jerry had changed his mind about the Eberlin house and was moving out. A closer look revealed the van to be a delivery van from Masterson's Music.

Jerry met me on the porch. I said, "What's all this about?"

He grinned. "A piano."

"A piano?"

"Yeah, you know. Big thing with keys. Makes music."

I couldn't believe it. "Where are you going to put it?"

"In the music room, of course."

Two men came out. One handed some papers for Jerry to sign. He signed and gave a copy to one man. "Thanks. Come have a look, Mac."

We went into the parlor. Gone were the séance table and chairs. A shiny brown baby grand sat at the side windows.

"Thought I'd paint this room yellow," Jerry said. "Brighten it up." He gave me a sideways look. "Or you could paint it."

"I don't do walls."

"How about landscapes?"

"We'll see." To me, the parlor already looked brighter.

Everything looked brighter. "This room's almost big enough to dance in."

"Almost." He sat down on the piano bench. "So, you want to hear a song?"

"You bet."

"Pull up a chair."

Instead, I sat down on the bench beside him and watched as he played. He was intent on the keys and didn't notice how my gaze lingered on his face, on his calm gray eyes. I didn't recognize the song. He was probably making it up as he went along. But that's what I loved about him. Maybe his imagination took some crazy turns, but I could live with that, if he'd let me.

I realized he'd stopped playing and was looking at me. There was so much emotion in his eyes it took my breath away. At last I knew for certain he felt the same way about me.

"Jerry," I said, "I have something I've been wanting to tell you for a long time."

"That's funny," he said. "I've been wanting to tell you something, too."

We sat for a moment. I could hear my heart pounding. I wasn't sure I could say anything. "Jerry," I began.

"Mac, let me go first."

I swallowed. "Sure."

"Since we've come to the house, a lot has happened, and I've been doing a lot of thinking." His grin was slight. "Yeah, I know. Thinking, what a concept. But I've been thinking and I've been paying attention even when you thought I wasn't. There's something I want you to know."

Oh, my God, he's going to say it!

"All that with Olivia. I'm not sure what I was doing. I knew she was all wrong for me, I just—well, you know. I'm a total screw-up and can't get serious about anything, especially about romance."

I wanted to disagree and assure him he wasn't a total screw-up, but I was afraid to speak. I'd never heard him talk like this, and I wasn't sure where he was headed.

Now he looked away. "There's a reason, Mac. I've never told you before, but you deserve to know."

What could he mean?

"It has to do with my parents." His face was unusually somber. He took a deep breath. "It's hard to remember what happened. But I think— No, I'm pretty sure I had something to do with the fire that killed them."

"Jerry…"

He put his hand over his eyes and gave them a quick swipe before looking at me again. "I can't believe I told you. I've been wanting to for so long, but I was afraid you'd leave, and you mean too much to me, Mac. I wouldn't be able to stand it."

I took his hand. This wasn't my moment, after all. The time before, he'd been ready, and I'd missed my chance. Now that I was ready, the time wasn't right for him. But what he needed was a friend, and for now, the relief on his face was all I needed. "I'm not going anywhere, Jerry. We're best friends, right? This is just another mystery for me to solve. You'll let me do that, won't you?"

He smiled. "I'd like that."

I smiled back and squeezed his hand. Hold on, I thought. Whatever secrets you have, I'll understand. Whatever happened to your parents, I'll be there.

Because I love you, Jerry Fairweather.

For a little longer, he would just have to read my mind.

* * * * *

REQUEST YOUR FREE BOOKS!

2 FREE NOVELS
PLUS 2 FREE GIFTS!

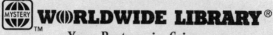

W(☉)RLDWIDE LIBRARY®
Your Partner in Crime

YES! Please send me 2 FREE novels from the Worldwide Library® series and my 2 FREE gifts (gifts are worth about $10). After receiving them, if I don't wish to receive any more books, I can return the shipping statement marked "cancel." If I don't cancel, I will receive 4 brand-new novels every month and be billed just $5.24 per book in the U.S. or $6.24 per book in Canada. That's a saving of at least 34% off the cover price. It's quite a bargain! Shipping and handling is just 50¢ per book in the U.S. and 75¢ per book in Canada.* I understand that accepting the 2 free books and gifts places me under no obligation to buy anything. I can always return a shipment and cancel at any time. Even if I never buy another book, the two free books and gifts are mine to keep forever.

414/424 WDN FEJ3

Name _____ (PLEASE PRINT)

Address _____ Apt. #

City _____ State/Prov. _____ Zip/Postal Code

Signature (if under 18, a parent or guardian must sign)

Mail to the **Reader Service:**
IN U.S.A.: P.O. Box 1867, Buffalo, NY 14240-1867
IN CANADA: P.O. Box 609, Fort Erie, Ontario L2A 5X3

Not valid for current subscribers to the Worldwide Library series.

Want to try two free books from another line?
Call 1-800-873-8635 or visit www.ReaderService.com.

* Terms and prices subject to change without notice. Prices do not include applicable taxes. Sales tax applicable in N.Y. Canadian residents will be charged applicable taxes. Offer not valid in Quebec. This offer is limited to one order per household. All orders subject to credit approval. Credit or debit balances in a customer's account(s) may be offset by any other outstanding balance owed by or to the customer. Please allow 4 to 6 weeks for delivery. Offer available while quantities last.

Your Privacy—The Reader Service is committed to protecting your privacy. Our Privacy Policy is available online at www.ReaderService.com or upon request from the Reader Service.

We make a portion of our mailing list available to reputable third parties that offer products we believe may interest you. If you prefer that we not exchange your name with third parties, or if you wish to clarify or modify your communication preferences, please visit us at www.ReaderService.com/consumerschoice or write to us at Reader Service Preference Service, P.O. Box 9062, Buffalo, NY 14269. Include your complete name and address.

WWLI1B